rachel schneider

FORFEITING
decency

Cover Design: Murphy Rae with Indie Solutions

Editor: Murphy Rae with Indie Solutions

Interior Formatting: Wendi Temporado of Ready, Set, Edit

Please note:

Forfeiting Decency is a spin-off from the *Breaking Habits Series.* While it can be read as a standalone, it does contain spoilers from book one in the series, *Taking Mine.*

To Sara, for making this a possibility.

prologue

IT'S IN THIS MILLISECOND of a moment that I know I'm seriously convoluted and completely fucked up. I feel victorious. I keep my chin jutted out, defiant, refusing to back down. I want this. My body is humming with anger, hurt, and the adrenaline of goading him.

And it sickens me.

one

SMACK

Everyone seems to freeze as the sound of the girl's palm meeting a man's face reverberates throughout the bar, and the silence that descends makes it that much more awkward. Most assume he's her boyfriend, but whatever their relationship may be, this isn't the place to cause a scene. Hudson's is a members-only, high-end cocktail bar. Admittance requires some serious name-dropping, a six-figure minimum annual salary, and a non-disclosure agreement signed upon entry. How this particular couple got in is a mystery, but it's evident they're new. There's rarely a need for him, but the security guard makes his way toward the couple as the rest of the bar falls back into routine.

Mondo shakes his head. "Puppy love," Mondo says, shooting Kaley a smirk as he dries a glass behind the bar.

Kaley returns his smile. "If you want to call it that."

The girl's boyfriend spent the last hour checking Kaley out, as well as anything else within spitting distance. Not just the women, either.

"He's late."

Mondo doesn't have to say who; Kaley already knows. A glance at her phone tells her he's exactly one hour late. There's a good chance Peter isn't coming. It's not uncommon for him to be a no-show. Maybe the wife gets a little needy from time to time, or maybe he actually has to work. Either way, Kaley has seen him once since he left for vacation three weeks ago.

Kaley twirls the stem of her empty wine glass, too scared to order another and not be able to pay for it.

"Has he messaged you?" Mondo asks.

She shakes her head. She's adorned in one of her most expensive dresses, waiting for a man to come and pay for her twenty-dollar glass of wine. The irony isn't lost on her.

Mondo sets down the dishrag, leaning across his folded arms on the bar top. "Who's on the radar, then?"

Casually, Kaley pulls the hair from her neck, making eye contact with the man sipping scotch in one of the alcove booths. He's mid sip, but there's a knowing look in his eyes.

Noticing her gaze, Mondo says, "Senator Landry. Oddly single in the political world at the ripe age of thirty-four. Currently resides in Bristle and attends mass every Sunday."

Mondo is Kaley's go-to background check. Kaley's never gone home with a man that Mondo didn't approve of first. He has details on anyone who's been in this bar. So far, he hasn't steered Kaley wrong.

"Democrat or Republican?"

Mondo gives her a look. "Does it matter?"

No, no it doesn't.

Pushing the wine glass away from her, Kaley uncrosses her legs, turning to where Senator Landry is just within view. She wonders if he'll make her call him by his title when they're together. Some powerful men are narcissistic like that.

Every man is a little different, but essentially, they all want the same thing: to feel needed. Some are funny, some are serious, and there's everything in between. Whether they prefer to dress in a three-piece suit or jeans, they're all needy bastards. They take until there's nothing left, and that's the scariest part of the life Kaley leads. One day she might not have anything left to give, and she'll have nothing to show for it.

"Is he nice?" Kaley asks.

"He's never gone home with anyone, so I can't say for sure. He hasn't had any bad press so far."

That's tricky. "He might not be into it."

Mondo clicks his tongue, a wry smile on his face. "He's a politician and comes from money. He's here for a reason, probably really good at hiding it. Besides, have you ever met a man who turned you down?"

Can't argue with that.

Kaley keeps an eye out for the senator in her peripheral vision. Occasionally, he glances in her direction or at his watch, but Kaley remains seated. She really should be making the first move, but she wants to give him the opportunity to come to her first. Usually, she likes to stick to her regulars, someone she knows what to expect with. But tonight is particularly slow. If he's looking for what she's selling, he'll have to make the first move.

This isn't new to her. She comes from the same money that's sitting in this room. It's full of corruption and lies and self-fulfillment—everything that she was taught how to master—and it's easy. Her family's money may be gone, but she doesn't have anything to prove. Hudson's fits her like a glove—like coming home.

When Senator Landry finally does grow the balls to approach, Kaley doesn't let her haughtiness show. He takes the seat to her right, but she doesn't move or acknowledge his arrival. Mondo takes his second order of scotch.

Then he speaks. "It's after nine. Does that mean I'm in the clear?"

Kaley immediately knows he's referring to Peter. Peter meets her here every Tuesday and Thursday at the same time. Realizing he's aware of this tells her he can't be that new to the scene.

Proficiently, Kaley looks over her shoulder at him. "What happens after nine?" she asks, playing coy.

He shrugs, looking a little too smug for Kaley's liking. "You tell me."

"Okay, you have my attention."

"Do I? Someone isn't going to come sweep you away?"

She gives an impish smile. "Only if you're too slow."

He's amused, but still cautious. "I didn't realize it was a race."

"Isn't everything a race?"

He weighs the point back-and-forth. "That's a valid but sad position on life."

"It's only sad if you don't accept it." *Especially as a politician*, but Kaley doesn't voice her thoughts.

Mondo sets the senator's drink down in front of him, and he takes a sip, giving her a satisfied nod. "You've got an interesting view on things."

Kaley shrugs, indifferent to his opinion. To her, life is the way it is. You adapt and move forward, or break in the process.

She swivels toward him, finally giving him her full attention. "I do a lot of interesting things." She re-crosses her legs.

He smirks, but his smile gives away his desire. Taking one last swallow of his drink, he drops a bill on the bar and stands, reaching for her hand. "Care to show me?"

"Where to?"

He pulls her to his side, looping an arm around her waist as he guides her to the back of the bar and toward the hotel lobby. "A room is closer, don't you think?"

"You already have a room?"

They step into an open elevator, congregating to one side, letting another couple occupy the other. "I occasionally book a hotel when I know I'm going to be working late in the city."

"Sounds like you work too much.'

"Depends on who you ask."

Kaley smiles, a tad impressed by his charm. Only a little, but that's more than she can say about her other clients. Senator Landry is handsome in the classic politician style. Slick hair, clean shaven, medium build. The prospect of the night doesn't look too bad, considering she might actually enjoy it.

They exit on the tenth floor and enter a small suite with a king-sized bed, the furniture and décor a familiar sight. Kaley runs her hand over the dresser, taking note of the clothes tossed across the bed and shaving kit perched on the nightstand. Her heart thumps against her chest, trying to remind her to be cautious, but sometimes she doesn't think she remembers what it feels like to be scared. She turns to face him as he shrugs out of his coat.

He briefly makes eye contact, allowing his gaze to travel the length of her body, blatant lust evident on his face. "This isn't where you give me the I-never-do-this speech, is it?" he asks frankly, but with that same charm that had appealed to her from the beginning.

She smiles, thankful for his bluntness. "I couldn't pretend to give that speech if I tried."

"We're both in understanding, then," he says, looking at her meaningfully.

"I think we are."

A look of relief flashes across his features, quickly replaced by one of desire. He takes one long step toward her, placing one hand around her waist and another firmly behind her neck. Tilting her head to the side, he places his lips against her throat, trailing down to her clavicle. She wills her heart to respond, wanting to desire his touch, aching to feel some sort of excitement, a hint of arousal, anything. But…

…nothing.

All she feels is the wetness of his tongue dotting across her skin as he pulls the zipper of her dress down, yet the steady knock of her heart never changes pace. Time seems to skip with every blink. Like the shutter of a camera, things move in fast forward. Every time she opens her eyes, the scene changes, forcing her to refocus.

He pulls off the remnants of her dress and drops it on the floor.

Blink.

He's climbing over her as her hands and knees meet the sheets.

Blink.

He retrieves a condom as he kneels between her legs, smiling like he's won the lottery.

Blink.

He enters her and she voluntarily moans at the feeling.

Blink.

Repetitive movements, sounds, breaths.

Blink.

And it's over before she even realizes it, the warmth of his body replaced by the cold as he rolls off of her.

"Are you going to lie there all night or what?"

Kaley turns and sits up on her elbows, pulling her gaze from the bedding, concerned by how much time has passed. "Well, that depends."

He laughs, pulling on a pair of boxers. "That's assuming I'd even want you to spend the night." He slides onto the bed, propping his head up on his elbow near her. "Although, morning sex would be a bonus."

"You don't pay me to stay; you pay me to leave. That would be counterproductive."

It takes a moment, but his smile wavers when he realizes she's serious. He pulls back, giving her an incredulous look. "Pay?"

The word hangs in the air between them.

She points at him. "You," she says, slowly turning the direction of her finger to herself. "Pay me."

"Uh," he hesitates, shaking his head. "No?"

She sits up. "Yes. That's what we do. We have sex, you pay me, and no one finds out."

He looks up at her from his position, now completely at ease, all hesitation gone. "I'm single. Why would I care if anyone finds out?"

"Because you're a senator," she says, voice rising with her panic.

"And I'm not allowed to have sexual relations because of that? I can assure you, that's not how this works."

"That's exactly how this works." Kaley stands, quickly pulling on her underwear. "Hudson's is a bar for secrecy. You signed a non-disclosure upon entering."

He smirks at her, his cockiness hitting an all-time high. "The non-disclosure is an insurance policy instilled for anonymous business decisions between public figures. Just because other men pay for sex doesn't mean I do. Give me some credit."

She's astonished. Flabbergasted. At a complete loss as to how she found herself in this position. "You knew I was an escort," she says, working to keep calm. "You said we were both in understanding."

"Of where the night was headed, not that I'd be paying for it."

Tears threaten to break as Kaley gets dressed, ignoring the obscene pounding of her heart, annoyed by its renewed vigor.

"Oh, come on. There are worse things you could have been doing for free."

His words grate against Kaley's ears as she attempts to block them out.

"And it's not like it wasn't good for you, too."

Sitting on the corner of the bed, she stops to slide on her heels. "You knew." She turns facing the him. "You knew this is what I do, and you took advantage of me."

He sits up. "If you're looking to get paid," he says, a new level of seriousness taking over his features. "I have a better proposition for you."

two

ONE DAY I'LL DIE, but I'm really, really hoping it's not today. I'm not sure if it will be the car or Lilly that does me in. My tiny car is running on its last leg and it might blow up. Soon. The longer I drive, the more I regret not eating that chocolate croissant from Starbucks. The five-dollar cup of tea was already pushing it, but if I'm going to die, I'd rather be stuffed with the yummy gooeyness of a warm baked good. I hold the cup up, reading the misspelling of my name.

Kaleigh.

I roll my eyes and take a sip. There's a chance Lilly might actually kill me when I arrive. It's up in the air. She might be happy to see me, but I'm almost positive that once she learns I've been living less than an hour away, she'll quickly change tune. No contact. Not a phone call, a text, or a handwritten note for the past four years. Unless you count the picture I sent her on a whim from Paris, along with the two gifts she had bought for Kip and Justin which she left in my car. I don't know why, but I felt like she would need them.

In my defense, she hasn't tried to contact me either. The last time we've spoken in person was right after the verdict was read and the trial was over. Our lives had both changed drastically, but Lilly took it way harder than I think I realized at the time.

Lance gave me her address. A British voice comes over my phone, telling me to turn right and I will arrive at my destination on the left.

This is it.

I park in the driveway of a stout townhouse. The familiar weathered truck that's parked out front gives me conformation I'm at the right place. I turn off my car, letting out a breath as I do so. The probability that it starts back up is slim. I check my face in the side-view mirror, grimacing at the bluish bruise on the apple of my cheek. No amount of concealer will cover it up. With shaky legs, I walk to the door and knock.

There's no reply.

I knock harder, squinting through the blinds to see if there's any movement. Still nothing.

I groan. Just my luck. I finally grow balls to visit, and she's not even here to see them. I turn around and look at my car. Yeah...I'm not getting back in that deathtrap.

I try the knob and it gives. "Hello," I call, listening to my echo. "Anyone home?"

The front door opens to a staircase, separating the kitchen and living room. I take a look around, double-checking that I'm in the right house, and spot a couple of pictures of Justin and Lilly together. A noise sounds from upstairs.

"Hello?" The stairs creak as I walk up them. "Yo, anyone home?"

There's a small landing at the top of the stairs, which leads to three different bedrooms. The door to my left leads to an office slash storage room, the master bedroom is positioned straight ahead, and they both come up empty. Shuffling comes from the room to my right. The door is slightly ajar, so I push it open.

And I'm struck dumb at the sight before me.

He has a body to die for. I lied when I said I didn't want to die today. If dying meant I'd been killed while ogling this man's naked flesh, I'd die every day over. He's wet, fresh out of the shower, and toned everywhere. My eyes travel over his strong shoulders, his chest, abdominals, happy trail, down to what's hanging between his legs. And it's as if his dick already recognizes I'm in the room, already sporting a semi. It's not until the towel lowers, uncovering the man's face, that I scream.

"What the fuck," Kip roars, hurriedly covering his junk.

Then I start laughing. Kip's face morphs from rage to confusion to annoyance all in the span of three seconds, and it only adds to my hysterics.

"What the fuck are you doing here?"

"I'm sorry." I wheeze through laughs. "I guess this is payback from all the times you walked in on me naked in Lilly's room."

His eyes cloud over in mirth. It's a familiar look he used to give me throughout my teenage and college years but always tried to cover it up, clearly not wanting his little sister's best friend to know he thought she was amusing.

"It was my house," he says in defense. "And it's my house you're in now. Get out."

"This is your house? Where's Lilly?"

"She and Justin went to go pick up her cap and gown for graduation. They'll be back in a while."

She's graduating? A ping of sadness registers before I push it away. Of course her life goes on without me.

Kip stalks toward me and I lose the ability to breathe. He stops centimeters from where I'm standing, and I can feel the lingering heat on his skin from the shower. Moisture surrounds the air around him and the humidity makes it that much harder to suck in air. He looks me over, starting at my feet, his gaze traveling up over my body like I just did him, eventually meeting my eyes. *Kip just checked me out.*

I cock an eyebrow at his audacity.

"Wait," I say, my mind finally catching up. "Aren't you supposed to be in prison?"

I don't get a response before the door slams in my face.

I rub the tip of my nose. "I'll just wait downstairs," I call through the door.

"Great," he replies, sarcasm evident.

I snicker as I descend the steps. Prison has done Kip well. He used to keep his hair long, tied back when he worked under cars. Now it's short, cropped close to his skull, and it does nothing but enhance his features. It no longer distracts from the stark color of blue in his eyes or the slight hollow of his cheeks. And those muscles.

Oh my god.

I just saw Kip's dick.

And it was glorious.

As I wait in the kitchen, I scope out the fridge, deducing that Lilly and Justin eat like pigs. There are three different take-out boxes, a surplus of soft drinks, and a full block of cheese. I settle for a glass of water.

Kip's feet pound down the stairs and I can hear his annoyance in every step. "Enjoy the show?" he greets me.

"I see prison only added to your deep need to be super surly all the time. But yes, I enjoyed the show. How come you never mentioned how well endowed—"

"Kaley," he interupts, gripping the bridge of his nose.

"There's nothing to be ashamed of. Most men would be ecstatic to be so…" I take a moment to hold my hands up, exaggerating by a foot or so.

"I swear to god, if you mention this to Lilly…" He trails off.

"You'll what?"

He breathes out, turning away as he opens the fridge. "Jesus Christ, do they eat any real food in this house?"

I guess we're letting the penis topic go. He rifles through the fridge's contents, coming up with a pack of yogurt he must have dug out of Narnia, because I'm positive there's no way that fridge produced it. He sets it on the counter and starts opening and closing drawers, finally finding the utensils.

"This yogurt is expired."

Peeling back the lid, he sniffs it before planting a spoon into the container and taking a bite. "Can't be worse than what I've been eating." Deeming it acceptable, he takes another bite, pointing at my face. "What happened to your face?"

"Nailed myself in the face with the freezer door last night." He gives me a dubious look and I laugh. "Believe me, I wish I had a cooler story to tell."

He replies by taking a bite of his yogurt.

"So, you're fresh out, huh?"

He nods.

"Since when?"

"Yesterday."

"Good behavior?"

"Something like that."

"No gang fights or shanking someone for calling you a bitch?"

He laughs through his nose, shaking his head. "No. Federal prison is nothing like television or movies portray it to be. It's equivalent to an all-male, adult daycare. Although, I've seen some guys do some weird shit for a roll of toilet paper."

I laugh. "Sounds like you know from experience."

He smiles, bracing his arms on the counter. I'm almost positive he's going to tell me a borderline homoerotic prison story when Lilly's voice cuts through the air. "Whose car is in the driveway?"

Kip leans back, shoveling more yogurt into his mouth. Air lodges in my throat as I wait for Lilly's arrival. The front door shuts and two sets of footsteps march into the kitchen, coming to a halt when we finally make eye contact.

"Kaley," Lilly says in surprise, caught off guard by my presence.

She looks exactly the same, blonde hair pulled up and worn out Chucks on her feet. But she's also different. Taller, maybe? She's always been pretty, but it's more than that. It's…deep rooted. Happier, for sure.

"Hi."

Justin's the first to break the moment, hanging a garment bag on the doorjamb. "Hi, Kaley."

Lilly spurs into action, pulling me into a hug. "Where have you been? And what did you do to your face?"

I don't know if it's her question that makes my throat close up or if it's the human contact, because I suddenly can't remember the last time I hugged someone. Squeezing my eyes shut, I hold on to her presence. She smells like shampoo, but there's still the familiar underlying scent of motor oil.

"You know me," I answer with a shrug.

She smiles and shakes her head. "When'd you get into town?"

I pull back, well aware of Kip and Justin watching. Clearing my throat, I force out a smile. "You have to promise not to get mad."

Her face drops. "Why?"

Justin coughs and it must be man code to give us space, because Kip follows him out of the room.

15

"Where have you been?"

"Promise not to get mad," I reiterate.

She thumps me on the forehead.

"Ow." I rub the spot. "What the hell?"

"If I can't get mad at you after, I'm going to do it now, before." She flicks me again. "Whatever you did or are going to do is probably the dumbest, craziest shit I've ever heard of. You're a fucking idiot."

I smile. "I can't argue with that. Are you done?"

"I suppose, since I don't actually know what I'm supposed to be mad about."

I rush out the words, hoping if I say them fast enough it'll lessen the blow. "I've been living right outside the city."

I can see the inflation of her chest as she breathes in. Some things never change. Anytime Lilly gets overwhelmed with any one single emotion, she inflates like a balloon. "You sent me a picture from Paris," she says, disbelieving.

"Yeah, that's a long story."

"So you've been living not even an hour from here," she clarifies.

I nod, grimacing.

"You—"

"Uh-uh-uh," I say, shaking my finger back and forth. "You promised."

More inflation on her part.

Justin reemerges seemingly out of nowhere, massaging her shoulders in an effort to calm her. "Breathe, babe."

Lilly turns on him like a whip. "You knew."

It's his turn to grimace. "I mean, I didn't know the exact address—"

That's all he gets out before Lilly attacks, punching him anywhere he's vulnerable, which constantly changes due to his flailing efforts to avoid her assault. His laughter only antagonizes her more.

"Hey, children," Kip admonishes them, pulling Lilly away by swooping an arm around her waist. "Let's use our words."

That was a mistake on his part. Lilly unleashes every cuss word in the English language with a weird mix of Spanish thrown in. Kip rolls his eyes, releasing Lilly and sitting on the stool next to me.

"She minored in Spanish," he explains.

We watch Justin poorly defend himself, half laughing and half trying to take Lilly seriously. He could take her down if he wanted, but she's not really, really mad. Just enough to be cute-angry, and he kind of loves it. It takes a few minutes, but she eventually calms down, traipsing up the stairs to deposit her gown in her room.

"Why didn't you tell her where I lived," I ask Justin once she's gone.

"I don't know," he says, releasing a breath. "At first I figured you both needed time to figure out things on your own. As time went on, it seemed like you didn't want to see her. Why would I add to her heartbreak of losing her brother with losing her best friend?"

Kip speaks before I can register the verbal slap in the face Justin dished out. "That's not fair. She didn't lose me. It's not like I died. I went to prison. And Kaley was going through her own shit."

"Lilly was there for Kaley every day of the trial, and Kaley walked past her every day like she didn't exist. It takes one freaking second to acknowledge someone."

"Contrary to popular belief," Kip spits, surprising Justin and me with his anger. Maybe even himself. "The world doesn't revolve around my sister."

Justin's face grows red.

"Kip's right." All three of us turn our heads in Lilly's direction. "The world doesn't revolve around me. And this was four years ago, so why are we arguing about it?" She braces her elbow on the counter, propping her chin on her hand and cocking her head in my direction. "The real question is, why did you just decide to show up out of nowhere?"

Oh, the sass is real.

"Well, I, uh." They're looking at me, waiting. Except for Kip, who seems more interested in his yogurt.

"Since when did you become shy?" Justin remarks.

Kip snorts. "She's not, trust me."

Lilly and Justin both look to Kip for an explanation, so I force words out of my mouth to distract them. "My car is broken."

Justin suppresses an eye roll but Lilly ignores him, unsurprised that I came to her because I needed something. "Broken how?"

"All I know is it sounds like it's dying and I don't want it to blow up while I'm in it."

"I'll go take a look at it." When Justin makes no effort to move, she grabs him by the collar of his shirt, hauling him behind her.

"Could have been worse," Kip says, taking one last bite of his snack.

"You didn't have to stick up for me."

"Justin is always going to be Team Lilly. It didn't feel fair to leave you hanging."

"Aren't you Team Lilly?"

"And because of that," he says, shooting the empty yogurt cup into the trash bin like a basketball. "Lilly's always had someone in her corner, rooting for her. But who have you had?"

I roll my eyes. "My life isn't that dramatic, Kip. I'm a grown-up."

He gives me a cursory glance, stopping for a split second on my chest. It's so quick I would have missed it if I hadn't been paying such close attention. That's twice in the last thirty minutes, twice *ever*, that he's looked at me with any interest. Not just in fascination, but with sexual connotation. I don't shy away from his attention and I don't bother to hide my interest, either. He doesn't react as he turns away and stomps up the stairs, away from my smile.

Prison must be as lonely as people say it is for Kip Foster to suddenly show interest in me. I mull it over in my head. He's definitely stupid hot—and I've seen what he's packing—but it's confounding to think of him as anything other than Lilly's brother. The same older brother that used to shield his eyes like the sun was blinding him anytime he saw me in a bathing suit, or convinced Lilly I was a bad influence because I drank all of his beer freshmen year.

But I'm not that girl anymore. And I don't think Kip is that big of an asshole anymore. I think Kip's noticing me in the same way I'm noticing him: as a good lay.

I take my time to tour Lilly's living room as I wait, checking out the framed pictures situated throughout the space. They document Lilly and Justin's relationship over the past few years I've missed. Most selfies, some from afar at various places they've traveled, and a few with some people I don't recognize but I assume are Justin's family. Various knick-knacks are scattered across the mantel, matchbox cars mixed with candles and tiny army men.

After a half-hour, Lilly and Justin return inside to give me the bad news. My car is fucked. It's so fucked that Lilly refuses to let me drive it home. It has a leak in the transmission, but she thinks it can be fixed. If it's not what she thinks it is, it's likely it'll need to be replaced. I'm too broke to pay for a new transmission, and it brings on the question whether or not it's even worth replacing, considering the car's value.

Justin's drives me home because Lilly had to study for her exiting finals. She's always been a religious studier, but I can't help but wonder if it's because she didn't want to be in a car with me. She's probably madder than she's letting on.

That or I'm just really paranoid.

"Lilly seems happy," I say, finally cutting through the tension.

"She is," Justin agrees, a small smile on his lips. "She's even happier because graduation is right around the corner."

"Senioritis."

He agrees. "She's ready for it to be over."

I nod like I understand, but in reality, I have no idea what it's like to accomplish what she has. I left school when the news of my dad's arrest broke. Stomaching the stares from other students, as well as my professors, was too much to bear.

"I can get you a ticket if you want to go."

It takes me a few moments to figure out what he's talking about. "To graduation?"

He nods.

"I don't know," I say noncommittally.

He says my name, making sure he has my attention. "She misses you."

A smile tugs at my lips. "She no longer needs outside validation."

An even prouder smile spreads across his face. "No." Ne shakes his head. "Not anymore."

Justin drops me off at my apartment and I enter my address into his phone to send me a ticket, just in case I decide to attend. He insists.

I traded shifts with a girl from work, trying to make up for the compensation I was gypped from last night. But that was before I was sans car, and walking thirty-five blocks isn't nearly as fun as it sounds. I would have taken the bus, except…well…I'm scared of the bus. So much bodily flood and mucus and germs not visible to the eyes…I just can't. On the bright side, walking is good for the body. Never mind I nearly get bulldozed by an asshole in a jacked-up truck, step in two mystery puddles, and have to fend off a homeless woman trying to sell me knock-off flip-flops.

Still less traumatizing than the bus.

"You're late," Janine says, passing me a tray of chicken tacos the minute I clock in.

"I'm not late, just behind," I say, shouldering the mass of food. "Three minutes, tops."

She's not swayed by my ability to talk in circles. "Deliver these to table twenty-seven and take twenty-two's order. He's been waiting for fifteen minutes."

I drop off the tacos to a rambunctious group of college students, already tipsy before the sun has gone down. It takes way longer than it should for them to remember who ordered what, and I can already tell this night is going to be hell. As I approach the second table, my pen is already poised over my notepad, ready to go.

"I'm so sorry for your wait. Can I start you off with an appetizer?"

"That wasn't very sincere. Want to try again?" The familiarity of his voice makes me look up.

"Lance," I exclaim, throwing my arms around his neck. "When'd you get back?"

"Yesterday. Went by your apartment this morning, but you weren't home."

"Yeah. I drove to Lilly's to get my car looked at."

He lifts his eyebrows. "Really?"

I nod.

"And how'd that go?"

I shrug. "Could have been worse. Did you know that Kip's out?"

"No shit," he says, smiling. "That's good. Does he still have a stick up his ass?"

An image of Kip naked skips through my mind and I smirk. "No, definitely no stick. At least not in that area."

"I'm glad he got it removed. Maybe becoming jail bait isn't so bad."

I shake my head. Lance may not have been the exact reason Kip went to prison, but he definitely played his part. For him to joke about it so lightly is very low class. "When was the last time someone told you that you're an asshole?"

His smile only grows. "Give me whatever's on draft and the cheese sticks."

I hit him over the head with a menu as I walk away.

Janine gives me a look. "I'm not in the mood to fire you again."

"Jan, you never fire me. You suspend me until you're ready to take me back. He's a friend."

"Just don't cause a scene. The last time you hit a customer I had to talk him down from a lawsuit."

I've had my fair share of gropers—it's almost an everyday occurrence—but when a man tries to stick his hand up my shirt, things are going to get ugly. Only a chauvinistic bastard would threaten suit when there's cameras.

The night runs just as horribly as I predicted. A screaming three-year-old at table thirty is up way past his bedtime, a group of teenagers take up the banquet room after a school dance and leave a stingy tip, more drunken collage students come in, and an old lady attempts to bring her Chihuahua in, claiming it's her guide dog.

Lance stays, munching on appetizers and watching whatever sports game is playing tonight. He only does this once or twice a year, depending on how often he gets to come home. He stays gone, on whatever missions the DEA sends him on sporadically. So he likes to relax the few weeks he has off a year. Why he does it in a rinky-dink restaurant, I have no idea.

There's only a couple of stragglers left when I clean off his booth, taking the seat opposite him so I can wrap utensils for the next day shift.

"Busy night," he remarks, sipping his beer without taking his eyes off the TV. "Any good tips?"

"Some. How long are you home for this time?"

"A couple of weeks, give or take some."

We fall into silence, the only sounds coming from the TV and the silverware clinking together as I roll them into napkins. Lance and I didn't always have an easy friendship, if you can even call it that. We met at a frat party between school semesters, had a one-night stand which later turned into a friends-with-benefits relationship. That is, until I found out he was working with my dad as an undercover narc who would eventually deracinate everyone's lives.

It wasn't Lance's fault. I was, and am, very well aware that my dad is a piece of shit. Finding out my dad was a drug smuggler who had inadvertently hired Lilly, not realizing Kip was her brother to unknowingly transport drugs for him was a shocker, to say the least. All the money I grew up with, the fancy dinner parties, private planes, luxury vacation homes, was all dirty.

In essence, people went to prison—my father and Kip included—and Lilly and I lost everything we knew. Add in the fact we found out Lance and Justin were partners working for the DEA to take down my father's drug ring, I think it's safe to say it's not a surprise we went our separate ways. At the time, I think it was too much for us to deal with on top of everything.

"What's wrong with you?" Lance says, not unkindly.

I laugh. "That's a loaded question," I say.

"You're oddly quiet."

"So?"

"So…talking and breathing are synonymous with you."

I sigh. "Justin gave me a ticket to Lilly's graduation."

He finally looks away from his game, giving me his full attention. "And you don't want to go?"

"Yeah?"

He cocks his head, confused.

"No? I don't know. If she wanted me there, she would have invited me herself…right?"

He takes a sip of his beer and sets it down. "Who knows Lilly better than anyone?"

At one point in our lives, I would have said me.

"Justin," Lance answers for me. "Would Justin invite you, knowing Lilly didn't want you there?"

I roll my eyes, hating how right he is. "No."

Picking up his beer again, he smiles. "Right. So stop being a pussy and go."

There's only one problem.

Peter.

three

KALEY HAS BEEN WAITING thirty minutes for Peter's arrival. It's been almost a month since she's received any kind of payment other than her measly tips from the restaurant, and money is tight. She's starting to feel desperate—itchy.

There's a man down the bar Kaley knows she's slept with before. He spins a coaster on the bar, smiling devilishly in her direction. For the life of her, Kaley can't remember his name, and Mondo is busy taking another patron's order. Nicknames usually help, but she can't remember if it's Spit-talker Fernando or Ear-sucker Tucker. Both equally unpleasant.

She twirls the stem of the glass and decides to give Peter a few more minutes. When the seat next to her fills, she assumes it's the man at the end of the bar, but is surprised to find someone much more enjoyable.

"Julia," Kaley greets her.

Mondo catches a break between customers, holding up a bottle of wine in response to Julia's arrival.

"Jesus, yes," Julia answers.

Kaley smiles, amused by Julia and all her ways. "It's been a while."

Mondo pours Julia's drink, resting both palms against the bar when he slides it over to her. "What's been happening?"

They wait to hear Julia's explanation as to why she's been absent lately.

Julia hums around her fresh glass of red wine. "I was living with a trust fund baby in L.A. for a few months."

"And you're not anymore because...?"

Mondo may need to ask, but Kaley doesn't. Julia comes from money, a trust fund baby herself. She doesn't have sex for money because she needs it, or because she wants to piss off her daddy. No, Julia does it out of sheer boredom.

"There's only so much money can buy," she tells Mondo.

Julia and Kaley share a knowing smile.

Mondo gives them an incredulous look. "Pft. Do you think I'd work here if I could find another way to solve my problems?"

"Different problems," Julia puts simply.

Kaley remembers those days, when the day's main objective was finding something to do just to stop thinking. First came boys. They were easy and fun. Then they, too, lost a smidgeon of luster. Alcohol, followed with some recreational drug usage, and then she slowly went back to boys once she realized drugs do their own special form of damage. Boys are safe, easy, fast creatures. There was once a time Kaley enjoyed her nights at Hudson's, thrilled by the idea of someone new and exciting. The adrenaline and desire and love of keeping men on their toes.

In a lot of ways, Kaley envies Julia. She wishes Julia's enthusiasm still found her on nights like tonight. Over time, being an escort became one of the most boring professions in the world. Same men, same game, different night. She's ninety-nine percent certain medical filing would be more riveting.

Julia runs her fingers through her perfectly tousled waves, tilting her head in Kaley's direction. "I'm glad you're here tonight. I need to ask you something."

Kaley's defenses shoot up. Her relationship with Julia is friendly, but strictly limited to Hudson's. "Yes?"

"What's your business with Senator Landry?"

Kaley concentrates on keeping her face neutral as she replies, "I'm sure I've slept with him. Why do you ask?"

Julia smirks, not at all swayed by Kaley's aloofness. "Lousy lay."

Kaley nods her head in agreement, a small smile playing on her lips.

"Is there a reason he would pay me to out you to Peter?"

"He did what?" Kaley nearly shouts.

Julia makes a hand motion to lower her voice, glancing over her shoulder to double-check no one is listening. "He offered me money to tell Peter about you sleeping with other men at Hudson's."

Tension roles down Kaley's back as she struggles to keep her posture relaxed. As if Julia and her having a hushed conversation isn't already a dead giveaway.

Kaley shakes her head. "It doesn't make sense. Why would he need you? Why wouldn't he just do it himself?"

"He offered a lot of money, Kaley," Julia emphasizes. "Maybe he thought it would be enticing enough for me to go through with it."

"Little does he know, you don't do this for the money."

Julia returns Kaley's smile. "Exactly. But someone else might be a little more desperate than I am."

Kaley glances around the bar. At this very moment, there's roughly fifty men in the bar, outnumbering the women five to one, and nine out of ten women are escorts. Most of them work for an escort company and use Hudson's as a discreet meeting place. The good side of working under an escort company is the money. Married or successful men are willing to pay more for an NDA agreement. The bad side is an escort doesn't get to choose who they get paired with. It can literally be anyone.

"Thank you," Kaley says, putting as much sincerity behind it as she can.

Julia cocks an eyebrow, mid-swig of her wine, and Kaley knows it's her way of saying welcome.

A man sidles up next to Julia, leaning his hip against the edge of the bar. "Julia, Julia, Julia," he says, a predatory gleam. Julia winks at Kaley, turning her attention to the man. They stand, and Kaley follows their departure with her eyes, accidentally making eye contact with Senator Landry in the process.

He's in a booth with a pretty brunette sitting on his thigh, whispering something into her ear. He doesn't break eye contact with Kaley as he takes a sip of his drink, rubbing a hand up and down the girl's arm. He doesn't come in every night, but he's been making a regular appearance.

He wanted her to know, Kaley surmises. It's the only explanation she can come up with. He wants her to be paranoid, afraid of his power. And damn it, he's succeeded.

Giving in to the fact Peter isn't going to show, she's poised to make her approach to the man yet to be named, when Mondo snaps his fingers to get her attention in the middle of pouring a martini. She follows Mondo's gaze to the man walking towards her. He swoops his right hand around Kaley's waist as he leans in for a kiss on her cheek.

"Kaley," Peter greets her, his tone a little harsher than usual. "Sorry I'm late."

"Peter," she breathes his name, smiling through her surprise. "It's okay. I was about to call it a night."

Peter's eyes flicker to the man down the bar, now typing away on his phone, all but forgotten about Kaley's interest. Kaley's a good liar, but Peter is better. He makes a living lying as a defense attorney. She tries not to give away the fear he almost caught her mere seconds away from advancing on another man. Kaley doesn't try to talk through her nerves, knowing he would see right through it. Slowly, he lets his hand slide from the nape of her neck, caressing her arm on the way down. It's then she knows she's off the hook.

Peter is a hot commodity at Hudson's. The girls know he pays well and they'll do about anything to sink their claws into him. But Peter doesn't pay to be with a woman; he could be with a lot of women for free. He pays for routine. He knows what he likes and he'll pay nearly double for it, asking for monogamy in return. Normally, that isn't a problem for Kaley. But Peter's been more MIA than ever lately, and the money doesn't stretch that far.

Mondo finds his way to their side of the bar, setting down Peter's usual with a napkin folded under the glass just how he likes it. Peter doesn't speak, not even a nod of acknowledgment as he drops a fifty on the bar. It's the same tip he gives for the same drinks he always orders: one glass of sauvignon blanc and one glass of vodka on the rocks.

Kaley hates this habit of his. He thinks his money is generous enough it doesn't require him to actually speak to anyone. And he doesn't. His fingers lace with hers as they leave the bar, into the lobby, and to the elevator. Kaley automatically pushes the button for the thirty-fourth floor.

"I've missed you," he says, finally feeling free to show her affection away from wandering eyes.

"You needed a vacation," she says in turn.

He hums. "If only I could have spent it holed up with you."

Their reflection shows the girl in his arms smiling, but only Kaley can feel her bitterness. "I'm sure the kids enjoyed you away from work."

His lips leave her skin as the doors open. "Yes, but work still reaches me when I'm a thousand miles away."

He struggles to retrieve the key from his pocket, so Kaley takes the glass from him, freeing up his hand. He smiles once he finally gets the door open. When they're alone, Kaley takes a sip of his drink, and Peter's eyes hold a hint of examination.

"Thirsty?"

She smiles around the glass. "That glass of wine made me sleepy. I need a pick-me-up."

He slides off his jacket, popping open the buttons of his white shirt in follow. "I thought our first night together in weeks would be enough to keep you on your toes."

There's a tinge of anger in his words. "Peter," she says, holding the glass up to his lips. "Of course I'm happy to see you."

He opens his mouth as Kaley tips the glass forward, letting her cater to him. Pulling away, he takes the glass from her, setting it on the nearby table. Kaley runs her hands up each side of his neck, angling his head down to hers. His kisses are the same as they've been for the past four years: demanding, straight to the point, a means to an end. There are no false pretenses with his body language, never have been, even when hiding ulterior motives.

Releasing her, he turns her body away, pulling the straps of her dress down her arms. It's when his hand threads through Kaley's hair, pulling it tight at the roots, she realizes the extent of his anger. "You know this isn't an open-ended deal."

"Why would you say that?"

"There's been rumors."

"Rumors?" She turns around to face him, trying to judge the amount of animosity in his voice.

"That there's a brunette escort who meets Peter Baranski every Tuesday and Thursday at Hudson's."

Kaley smirks. "That's not a rumor, that's true," she says, pushing her hands inside his shirt, trying to rid him of his insecurities.

"No, the rumor is that the same brunette escort has been seen leaving with other men."

Her hands still.

"Regularly," he tacks on.

"Peter," she says, trying to leak amusement into her tone. "You know better than that." Trailing her fingertips over his shoulders, she places a soft kiss to his chin.

It takes a moment, but eventually the stinging pull of her hair withdraws, and his lips lose the tightness in them, a smile taking its place. "I know."

Kaley smiles, happy to have placated him, even though renewed fear has settled deeper into her bones. Peter's been more sporadic lately, canceling last minute, leaving for vacation on the drop of a dime. She'll have to be more discreet. The Hudson may be secretive, but not immune to gossip.

Peter moves her back toward the bed, pulling her dress down along the way. He's never been gentle with her, and she knows it'll be the same routine tonight. He removes his wedding band, placing it on the end table, as if there's a loophole that comes to marriage and rings. If you're not wearing it when you actively put your dick in someone, it doesn't count, right?

Kaley turns over, onto her hands and knees, listening to the sound of Peter's movements as he unbuckles his belt. Her eyes stay locked on the gold band. For some reason its presence bothers her more than usual. She's met Peter's wife, Lydia. Not a spectacular lady. Not in the slightest. Lydia and Peter both have the tendency to look down at people, and Lydia is especially good at looking down at Kaley. She's always theorized that Lydia knows who she is, but never cared enough to address the issue with her.

But tonight, as Peter enters her…

…touches her…

…she works extra hard to stay focused on the movements. She ensures that she's engaging, her usual sounds of pleasure, same push and pull. But for some reason, she can't think about anything other than that ring. Even after he's finished and he's pulled her body close to his, spooning in their regular position for the obligatory fifteen minutes or so, she still can't tear her eyes away from the shiny metal.

After he catches his breath, Peter pulls away to get dressed. Kaley watches as he slides the gold band back onto his left ring finger, replacing it with folded envelope that she knows holds a stack of crisp one-hundred-dollar bills inside.

He leans over her, placing a kiss on her lips. "You're so fucking beautiful."

He says it as if there's no better compliment he could ever bestow upon her. Kaley covers herself as she watches Peter get dressed, scooting to the edge of the bed. It's now or never. She knows she needs to speak now or forever hold her peace.

"So, uh, I have a friend that's graduating Thursday."

The drone of silence echoes in her ears as she berates herself for stumbling, forcing herself to meet Peter's gaze. She rehearsed her words, perfected them, determined for them to be straight and to the point. It's easier said than done when faced with the look of Peter's indignation.

"I didn't think you had any friends."

It's true—she doesn't—but it's the way he says it that irks her.

"She's an old friend from college."

He trails his finger over her chin, eyes jumping back and forth between hers. "Thursdays are our days. You know that."

"I know…but I would really like to go."

She mentally shakes herself. This isn't a question. She isn't asking permission. She's *telling*.

"We can always meet on Friday or maybe even a day later this weekend."

There. A compromise.

Peter doesn't say anything. Why would he? He doesn't need to. He lets his money do it.

Reaching behind her, he picks up the envelope and shoves it back into his pocket, leaving without a second glance in her direction.

The sound of the hotel door slamming shut ricochets throughout the room, and Kaley closes her eyes, willing the tears to reside. Walking away empty-handed twice in one week is devastating. Not only to her bank account, but it finally makes he feel like maybe she's not doing something right.

Standing, she peels off the dress they hadn't bothered to completely remove, preparing to wash away the night. This time it's not Peter's smell or touch that she's trying to rid herself of, but the way he made her feel; like her own wishes aren't anywhere equivalent to his, and how incredibly selfish it was of her to ask.

four

HOLY FUCK. I'M LATE. My taxi driver speaks all of three words in English. Yes, no, and thank you. Okay, fine, it's *technically* four, but that's irrelevant. Anytime I make a comment about how big of a hurry I'm in, he nods, smiles, and maintains his breakneck speed of two miles per hour. Maybe three—it's hard to tell because we were going *that* slow.

I hurry through admittance and the security guard gives me a curious glance. It doesn't stop me from bouncing on the balls of my feet from impatience as he checks my purse. When I'm through, I sprint down the hall and into the amphitheater. The ceremony has already commenced and the stadium is packed.

They're still announcing students with last names starting early in the alphabet and I finally breathe a sigh of relief. My eyes jump around the audience, but I don't spot Justin or Kip anywhere. I get a few snarky looks from parents with cameras held high, but I act like I don't notice. As the names start to dwindle down the alphabet, I pinpoint Lilly's spot in the procession of graduates. I smile when I notice her Chucks peeking out from underneath her gown.

Finally, she's called, and I'm cheering before the announcer even finishes saying her name. Justin and Kip, who I can finally spot a few rows over, are doing the same. They make eye contact with me when they hear my cheers, and their faces split into smiles. It makes me feel more confident about coming.

We're louder than any other family here even though there's only three of us. Justin scoots over, making room for me between Kip and an older woman to his right. She shoots me a dirty look as I get situated.

"I'm sorry." I lower my voice, slightly breathless from all the excitement. "That's my best friend."

The lady barely maintains her sneer, turning her attention away from me. I roll my eyes and Kip smiles.

His lips brush my ear when he whispers, "I'm so glad you made it."

I shrug off the goosebumps. "Barely. My taxi driver was a nightmare."

"You took a taxi?"

"No car. Remember?"

It takes a moment, but he nods in understanding.

I smile. "Dumbass."

He smirks, not at all fazed by my insult.

We wait for the rest of the ceremony to play out in agony. Lilly's thirty seconds of fame are soon followed by an hour-long ceremony during which the rest of the students receive diplomas and listen to bullshit speeches about grabbing life by the horns. Though they fail to mention the humongous dick the bull has and occasionally fucks you with. Whatever. Let them believe life is tamable.

We skip out before the ceremony finishes, trying to beat the crowd to where the graduates meet with their friends and families.

I gawk at Kip and Justin's empty hands. "Where's the bouquet of flowers?"

Justin cocks his head. "The what?"

"Graduation flowers, you ignoramus. A huge bouquet of flowers you're supposed to gift your girlfriend on the greatest day of her life."

He and Kip share an amused look.

"You two are idiots," I sputter, already walking to the florist who's set up shop by the door.

Their arrangements are mediocre and overpriced, but I dig in my wallet for a twenty and hand it over for some lilies. Kip shoots his hand out, replacing my money with his and picking a slightly larger grouping.

"You know Lilly doesn't care for flowers," he says.

"That's beside the point. It's the gesture that matters."

"Says the girl who was nearly an hour late."

The students start careening from the theater doors, spilling out into the lobby like water, a sea of blue gowns swishing through the crowd. Kip's the tallest and spots Lilly first, parting the way for her. He hands her the bouquet and she rolls her eyes, making Kip smile and point in my direction.

Her smile stops—it's the only way to describe it—before it eases back into place. She gives Kip a hug, saying something to make him laugh, and he keeps his eyes carefully averted as they separate. In a way, it's almost like seeing his own daughter graduate. He's worked his butt off to make sure she's arrived where she is today. I can't imagine the level of pride he has for her.

Justin's turn is slightly more dramatic and he lifts Lilly from the ground, kissing her from below as he holds her up. A few people smile at them from afar. It's hard not to notice their happiness. They speak in hushed tones, a moment between them, and this time it's Lilly's turn to hide the moisture in her eyes.

Eventually, Justin releases her, and we're forced to address each other. "You're buying the first round of drinks."

I laugh. "Since when do you drink?"

"Since 1L."

If this is an olive branch, I'm grabbing it. "Then drinks are on me."

We agree to meet at a restaurant Justin mentions and we sort out the directions. Justin and Lilly ride in her car together since she had to arrive early, and I ride with Kip because I don't want to be in the middle of them quite yet.

The smell of Kip's truck hits me when I sink into the seat, and I relish in the nostalgia.

"Remember when you tried to teach Lilly how to drive a stick?"

He quickly shakes his head, a small smile playing on his lips. "I thought the transmission was going to fall out."

"We were stuck at that intersection for half an hour."

"I almost went to jail because some asshole decided he was going to ram us."

"Oh, yeah," I drawl, remembering how Kip's face turned a deep purple. "But he only managed to cave in his front bumper."

Kip's lips twitch as he rubs the steering wheel. "No sports car can go up against this truck."

His reverence for his truck is kind of endearing. Maybe because I'm kind of attached to it too. This truck has gotten Lilly and me into a lot of trouble. Or out of trouble, depending on the way you look at it.

"It's nice that Lilly took care of it for you."

"Yeah," he says quietly. "I'm proud of her."

I'm not sure if he means the truck or his sister, but it makes me smile nevertheless. His eyes kind of glaze over and I take the moment to admire his body—I mean attire…to admire his attire. He's dressed in slacks with a grey button-down, un-tucked with the sleeves haphazardly rolled and pushed up. Even though the clothes are cheap and slightly wrinkled around the waist, he pulls off the business casual look quite well. I don't know why or how, but I focus on the area below his belt. His legs are relaxed, splayed at the perfect angle to drive comfortably, and all I can do is stare at his crotch.

Why can't I stop? Oh, yeah. I know what's hiding behind that zipper.

He ducks his head into my line of view, breaking my perusal. There's no point in trying to hide my examination, so I smile wider, cocking an eyebrow until he's uncomfortable enough to look away first.

"Some things never change," he says.

"And some things change a whole lot," I dispute. He doesn't take the bait. "I'm surprised you got so dressed up for the graduation."

"I had a few job interviews earlier today," he explains.

"That's great," I say, confused by his lack of enthusiasm.

He takes a moment, turning into the parking lot of the restaurant. "No one wants a convicted felon working for them."

Silence. So much silence.

What am I supposed to say to that? I don't have to worry for long because he's out of the truck before I can think of a logical, uplifting reply. Especially because it's my father's fault he's a felon in the first place.

The restaurant is nice. Way nicer than I'd think Lilly would be comfortable with. But then again, she drinks now, so things have obviously changed. Justin and Lilly are already seated, smiling at our arrival.

"I went ahead and ordered some celebratory shots," Justin says, pushing the two stout glasses in our direction.

I sniff it and cringe. I can't recall the last time I did a shot of hard liquor.

Lilly smiles, a touch of a challenge beneath it. "Just drink it."

I discreetly double-check and make sure pigs aren't flying. But Lilly is encouraging me to drink, so I do.

Kip is a little more hesitant. I nudge him with my elbow and he swats it away, tipping the glass back and coughing as he swallows.

Justin pats him on the back. "Prison's made you soft."

Kip takes Justin's ribbing good-naturedly, giving a small laugh in reply. "I haven't had anything other than a few sips of pruno in four years."

Justin smiles, eyes crinkling at the corners at Kip's admission to sneaking alcohol into prison. They start debating the different ways it's made, and how people hide the contraband, Kip even mentioning some techniques that take Justin by surprise. Which is hard to do, considering Justin's pretty much seen it all, working alongside Lance for the DEA.

Justin had confided in Kip while he was undercover, admitting his plans to take my father down, and recruited his help to do so. I imagine it must have been hard for Kip to wrap his head around at the time, especially because Justin had already gotten involved with Lilly without her knowledge of his espionage. Lilly's protection has always been first priority for Kip, and I know he didn't make the choice to keep it from her lightly.

Justin orders another round of shots, but Lilly quickly pushes hers away when they arrive.

"I still have to work tomorrow."

"Work?" I ask. "You just graduated."

"I intern at a law office as a clerk, but I've already applied to a few places downtown."

"That sounds...boring as shit."

She laughs. "Yes, yes it is."

We order dinner and Lilly gives me a rundown on her life as a clerk, and how stressed she is over taking the Bar Exam. Justin intervenes to tell her she's going to do great, and she barely maintains her eye roll. He's obviously told her this entirely too many times already, but she humors him. It's so cute its barf worthy.

Kip, however, is quiet. He's always been that way. More comfortable in silence than chatter. Neither Justin nor Lilly find his silence out of the ordinary, but for some reason it doesn't sit well with me. There's something about the way he's sipping his drink, solely focused on his food, avoiding small talk like the plague.

Justin clears his throat and Kip finally lifts his face up from the plate in front of him.

"I, uh," Justin says, gathering our attention. "I have something I want to say."

Lilly's eyes move in on him, slowly, narrowing in suspicion.

He acts like he doesn't notice. "Lilly."

Just by the way he says her name, she knows. Whatever it is, she knows, and she starts shaking her head. Kip and I trade glances. Justin's eyes soften as he gently shoves his chair back. "It's going to happen eventually, whether you like it or not."

"No." She says it with as much authority as she can, voice firm.

"I know you didn't want this in a restaurant," he says. And slowly, almost in slow motion, he falls to one knee.

My eyes widen in horror, and I look to Kip for clues that he knew, but his unwavering attention on his sister gives nothing away.

"But I've been holding this ring in my pocket for weeks, waiting for the right time, and I can't seem to find it." His hands are steadier than I expect them to be as he opens the velvet box, showcasing a simple wedding band. "If you can forgive me for doing this in public, I can't imagine—"

Lilly cuts him off with a hand over his mouth. "Quit talking."

Everyone, including the wait staff and patrons, stills at Lilly's response. This is going bad, and it's going bad fast. Justin's eyes are wide with caution. He doesn't move or speak as Lilly slowly removes her shaky hand from his face.

"I can't hear a damn thing you're saying over the sound of my heart. You're going to have to tell me later."

He blinks, slowly. "Is that a yes?"

She nods, linking her hands behind his neck. "Yes."

Patrons clap, and out of obligation I clap along with them, pasting a smile on my face. I look over at Kip and he looks as uncomfortable as I am. The restaurant's cheers eventually taper off, and after everyone turns back to their dinner, Lilly slaps Justin across the back of the head when he eases into his seat.

He rubs the back of his head, but it does nothing to erase the smile on his face.

"Why does everything you do require a fucking audience?"

He cocks his head, kissing her. "But did you say no?"

She can't argue with that. Her stupid smile gives away how much she actually loves it.

And then reality sets in.

Lilly is getting married. Holy. Fucking. Shit. This is happening way too fast. But really, for them, this is years in the making. It only makes sense that this is the next step in life for them. This is what normal people do. They meet, fall in love, finish college, get married…have kids.

Suddenly the air is sparse. My gaze wanders to the vents in the ceiling, and I wonder if anything is actually being pumped through them, because I'm really freaking sweaty. I take a sip of my drink, hoping the alcohol gives me clarity. Why is my hand shaky? It's not like I'm the one who was just proposed to in front of an entire restaurant. Yet, it's my life that feels like it's running away from me.

"Kaley."

My attention snaps to Lilly. She's standing and waving a hand in front of my face.

"You're leaving?" I ask, my voice sounding small in my ears. I clear my throat.

"Yeah. It's getting kind of late."

I blink, trying to figure out how long I've been spaced for.

"Are you sure you're feeling okay?"

I half-nod, half-shake my head. I'm pretty sure I look demented. "Yeah, yeah. Of course."

"Okay," she draws out. "I guess I'll see you?"

I blink again, fully pulling myself out of my stupor. "Here," I say, retrieving my phone from my purse. "Give me your number."

She smiles, one of the rare ones that aren't just for show, and punches in her digits before calling herself. Hesitating for a moment, she hugs me, followed by Justin before they depart. Kip and I stare at each other in confused silence. My ears ring above the clatter of the restaurant.

"I should call a cab," I say, but my feet remain unmoving, ass glued to the chair.

Kip breaks from my stare as he motions to the waitress, "Two vodka sodas, please."

The waitress picks up our empty glasses. "Single or double."

I answer, "Double."

Kip doesn't speak while we wait for the waitress, both of us taking healthy doses of our drinks when they arrive. I'm not a big fan of vodka because it reminds me so much of Peter, but I push the thought away as I take another sip. There's an aura of melancholy surrounding Kip as he swirls the liquid in his glass.

"How much pruno did you *actually* drink during your sentence?"

Kip accepts my ice breaker, lips tipping up at the sides. "Not enough. Not nearly enough."

We share a smile and he tips the rest of the liquor back. Tonight is about to get real interesting.

Kip already has the truck door open before I'm able to park it in Lilly's driveway. I jump out, barely catching him as he stumbles onto the pavement. He pukes and it splatters everywhere. Groaning, I jump back as wetness hits my shins.

"How did I get this drunk?" he asks, surprisingly coherent.

"I lost count, but I'd say about ten, twelve, umpteen drinks ago."

I brace one of his arms around my shoulders, pulling as much of his weight as I can handle, laughing at the effort it takes for his feet to catch up.

"I'm glad you think thiss iss funny." His words finally reveal his state of intoxication, slurring at the ends.

"I'm just thinking about that old lady that swore you looked like her late husband Eddy."

He groans as I shift us through the front door. "She kept touching my face."

Figuring the couch is a much easier destination, I unhook his arm from around my neck, letting him fall back into the cushions. "It's only because you're so pinchable." I reenact the old lady's tone, pinching the apples of his cheeks.

He tries to swat my hands away, tilting him on his side from the effort. I pick up his legs and place them on the couch, positioning a throw pillow under his head. I stand, slightly breathless from the effort, and notice his eyes are already closed. I tip-toe back toward the stairs. The bathroom light is harsh as I blink against the monochromatic white tiles. The vomit covering my legs isn't visible, but I can feel the stickiness. The pipes screech when I turn the water on, and I hope Lilly and Justin are hardcore sleeping.

After they left, Kip and I moved from the restaurant to a bar down the block for happy hour. Quickly realizing Kip was on a mission to kill his liver, I quit drinking, letting him drown whatever he was attempting to kill. He's surprisingly good at pretending to be sober, though. I didn't realize exactly how drunk he was until he tried to pee in a mop bucket next to the bathrooms.

I find myself smiling under the spray of water. I had fun. We laughed. A lot. More than I can remember laughing in what feels like forever. He told me how Lilly only downloaded romance novels onto his Audible account the last six months of his sentence. He insists they're actually not that bad, and I told him about Mrs. Cecile who lives next me, and how the woman swears I'm the devil incarnate, always shoving pocket Bibles at me when I come in late.

Somewhere between the restaurant and here, he spoke more than I've heard him speak since I've known him. Kip has always held a label in my mind as Lilly's over-protective brother. But he's so much more than that. He's sarcastic and funny and kind of…sweet. I nearly choke on my own thoughts, unbelieving I even had them.

It's not until I'm toweling off that I realize I have no clothes to change into. I peak my head out of the bathroom and scurry across the hall to the spare bedroom Kip's been crashing in. I close the door and scour the bare drawers of Kip's dresser. There are only a couple pairs of jeans and T-shirts, maybe three pairs of underwear. This is what I get for being unprepared.

I laugh at myself as I drop the towel and shove my legs into a pair of boxers. My life is a giant test I've never studied for.

"What the fuck are you giggling at?"

I scream.

Kip has somehow made it up the stairs and into his bed while ungodly drunk. I hold the T-shirt up to my chest, trying to cover the important parts. I let out a relieved breath when I realize he's facing away from my direction.

"How'd you get up here by yourself?"

"Took a magic train." There's a moment of silence before he says, "How do you think? With my fucking legs."

He starts to move, and I finish getting dressed just in time for him to turn and face my direction.

"Did I miss seeing you naked?"

I smile. "It's not like you haven't seen it before." I walk toward him and start untying his dress shoes.

"How come I can't remember how many drinks I've had in the past five hours but can still count every single one of your freckles?"

He keeps trying to kick the heels of his shoes as I untie them, and I smack his leg for him to be still as I slip his feet free. I place a knee on the side of the bed, leaning over him to lift his head and situate a pillow beneath it.

"I think you're confused. I don't have any freckles."

"Six," he says, holding up five fingers. "You have six."

"Five?"

He nods and peels his eyes open, barely enough for them to go in-and-out of focus. "Plus one." We stare into each other's eyes for a few moments before he says, "My baby sister is getting married." His voice is a mixture of melancholy and amazement.

"I know," I say.

"He's a good guy."

"Supposedly."

He smiles, but it quickly wanes. "Do you ever feel worthless?"

The words slur as they escape his lips, almost like he didn't want to say them but they fell out of their own accord. He's so drunk that I doubt he'll remember this conversation in the morning, and it's to no surprise when his breaths fall into rhythm almost immediately.

I wait a few breaths before whispering, "All the time."

Standing, careful not to jostle him as I step back, I assess him. His dress shirt is unbuttoned down to his navel, stretched at the collar like he struggled to release himself from the wrinkled garment. He's a mess. A cute mess.

But never worthless.

five

I WAKE UP TO the sound of someone opening and closing cabinets in the kitchen. The flood of morning light is harsh as I slowly peel my eyes open, and dust motes swirl in the air as I sit up on the living room couch. I've lost track of how many times I've crashed on Lilly's couch. Different couch, different house, but same feeling. Almost a lifetime ago and yesterday all at the same time.

I find Kip in the kitchen fumbling around the cupboards and cooking utensils, a piece of bread clamped between his front teeth, an unrecognizable car part in his free hand. Black smudges of grease are streaked across every surface he's touched, not limited to his own face.

"Are you looking for your sanity? Because it disappeared sometime last night."

He jerks his head in my direction and bites off a piece of the bread. "Can you hold this, just like this, while I look for some vinegar?" He gestures to the part in his hand.

"Eh." I hesitate, noticing the atrocious amount of gunk covering it. "I'm not touching that."

Annoyed, he grasps my wrist and dumps the part into my hand, forcing me to catch it with my other. "Don't let it tip too far over or you'll only get more rust in the—you know what? Just don't move." He pauses, looking me over. "Are you wearing my clothes?"

I look down at the solid covered boxer-briefs and grey t-shirt. "It looks as though I am." I swear, his gaze lingers a second too long before he looks away. "How the hell are you up this early and not hung over?"

"My body is used to getting up early, and working out helps to release the toxins."

He's not lying. He's saturated in sweat. The bandana tied around his forehead catches my attention. Before prison, every memory I have of him includes a bandana tied like he has it now, folded to keep sweat from dripping into his eyes. I used to make fun of him for it, but now it's kind of comforting to know he's kept some of his idiosyncrasies. Prison might not have been as hard on him as Lilly feared it would be.

He slams a cabinet, cusses, and then angrily places his hands on his hips. "I have to go to the store."

"Okay," I say, unsure of what he needs from me.

"I'll be right back." And then he starts for the front door.

"Wait. What am I supposed to do with this?" I say, holding up the part.

He gives me a dumb look. "Hold it."

"Hold it until you get back?"

More dumb staring.

"You've lost your mind. I'm not holding this until you get back from whatever mission you're on."

He shrugs. "It's your car, do what you want. But if you let any more moisture get into that valve, you're going to have bigger problems than your car just making noise."

It hadn't occurred to me that he'd be working on my car. "Oh."

"Yeah, *oh*." Only he can say that with equal parts sarcasm and seriousness.

"Let me change and I'll come with you. I can pay for whatever you need."

I hand him back the part before he can protest and climb the stairs to Lilly's room. She's shorter and a little curvier than I am, but I find an appropriate pair of matching sweats to wear in public. When I finally meet Kip outside, I find my car is jacked up on bricks, and it looks entirely too hazardous for Kip to be working under. I say as much, but it's like the easygoing Kip from last night was nothing but a hazy dream. He's reverted back to the formidable, serious version of Kip, and I'm more disappointed by it than I should be. Capable, yet intimidating. Fun, but only secretly. All hell would break loose if anyone found out he actually smiles.

He hands me the part once I'm inside the cab of his truck. It's such a small part of a much larger machine. I'll never understand cars.

Or country music.

"We're not listening to this," I say.

He doesn't look at me. "Yes we are."

"You actually like this shit?"

"I actually like this shit," he confirms without a single drop of remorse.

It's shameful.

He turns up the volume.

Sitting in silence is one of my biggest pet peeves. Lulls in conversation irk me to the point I'll literally blabber about anything to avoid it, but I think this music might take the cake. Radio silence is better than country music any day.

"What do you need vinegar for?"

"Removes rust."

"Don't go into too much detail or anything," I say with as much sarcasm as I can muster.

He barely looks at me out of the corner of his eye, but I catch it, along with the effort he takes to conceal it—a hint of a smile. My arms get tired so I end up balancing the part between the crevice of my thighs, giving up trying to avoid the oil. It's like grease spreads. Every few minutes, I'll find a new spot it migrated to and no recollection of how it got there.

"We'll buy some Gojo."

"Some what?"

"For the oil," he says, nodding to my lap and all the surrounding areas of my thighs. "It's soap designed to remove grease from skin."

"That'll be great because I have work tonight."

This piques his interest. "Work?"

"Yeah," I draw out.

"You?" he says like he can't believe it. "You work?"

"Yes. I work."

"Where?"

"A sports bar on the East Bank."

He cocks his head in thought. "The place where the girls where underwear as shorts?"

"Hey, those shorts make me a killing in tips."

"Bet they do."

We arrive at a convenience and hardware store mixed into one, and I follow him up and down aisles as he fills the basket in his hands. Scrub pads, vinegar, beer, Gojo, rags, rubber O-rings, and other car related things that I've never seen before. We're in aisle nine before I can't handle another second of silent torture.

"So, you can fix my car?"

He turns a bottle over in his hands, inspecting the backside. "I'll do what I can from Lilly's, but it's not much. All of my tools were at the shop."

Toby's. The auto shop Kip helped run with his childhood best friend, Taylor, which doubled as an underground chop-shop. Last I heard the building and all of its contents were seized by the state and later put up for auction. It's also where everyone's lives changed because of the actions of my father. Effectively killing my small effort of conversation, we don't speak as we finish and checkout. It's when I'm climbing back into the cab of the truck, my reflection catches my attention in the side mirror.

"My face is covered in grease!"

Black smudges cover most of my nose and my forehead. Only my chin and right cheek is spared.

"People touch their face about three and a half times an hour," Kip's smile finally makes an appearance, tipping to one side. "I'd say you're slightly above average."

"You let me walk around a store looking like this?" I point to my face just in case he's confused.

He walks around the truck to get in and turns on the radio. "You shouldn't talk bad about my music."

I'm pretty sure I growl. We ride back to Lilly's in more insufferable silence with only banjos as a buffer. Every time he glances at me, his smile makes its appearance, and it's infuriatingly cute.

Once we're in the kitchen, he instructs me to wait, taking the stairs two at a time. "Try not to touch anything."

"Go fuck yourself."

Returning with a pillow, he sets it against the counter. "Here," he instructs. "Set it down, right in the middle."

"On a pillow?" I ask dubiously.

"Or hold it for the next few days. Your call."

I hold back an eye roll as he helps me situate the part in the best position. Both of us exhale a sigh of relief when it doesn't waver.

"Why didn't we do this before we went to the store?"

He shrugs. "I don't know. Why didn't you?"

I suck in my lip, shaking my head in annoyance. "You're a special kind of mean, you know that?"

He gives a half nod, not refuting it. "Let's get cleaned up and I'll drive you back to your apartment."

"So you can torture me with more music?"

He rolls his eyes, smiling down at his hands as he open up a tub of Gojo. "It's not that bad and you know it. In fact, I think you might actually like it."

"Sure. As much as I like bikini waxes."

He leans against the sink and positions me in front of him. "Stay still."

We're close. I can smell him and the hint of motor oil lingering between us. He dips his fingers in the tub of soap, rubbing them together as he brings his hand toward my face.

"Close your eyes."

"Not a chance."

"This stuff burns like hell if you get it in your eyes. I know it's hard for you to do what you're told, but try."

My heart trips.

Obeying, I let them fall shut. It's when I don't feel the touch of his hand that I open my eyes. "What?"

He doesn't answer. His eyes falter, but he tentatively brushes his thumb across the bridge of my nose. The touch is soft, barely there, gentle. He moves on to my forehead and then my right temple. His eyes follow the movement of his hand, but mine never leave his. He wanted me to close my eyes so I wouldn't see it.

To see the way his sole focus is on touching me.

It's wholly intimate in a way that makes me hold my breath. I don't dare inhale, afraid of taking in too much. He has to realize what he's doing, and he's doing a damn good job appearing innocent. I've spent the better half of my life perfecting seduction. Body language goes a long way, followed by verbal cues, laughter. But there's not a single drop of insincerity in the push of his fingers, or the steady rise and fall of his chest.

His eyes connect with mine momentarily as he turns toward the sink, allowing me a reprieve to breathe. Thoughts scatter through my mind as I watch him wet a cloth rag and wash his hands underneath the running water of the faucet. This is…this is strange. We're strange. What's happening is strange. It doesn't feel…fair.

I need to make a joke, right now before he turns back around.

"You're good with your hands," I say, internally cringing at the sexual innuendo.

He wrings out the cloth and turns back toward me, suppressing an eye roll at my attempt to lighten the mood. Swiping the cloth along the same path he'd taken before, he doesn't take the bait.

And the silence grows.

And so does the need to break it.

"Does this feel a little outré to you?"

This catches him off guard. "Oo-what?"

"Oo-trae," I sound out for him.

"If the meaning is as strange as it sounds, then yes, probably."

I smile and he smiles in return, meeting my eyes for a split second.

Living is so much easier when I can breathe.

After he finishes washing my face, he drives me home in record time, probably in a hurry to get away from my failed attempts to annoy him as much as country music annoys me. It's as we're pulling into the parking lot I'm reminded I'm going to have to walk to work.

I groan.

"What?"

"I forgot that I have to walk to work."

"Oh, the lack of car issue," he says. "It's…what? Forty blocks?"

"Thirty-five."

"Why don't you ride the bus?" He looks at my scowl and a smile forms. "Right. So no bus. What about a bike?"

"It hadn't occurred to me, but it wouldn't be a viable option considering I don't know how to ride one."

He blinks. "You don't know how to ride a bike?"

I shake my head, used to the surprised look I've gotten over the years when someone finds out. "I had a bike but no one ever taught me."

Try as I may have, I could never balance myself on my own. I lived with constant bruising on my shins as a preteen from where my feet would slip and the pedals would bang against my legs. Don't even get me started on the road rash.

"Okay, well, I guess I could hang out for a little while and give you a ride."

"You don't have to do that," I say out of politeness.

He already has his door open when he replies, "Stop pretending to be courteous. I owe you anyway."

"For what?"

"Taking care of me when I was sloppy drunk last night." He stretches and then lifts the hem of his shirt and sniffs it. "Can I take a shower?"

I laugh. "Yeah," I say, leading him up the stairs.

Mrs. Cecile's door opens a smidge, and I wave at her through the crack. "Hi, Mrs. Cecile. How are you today?"

She slams the door in answer. Kip gives me an amused look, and I shrug, not interested in explaining the effects of getting old. He has enough to worry about as it is. Kip steps into my tiny apartment and immediately his presence seems to dwarf everything in it. He takes two strides into the living room and perches on the arm of the couch.

"You don't make a habit of picking up after yourself, do you?"

There are dishes left on the counter and an empty bowl of cereal on the coffee table. A few clothes are strewn down the hallway from where I got home the night before, and the trashcan in the kitchen is starting to reach a dangerous height, near toppling.

"I'm sorry my cleaning habits aren't up to your par. I don't usually have people over." In fact, Kip is the first person who has stepped into my apartment except for Lance. Well, and Peter, but he owns the building.

"No, it's not that," he says, looking around, arms folded. "It's exactly how I imagined it'd be."

I start picking up the empty glasses and rearrange them in the sink to fit. "What the hell does that mean?"

He smiles. "You're a mess."

I stop, pivot, and glare in his direction. "I prefer the term organized chaos."

He right out laughs at my choice of description. I know I'm a tad delusional, but fuck him for thinking he has the right to classify me anyway.

"I didn't mean it in a bad way." He unfolds his arms, letting them rest between his legs. "It's who you are. You spit whatever pops into your mind out of your mouth, but you know when to shut up, too. You purposefully come up with ways to make people as uncomfortable as you are—"

"I am never uncomfortable."

"Just because you're not easily embarrassed doesn't mean you're not uncomfortable. It means you're shameless."

I can feel a twitch under my eye as he continues to talk.

"At the same time, you're not hateful; you just want to even the playing field."

I'm pretty sure I'm absolutely in reaching distance of a knife. "All I heard was you confessing that I get under your skin way more than you let on."

His lips barely hold place, showing his amusement. "Deflection."

I skirt past him, letting my fingers skim up his forearm. "The same could be said for you."

He looks down at where I've touched him, but doesn't counter. Feeling victorious, I pull a towel—one of the three I own that stays in constant rotation—out of the dryer, and lay it over the bathroom sink. Quickly, I do a double take to make sure my box of tampons is put away and I don't have any underwear draped over the shower rod. Kip's analytical side is out full force and the last thing I need is for him to psychoanalyze my personal hygiene.

"Shower's ready," I announce as I exit the hallway. "I'm probably going to make a sandwich for lunch. Want one?"

He doesn't move, and the smile that was on his face thirty seconds ago has disappeared. The awkwardness starts to feel like tiny pin pricks across my body, begging me to fill it. But I refuse, maintaining our eye contact, attempting to appear unfazed.

"I'd really appreciate that," he says, finally breaking the tension. "No mustard."

"Tons of mustard. Got it."

"You must really enjoy walking to work."

"Kidding," I say. "No mustard.

six

I CUSS, JAMMING MY key to the left a little to disengage it from its position in the lock. The sound of Mrs. Cecile's door creaking open adds to my agitation and I can't stop my eye roll.

"Are you ever going to call Tanya in the office to get that fixed?"

"I'll do it tomorrow," I reply, giving her the same excuse for the millionth time in the last four years.

She smacks her lips, making good use of them without her dentures. "I'm sure you won't, and I'll have to continue to endure listening to you bang away on that god forsaken lock until I die or lose the rest of my hearing."

"I'm real sorry 'bout that, Mrs. Cecile. I'll try to be quieter." Slamming the heal of my palm against the key one more time, the key finally pulls free, and I give Mrs. Cecile my sweetest smile as I turn into my apartment. "Goodnight!"

I hear her unappeased grunt as I close the door.

It's a little after midnight, and my body hates me. We had a large group of graduates come in last minute at work, and they stayed well after closing. After getting no sleep the night before with Kip, my body is refusing to stay upright any longer. I'm just glad a coworker agreed to drive out of her way to drop me off, or it would have been an hour walk home. I judge the distance to my bedroom and decide the couch is way closer. Grabbing the closest duvet, I drape it over the couch to save the cushions from smelling like stale grease in the morning. I'm in a strange place where tired meets drunk, and the world tilts on its axis when I lie down.

There's a knock at the door.

Peeling my eyes open, I check my phone still in my hand, and calculate I've actually been asleep for over an hour.

"Kaley."

I blink the sleep from my eyes, confusion setting in. It's been years since Peter's come to my apartment, and he's never come unannounced. I peek through the peephole to double-check and open the door once I confirm it is indeed him.

"Hey, is everything okay?"

Peter glances both ways before requesting to come in.

I step back. "Yeah, sorry," I say, closing the door behind him.

"Does the crazy lady still live next door?"

Mrs. Cecile has a habit of gossiping to Tanya in the office. She's part of the reason we decided to start meeting at Hudson's.

"Yes, but you should know this since you own the building," I smirk.

He takes in my apartment and shoves his hands into the pockets of his suit. "I'm sorry."

Wait...*what?*

"I'm sorry for leaving you like I did Tuesday. It wasn't fair for me to do that."

Struck dumb, I wait for him to continue.

"We've barely had any time together lately, but that's not your fault. Please forgive me for being such a jackass. You can't blame me for wanting to keep you to myself."

"Peter, it's fine. You work and have a family, I don't. It makes more sense for me to bend around your schedule than the other way around."

He closes the gap between us, and I let him pull me in. "This is why you and I work so well together. You get me. I need to pay more attention to you. Like how we used to be."

He's talking about the trips, the shopping, the times before our dates became confined to a hotel room. As twisted and fucked up as it sounds, we had a mutualistic relationship, but it was simple. We spent a lot of time together because it offered us something neither of us had. It offered me the financial stability to keep up with the lifestyle I was used to, and offered him an emotional connection that he had long ago lost with his wife. But oddly, I don't want those days back. I like our routine. The easy in-and-out of what to expect. No pun intended.

"You're overthinking this," I say, trying to put some affection behind my words. "I'm happy with the time I get with you. Any time is better than nothing."

He smiles, and it reminds me of the carefree person hiding beneath his harsh persona.

"Besides, you're almost too old to keep up."

He laughs and I can't stop my smile.

"I promise to make more of an effort," he says. "And I brought you a present. An apology, of sorts."

My smile slips as he pulls an envelope from his pocket, holding it out for me to take. I should turn it away, play nice after his apology. But it's right in front of me, and I can almost smell the sweet smell of fresh hundreds.

"I should have never put you in the predicament I did. Let me make it up to you." He shakes the envelope a little, tempting me. I take it absentmindedly.

He dips his head, placing his lips to mine, and all I can hear is the sound of the envelope crinkling between us as our bodies close the gap.

During the trial, my life started to change very drastically. Simultaneously, I lost the house, my car, and most of my possessions. Lance let me crash with him while I figured out what I was going to do. But even then, I wasn't all that worried. Losing everything didn't impact me like I thought it would. I was angry, sad, and confused, but not scared.

No, fear came later, when my bank account finally dipped to single digits and Lance was out of town working. I'd never had to worry a day in my life, then all of a sudden I didn't know how I was going to live, and it was terrifying. I realized fairly quickly, name brand clothes and jewelry don'tmean much when you're hungry.

When Peter stepped in, my worry slipped away in the blink of an eye. He immediately took care of everything I was scared of. He provided a place to live, money to live on, and then some. I wasn't just living comfortably, I was living like nothing had changed. It was easy to sink into him. I have always been attracted to men of all ages, and Peter is a very attractive businessman. There wasn't much to say no to, but I can't remember the last time I looked at a man and thought of him in any romantic sort of manner.

Until *Kip*. An image of the way he looked at me when we were in Lilly's kitchen flashes through my mind.

I'm no longer attracted to Peter. He's not really a bad guy. Okay, maybe a little, considering he's a shit husband, but he's just a typical asshole male: letting his penis do all the deciding. I've often wondered if there are other women besides me. Especially once he started limiting our dates to two nights a week, but I eventually realized how much freedom it awarded me. I have a job I like, binge watch as many Netflix shows as I want, and I only have to answer to myself. I like what I have going on, and the last thing I need is someone coming in and disrupting it.

Peter pulls my shirt over my head and I push all my thoughts aside. I feel lighter as I shove the envelope of bills into my purse on the counter, giggling when he runs his scruff up the side of my neck.

seven

"HELLO?"

"Yo, it's Kaley."

There's a beat over the phone before Lilly replies. "Yo'."

Might as well jump in head first. "How's life with that ring on your finger? Not getting too heavy, is it?"

"You know what?"

The way she says it makes me smile. "What?"

"It's kind of annoying. It's top-heavy, so it's always flipping upside down, and it clinks against my coffee cup every time I pick it up. Not to mention the freaking attention you get when someone sees it. Glenda from accounting basically screamed at me when she saw it. Screamed like she saw Jesus, I swear."

"Wow, the engaged life is not for you."

She slips out a laugh. "I'm just so fucking tired."

"Why don't you come over tomorrow? We can cook something and drink wine and watch some of those stupid car shows you love."

A long pause stretches over the phone line. "That actually sounds amazing. Since when do you cook?"

"I don't. We can figure it out together."

"Or order pizza."

"No, we're going to make a valiant effort."

I can almost hear her eyes roll. "Fine. I can make a mean chicken caprese."

"Now we're talking."

We agree on a time and I text her my address before we hang up. It's then I remember I don't have any groceries and no car to go grab some. I could call in for a delivery, but the upcharge is ridiculous. I could maybe swing it if I stiffed the delivery guy of a tip, but that would make me a hypocritical asshole.

My stomach sinks when there's a knock at my door. I check the peephole, expecting Peter, but am shocked to find Kip standing there instead. He's looking straight at the viewer, and I smile when he makes a hurrying motion with his hand.

When I open the door, he says, "Thought you were just going to stare at me all day."

"What's with the bike?" I ask, gesturing to a silver mountain bike propped next to my door.

"You said you never had anyone teach you." He says it like it explains everything.

"So you bought me a bike?"

He looks at me like I'm slow. "Yes."

I lean a hip against the doorframe. "This doesn't seem weird to you?"

"You mean outré? No.

"You Googled it?"

"I did," he says. "But I have some bad news."

I guess. "My car is kaput."

He confirms my suspicions by nodding, handing me a folded check. "I was able to get a pretty good deal for the parts."

I sigh. "Well, thank you for trying." I move to let him in.

"I'll wait right here while you go get dressed."

"Wait," I say. "We're doing this right now?"

"Right now," he confirms.

"Like, right now?" I emphasize my point by pointing to the floor.

"Hurry, we don't have all day."

"I have things to do."

"Like what? Wash your hair?"

Insulted, I pull a few strands of hair from my ponytail and sniff it. "No, asshole, I need to buy groceries. Lilly is coming over for dinner."

"Really?" This makes him happy. "That's great. We can stop by the grocery store on the way back."

It does solve my existential crisis of never being prepared. Without replying, I close the door on his stupid face, smiling at the fact I'm on the right side of the door swing this time. Skipping to my bedroom, it occurs to me I'm way more excited about this than I should be. Like, way too happy to be going anywhere with Kip. But I reconcile it's because I might finally learn to do something I've never been able to master.

My excitement quickly deflates after we've been at the park for thirty minutes and all I've succeeded in doing is falling. A lot. Eleven times I've hit pavement. One scraped elbow and a little blood later, I'm already over bike riding and ready to chunk the entire thing into the garbage bin.

"Kip, there's no way to stay balanced and push the pedals at the same time."

A smattering of children pass by, pedaling at super-speeds, and I've never wanted to drop-kick a kid like I have today. It's the fifth time they've passed us.

"I never realized how uncoordinated you are until now," Kip says, maintaining hold of the bike while I straddle it.

"Don't rub it in."

"Stop being so scared."

"I'm sorry," I say, holding up my elbow and pointing to it. "Did you miss me barely escaping my death? It's like I've put my arm through a cheese grater."

"That's a scratch, Kaley."

"It's a gaping wound."

Exasperated, he sighs. "Let's try one more time and then we can call it a day."

"Kip, I'm more of a luxury car girl anyway. It's fine. Really."

Breathing deep, he stands with his hands on his hips. "I didn't ask if you were fine. I said, one more time." His commanding nature is annoying and weirdly sexy at the same time.

I grunt, agitated with him and my own wayward thoughts. Bracing one foot on a pedal, I prepare to push off with my other foot, hoping I can magically find the spare pedal once I start rolling forward.

"Wait," Kip says, halting my actions. "Go ahead and place both feet on the pedals. I'll hold the bike upright."

"If you let me fall, I swear on my nicest—"

He interrupts me. "I'm not going to let you fall. Start pedaling when I let go."

"You're going to let me go?"

He doesn't give me a chance to question him further, already propelling me forward and I'm forced to match his speed with my legs. I'm absolutely certain this is going to end in catastrophe. He shouts for me to pedal a split second before he lets go of the bike, and I'm shooting forward without his help. I'm upright and I'm pedaling and the wind is in my hair…and I'm riding a bicycle. The absence of the pounding in my chest is so freeing. I have no heart, no pulse.

"I'm riding a bike!"

Almost immediately as the words fly from my mouth, the front tire slips off the path and I dart into the grass. I lose balance, landing on my side, trapped beneath the medal of the bike.

Kip jogs over to me. "You did it." He smiles, his face coming into view as he leans over me.

"I did it," I reiterate.

We hold each other's smile for a few beats until it starts to feel awkward, and I laugh to break the moment. Picking up the bike, he helps me to my feet.

"We can go now, if you like?"

"We can't leave now," I say through my excited breaths. "We just got started."

He laughs. "Whatever you say."

I skip to the path, not waiting for him to catch up, too excited to walk at his slow pace.

A kid in the little-league bike gang passes by. "'Bout time, lady."

I start to lift my hand to flip him off when I remind myself I'm in a public park.

Kip finally reaches me, shaking his head as he holds the bike up for me to mount. "You're irrationally angry with an eight-year-old."

"They're riding around on their condescending, rolling thrones of shame, mocking me."

"You just made all of that up in your head."

At the most opportune time, a kid happens to pass by and yells, "Try not to stop with your face next time."

Kip laughs and I shove his shoulder, but I can't stop my laugh, too.

"Are you sure you want to go again?" Kip asks.

"Yes," I say, straddling the bike. "I can't let them see my weakness."

He shakes his head, finally getting used to my commentary. We do a repeat performance, but this time I manage to stop by clumsily walking the bike to a halt. It wasn't flawless, but it was better, and no less exhilarating than the first time.

We practice kicking off on my own, but it proves to be the hardest part. Instead of successfully pushing forward, I keep missing the pedals. Kip stays near, catching me when I slip. His hands land on my hips, near my ribs, close to my breasts, and it creates a swimming sensation in my head. Over and over again it's the same motions, and I can't tell if I'm even falling on accident anymore.

"You're distracting me."

Kip gives me a look. "How?"

"You're breathing down my neck."

I've felt every single breath he's taken while hovering over me for the past thirty minutes.

"Sorry," he says, baffled, backing up another step. "I was just trying to keep you upright."

I heave a sigh, aggravated with myself more than him. "I know."

This is torturous. I don't know what's wrong with me. I'm flustered with a dozen other emotions I can't seem to pinpoint.

"Can we take a break?"

"Fine," he concedes. "I packed a lunch. Maybe we can try again once you're done freaking out about whatever you're freaking out about."

He runs to the truck and comes back with a blanket and a lunchbox, spreading everything out under the shade of a nearby oak tree. Suddenly, bike riding seems less intimate than having a picnic in the park. I look around, noting the other couples enjoying the spring air, knowing Kip and I look like one of them. He sets up a portable radio as I dish out the contents of the lunchbox, handing him the sandwich labeled with no mustard.

"More musical stylings from a donkey banging on banjos today?"

He unwraps his sandwich and takes a bite, chewing a few times, and I'm mesmerized by the way his jaw clenches with the motion. "Something needs to drown out the silence so you don't talk your lips off."

It takes a moment, but I start to feel the ends of my mouth inch upwards. "I can't help it."

His smile mirrors mine as he looks at me. "I know."

He knows.

We eat our lunch in relative comfort, and I feel like a dumbass for freaking out about Kip's carbon dioxide landing on me. He's Kip: Lilly's brother. And I'm Kaley: not the type to come unglued because of a boy. Never. Not in high school, not in college, not anytime I can remember. I've never understood it.

Sex? Hell yes. But relationships? Ehhh.

I tried them a few times in high school, once in college, and they were more work than people let on. There's so much stress that comes with them. Having to explain what I'm doing, when, and why to someone is dumb on so many levels. It's constantly monitoring someone else's feelings and desires, more than my own, and it's a chore. I always failed at putting someone else first. Every relationship I've had has ended because of something I did, and I eventually decided relationships aren't for me. If sex and relationships were synonymous, there's no doubt I'd be celibate.

Kip lays back, arms crossed behind his head, eyes closed against the harsh sunlight peeking through the gaps in the tree limbs. He's beautiful, I'll give him that. A man in every sense. His features are harsh and straight. From the lines of his lips, to the line of muscles under his khaki shorts and cotton T-shirt, his body is all harsh planes and divots. There's nothing soft or feminine about him.

It's different from any man I can recall being with. He's stronger, more confident than the boys in high school and college, and harsher, more rugged than the men I've been with at Hudson's. I've been with a wide variety of men, but somehow a man like Kip must have fallen through the cracks. It makes me wonder…

"Have you ever wanted to kiss someone just to see what it would be like?"

Kip opens one eye and looks at me, squinting against the light. "What?"

I curl my legs under me and lean over him so my form blocks the sun. "We've known each other for so long. You've never thought about it?"

This really gets his attention, worthy of opening both eyes now. "No," he says.

"Don't lie. Not even once?"

He looks at me, gauging my seriousness, coming to a conclusion before reclosing his eyes. "No."

"Oh, come on," I say, leaning a little bit closer. "Not even a single little kiss on the lips?"

"Kaley, I'm not kissing you."

"I'm asking if you've ever thought about it."

He opens his eyes again. "Where is this coming from?"

I shrug, pretending nonchalance. "Curiosity."

He narrows his eyes. "You're a bad liar."

"No I'm not."

"Yes you are."

"If that was true—which it's not—how have I gotten away with so much shit for all my life?"

"You're pretty," he says, matter-of-fact. "People believe you because they want to believe you, not because it's logical."

I lick my lips, drawing his attention to where I want it. "So you think I'm pretty?"

He rolls his eyes and leans on one elbow. "If I kiss you, will you shut up?"

I somehow manage to hold back my smile. "Kiss me and find out."

"Kaley," he says, voice deep in admonishment.

"Fine," I agree. "I'll zip it."

Scrubbing his hand over his face, he releases a breath. His eyes jump from my eyes to my mouth, and mine follow the same path, trying to keep up with his thoughts running rampant across his features. Normally, I'd make the first move. I don't like hesitation. It only breeds insecurity. But I have a feeling Kip needs to feel like he has control of this situation.

With one last shake of his head, he leans forward, barely grazing his lips against mine. They touch, separating for a split second before making full contact as he breathes into me. My lungs fill as his empty. He's breathing when it feels like I can't. It takes a moment, but slowly, he moves his lips over mine, and we're actually kissing.

My lungs burn as I force air in and out of them.

Finally gaining a sense of self-awareness, I open my mouth wider, driving our kiss to deepen. He follows me without hesitation, teasing with a slip of his tongue against mine, before taking it away. I push, wanting it again, this time my tongue searching for his.

The moderation of our movements disappears. Gripping the back of my neck, he holds me still as he presses his mouth harder against mine. It's rough, but followed with gentleness. His tongue delves in to feel, only to retreat. Lips cover mine fiercely, only to pull back a moment later. I'm no longer leading, only following…accepting.

When he finally pulls away, we're both breathing hard, eyes bleary as we make eye contact.

That was...

He licks his lips.

…the furthest thing from outré.

Releasing his hold on the back of my neck, he looks almost weary. Afraid, even. It's kind of awkward, but equally mesmerizing at the same time.

"You—"

"Nope," he says, cutting my words off. "No talking."

I laugh and he resumes his position, eyes closed. Lying back, I bask in his kiss. My body is warm and light, everything the sun supplies, but in the form of a kiss. He doesn't know it, but that is most definitely, absolutely fucking happening again. I turn my head to the side and catch him staring at me. If my smile wasn't obvious enough, it reaches ostentatious proportions when my eyes meet his. His face morphs from minor confusion, to maybe interest, a slight smile appearing before it disappears.

It's progress. Progress I intend to exploit.

He has no idea.

We eventually get sick of the sun and venture into the shade to try my luck at bike riding once more, and it goes much like the last time. My shins are blotted with dark shades of blues and yellows from the pedals nailing them every time my feet slip. It reminds me of my childhood, and it brings on a weird sense of sadness.

Kip catches on to my mood, because he pushes the sweaty hairs stuck to my forehead back as we take a water break. "You'll get it eventually."

I don't reply.

"Once you do, you'll never know what it's like not to ride again. There's nothing more universal than knowing how to ride a bike. You can't forget it."

I recap the bottle, squinting up at him. "When was the last time you've ridden one?"

He clicks his tongue. "Close to ten years, I suppose."

"How do you know you can still ride one if you haven't done it in so long?"

He smiles but doesn't look away when he says, "Because it's like kissing. You just know what to do."

And I'm reminded that I'm probably, most definitely, the first girl he's kissed since being released from prison. This shouldn't make me this happy. Merely an hour ago we were kissing, and it's as if I've gotten to glimpse into a part of Kip that's hidden. Almost like he's given it to me.

"Are you listening to me?"

I refocus my attention. "Uh, yeah."

"What did I just say?"

"That I have no balance and should give up."

He breathes out through his nose. "Try to kick off by yourself."

Beyond motivated and too distracted, it's not surprising when I miss the pedal. I cuss, checking for blood.

73

"I know what's wrong," Kip says.

"Oh, really? Please enlighten me."

"You're pushing off with your toes. Don't do that." He bends down, pressing my foot flat against the pedal. "Plant your foot, don't toe it."

"That feels weird."

"I promise it won't feel as weird when you do it."

"Kip—"

"One last time," he says. "I'll let you give up if you want to quit."

I place one foot flat on the pedal, finding one last ounce of effort, letting my weight push the bike forward. My body rises and falls with the rotation, and I lift my other foot to find the opposite pedal before I stall. I'm prepared to feel the familiar blow of the pedal when I bring my weight down again, but am shocked when my foot meets resistance. Taking a chance, I glance down and confirm my foot is correctly positioned on the opposite pedal.

I ride a few more feet before stopping, staring down at the handle. For some reason, I find myself choking back an emotion I can't find. This should be joyous. I should be jumping up and down in excitement. At the age of twenty-six, I've finally learned how to ride a bike.

But that's not what I feel like doing.

"It's not a big deal," Kip says, somehow finding words for me.

My voice is shallow when I speak. "I never said it was."

He tilts his head, his lips thinning in the process. "You don't have to. It's written all over your face."

I clear my throat, pushing past the ache lodged there, meeting his stare. "Thank you."

Pushing my ponytail over my shoulder, he allows his fingers to linger on the soft spot where my shoulder and neck meets. "This was all you."

My heart swells along with my lungs, and it's like they're fighting for space in my chest. I'm not sure which will win. I let out a shaky smile, past the point of pretending I'm not holding back tears. "I am pretty damn awesome."

He laughs. "Let's go again."

And just like Kip said, from that point on it's like I didn't ever know how not to ride a bike. I'm still wobbly at times, and stopping still proves to be challenging, but Kip lets me ride around the park to my heart's content. I even give one of the little shits a high-five in passing—that's how great of a mood I'm in when we leave.

Kip lifts my bike into the bed of his truck and I get in. There's a manila folder wedged behind the bench seat I hadn't noticed before and I pull it free, flipping through the copies of his resume. Kip catches me holding it and he takes it from my hands, shoving the folder into the glove compartment.

"Still no luck?"

He shakes his head. "If worse comes to worst, I have a friend who owns a shop on the east bank. It's nice, but he doesn't have any managerial positions open, and I'm too experienced to be a service technician."

"Like changing oil and tire rotations?"

"Yeah. I don't mind working on the floor, but I know I'm worth more."

"How many places have you applied?"

"A few," he answers vaguely.

Kip helped run Tobey's with his best friend, Taylor, after Taylor's dad passed away. And I think Kip was the one to legitimately keep the place afloat.

"Why don't you just open your own shop?"

He tilts his head in thought. "I've considered it."

When he doesn't continue, I say, "And?"

He shrugs. "I don't know. There's so much time and money involved, not to mention the years it takes to build a good clientele. The first few years are always touch and go. I don't need another failure under my belt."

"But you know how to do it. You've done this since you were a teenager. If anyone can make it happen, it's you."

His smile tips up to one side. "You think?" he says with just a touch of insecurity.

"I don't see why not."

He tilts his head in thought.

"Just think about it, okay?"

His chest rises and falls. He's a man of few words, but I'm finding that Kip talks a lot with his body. He'll tell you almost everything if you pay attention.

"And you're not, you know?"

"What?" he asks, finally looking at me.

"A failure."

eight

"THIS IS SOME SHODDY wine," Lilly says, taking another sip.

"Hey, it's free. Enjoy it for what it is."

We've finished prepping dinner and have thirty minutes to kill while we wait for it in the oven. From the minute Lilly stepped through my door, she's asked all the questions most people would deem inappropriate, insulted my job, and insisted on helping me organize my ridiculous amount of clutter.

God, I've missed her.

Lilly and my relationship always came easy to us. We never set unreasonable expectations for our friendship, or try to validate one another, and I've never felt like I had to walk on eggshells around her. It's nice to know that didn't disappear.

"So," I say, twirling the wine glass in my hand. "Have you gotten any replies on your applications?"

She nods, wincing through a sip of wine. "I've gotten a few, but not from the one I've had my eye on."

"Family law, right? That's what you want to specialize in?"

"Yeah, how'd you know?"

"Kip told me."

She raises her chin, assessing the source of information before nodding. "Yeah, that's the plan," she says. "Either way, we'll have to move to the city."

"You don't want to?"

She shrugs. "Too many memories, maybe? I don't know. I like being away from it all."

"Isn't Justin from the middle of nowhere? Like Backwoods, Virginia or something?"

She snorts. "Sort of, but he's fine with living wherever."

"He'll go where you go."

She doesn't object, just smiles and takes another sip.

"What's he doing now? You know, since he was let go from the agency?" *For spoiling the DEA's investigation against my father to save your life.*

"He's been working as a security manager at a hotel in the city."

"Catching more bad guys," I say, not at all surprised.

"Pretty much," she says, pausing a moment before continuing. "If I tell you something, promise to keep it a secret?"

"Who would I tell anyway?"

She cocks an eyebrow. "My brother?"

Befuddled, I scrunch up my nose. "Why would I tell your brother?"

"We're going to act like you two didn't stay out all night after my graduation? Or went on a date yesterday?"

"Whoa, hold up. It was not a date."

"So you aren't screwing my brother?"

I laugh, half amused and half horrified. "No way. Why would you think that?"

"Kaley," she says. "Name a guy that you've been friends with and didn't sleep with."

I stall and take a drink of wine, glancing at the timer on the oven. *Damn it.* Ten more minutes. "I might have loads of new guy friends you don't know about who are completely platonic."

She gives me a look.

"Okay, I don't, but I don't even classify Kip and me as friends. He's your brother." It's a reminder for me as much as it is for her.

After a second, she sighs. "I'm probably projecting. I didn't realize how much he isolated himself until after he went to prison. I was literally the only person connected to him from the outside world. I don't..." Her face morphs into a look of disgust as she spits out the next words. "I don't even know how long it's been since he's been with someone."

I laugh at her discomfort. "I doubt he'd tell you if he had."

"And now I have Justin..." She takes a moment and stares at the ring on her finger.

"You want him to have what you have, relationship wise."

"Yeah," she breathes out, a small smile in place. "That's not so wrong, is it?"

"There's no way Kip would blame you for that."

"I have a friend I could try to set him up with."

"Eh, he might blame you for *that*."

She twirls her ring, lost in thought. "I get the feeling he kind of resents Justin."

"For the whole undercover cop thing?"

"No," she says. "For taking his place."

We both let that sink in, quiet in our own thoughts. Kip has spent his entire life taking care of Lilly, and now she doesn't need him anymore. His drunken words float back to me. *Do you ever feel worthless?* A new level of emotion settles in my stomach, and I don't like it.

"Back to your secret," I say. "Are you pregnant?"

"Shut your mouth, right the fuck now." She points at me and I pretend to zip my lips. "I convinced Justin to elope with me in Vegas instead of having a traditional wedding."

"You can't *not* have a wedding."

"I don't want a wedding and Justin doesn't care as long as I don't back out."

"But…" I say, mildly outraged by her proposal. "What about the dress and walking down the aisle and the flowers and the—" I look up at her incredulous face and suddenly remember who I'm talking to. "Okay, so no big wedding," I say, deflating.

"Whoever wants to come is more than welcome, but we don't want to make a big deal out of it."

"Kip's okay with it?"

"He doesn't know yet." She's a little less affirmative when she says, "I want him to get settled before we do anything."

I think about mentioning Kip's struggle trying to find a job, but stop myself. Kip is protective of Lilly, and there's a good chance he doesn't want to burden her. He's always been like that—doing whatever needs to be done to make sure life was easy for her. Maybe it's time for someone to look out for him instead.

"You're home super late," Kip says, scaring the hell out of me as he leans against my apartment door. "Or early, depending on how you look at it."

It is early—seven in the morning early—and I'm arriving home after spending the night with Peter. While finding Kip outside my door is intriguing, there's absolutely no way to successfully lie about coming home this early and looking like an expensive hooker.

"And you're here because…"

"I have a couple of interviews later today. I figured we could swing by the park early."

I unlock my door and Kip follows me in. "You could have texted and checked if I was busy."

"I assumed you'd be home sleeping." He uses the heel of his shoe to kick the door shut. "And I don't have your number."

Last night was agonizingly long, and I'm surviving on only a few hours of sleep, but the idea of spending the day with Kip wakes me up more than the cup of coffee I drank back at the hotel. "Is it okay if I take a shower first?" I say, already unzipping the side of my dress. I look over my shoulder and find him following the movement with his eyes.

He closes his eyes a moment before looking away. "That's fine. I haven't had breakfast yet. Is it okay if I make something to eat?"

"Only if you make something for me while you're at it."

"How do you like your eggs?"

"Cooked."

Kip catching me mid Walk of Shame might be the first time I've ever actually felt shame for it. It's not that I think Kip is really disappointed—he has a pretty good grasp of who I am—but maybe that *I'm* disappointed in myself. Or at least in the face of Kip, I am. It irks me.

I take a quick shower, throwing my hair in a bun after I do my best to towel-dry it. There's a plate of scrambled eggs and toast waiting for me when I walk into the kitchen and Kip is already elbow-deep in washing the dishes.

"Yum, this looks amazing." I grab a bottle of grape jelly from the fridge and squirt it over my entire plate. Kip looks over at me in disgust and I smile around a large bite. "You didn't have to do the dishes."

He rinses the mug out and places it in the drying rack. "Gave me something to do while I waited."

I look around my apartment and nearly choke on my food as I begin to notice things out of place. The duvet is folded and lying across the back of the couch, the dishes on the coffee table are absent, the rug isn't skewed like it usually is, and…is the shelf above my TV dusted?

My eyes fixate on the laundry basket beside the couch. "You folded my clothes?"

His back is to me, but I see him squeeze out the sponge and place it next to the sink. "Is that okay?"

"You can't just fold my clothes, Kip."

"Why not," he says, turning around. He dries his hands on a dishtowel.

"It's like an invasion of privacy." A thought dawns on me, and my voice drops as I say, "Did you touch my underwear?"

He smiles. "You mean the black lacy underwear with the little pink bows?"

I say his name in warning.

"No, I didn't touch them. I left them in the bottom of the basket where I found them."

I set down my fork as calmly as I can and level him with a stare. "We need to set up some boundaries since you obviously don't have any idea what they are."

He points at his chest in question. "*Me*?"

"Yes, you. Peeking at my underwear while I'm in the shower."

"Speak for yourself. You were *wearing* my underwear without my permission."

"Completely irrelevant to this conversation."

"How?"

I take a moment to redirect the conversation. "Look, I totally understand why you might be mad about the whole walking in on you naked issue, but I promise you have nothing to be embarrassed about."

"What are you talk—"

"It was a freak accident, won't happen again."

"If anyone should be embarrassed, it's you."

"Really?" I lift an eyebrow. "Then why are you sniffing my underwear?"

I know Kip didn't actually hold my underwear to his nose and take a big whiff, but his lack of remorse for something he didn't do is annoying. He stands tall, unflinching as he decides his next course of action. Walking around the counter and into the living room, he digs the pair of said underwear out of the bottom of the basket.

"If I'm going to be deemed a pervert, I might as well own it."

Stalking towards me, he places an arm on one side of me, crowding my space. Then, like a strange figment of my imagination, he holds the material up to his face, and *sniffs it.* Nothing shocks me, but Kip sniffing my underwear is at the top of the list of things I never thought I would witness.

He hums, eyes closed as he concentrates. "Smells floral, like you've been sitting on a bed of…lavender? Lilac? Or is it fabric softener?"

"You've lost it," I say, finding my voice.

He opens his eyes, looking up at me. "I'm only demonstrating what I did while you were in the shower."

"Stop it right now."

He drops the material on the counter, now placing both hands against the ledge as he corners me on the stool. A satisfied smirk graces his face, and I fail at staring anywhere but at his mouth. "You know what I think," he says, voice rough.

"What?" My voice is small, shaky, completely out of my element with this side of Kip.

"You like the idea of me seeing your underwear, maybe even you in your underwear. And instead of trying to figure out why, you're projecting all those confused feelings onto me."

I didn't think it was possible, but his words are even more shocking than him sniffing my underwear. "You wish."

He cocks his head to the side. "Do I?"

We're still watching each other, refusing to break when our lips meet. I don't know who makes the move, or if it's both of us. But he pulls away before we actually kiss. His condescending smirk tells me everything I need to know.

"And you call me shameless," I say.

He shakes his head, reluctantly letting his smile remain in place. "Finish eating so we can go. We're on a schedule today."

I replay the argument in my head as I shovel the rest of my breakfast into my mouth. I expect the awkward to grow, manifest the silence until I admit every bad—or good, depending on how you look at it—thought I've had about him over the past few days. How I've replayed our kiss over and over and how I want to do it again. Worst of all, scariest of all, I'm scared to admit how I pretended I was with him last night instead of Peter.

But amazingly, Kip does a damn good job of letting everything slide back into place. Discreetly, I watch him as he moves through the apartment, putting everything in order, even putting away the clothes he folded—my underwear included—before we leave.

Something manifests inside me, something addicting. Something I don't want to stop, unsure I even could if I tried.

nine

"CAN I BUY YOU a drink?"

Kaley tilts her head toward Senator Landry's surprise appearance as he takes the seat near her. "I'll just go ahead and take the cash."

He smiles what looks like a real, genuine smile as he orders her a drink anyway. It's the very same smile that convinced the majority of his favoring party in his direction, winning him the election and the popular vote by a landslide. Kaley did her research, but she knows what's concealed underneath his squeaky clean behavior. Senator Landry is nothing but deceit, and he's very, very good at hiding it.

"Don't tell me Mr. Baranski isn't holding up his end of the deal," he smarts. "I know how much it bothers you to be left empty handed."

Kaley hums around her fresh glass of wine, nodding at Mondo as he moves on to the next customer to let him know she's okay with Landry's presence. "Do you need something," she asks, cutting to the point. She doesn't find his small talk entertaining.

"Only checking in, making sure you're withholding your end of the bargain."

"A bargain implies that I have a choice in the matter."

"Of course you do," he says, moving a little closer, just close enough she can smell the alcohol on his breath. "You have a multitude of choices."

"All in your favor."

"In our favor, if everything works out."

"One can only hope."

"I suppose I should move along. I'd hate for your banker to realize you've been giving away what's his." He stands, but before retreating, he leans one step closer. "For free," he whispers, a devilish smile playing on his lips. Satisfied with himself, he leaves.

Kaley's hands shake as she forces down another swallow of wine, aching to appear unfazed by Landry. Other than her father, she can't remember the last time she's hated a man so much. They're the type of men who only use their power to further their own agendas, leaving nothing but broken people in their wakes. The only silver lining Kaley holds on to is that all powerful men must die eventually.

The spot Landry vacated fills, and she's never been happier to have Peter by her side.

"I'm sorry I'm late. I had some business to take care of," he says, kissing her cheek.

"It's okay." She looks him over, noticing the tint of red around his eyes. Placing a hand against his cheek, she asks, "Are you feeling alright?"

He takes a healthy dose of the drink Mondo just poured for him, leaning slightly into Kaley's hand as he swallows. "I have a client who's intent on ruining his own case. He refuses to listen or keep his mouth shut to the press." He takes another gulp of vodka.

Kaley crosses her legs, settling in to talk. "The Nathanial Lacassan case?"

He sucks on his front teeth, nodding. "For being the son of a clergyman, he is an entitled little shit."

Kaley cocks her head in agreement. Peter is known for taking on high-profile cases, and Nathanial is about as high profile as it gets. He's about to go on trial for second-degree murder of a masseuse. His defense is shaky, at best, and Nathanial is digging his own grave with every tweet, meme, and douchebag picture of him in a lambo. The public is much more lenient with those who show remorse. Kaley's mood plummets at the thought of Peter defending him. Defense attorneys are especially slimy because they fight to keep power-hungry narcissists like Nathanial out of jail.

"Want to head to the room?" Peter says, breaking her from her thoughts.

"Sure."

And just like that, Peter drops the conversation, settling between her legs the second they enter the hotel room. Kaley doesn't even attempt to stop her thoughts when they turn to Kip, imaging it's his lips and body on her instead of Peter's. She keeps her eyes closed, not wanting to break the façade, fairly sure it's the only way she manages to get through the night with her sanity.

ten

"WHY ARE WE HERE?"

"To ride bikes." Kip retrieves an old, battered bike from the bed of his truck, followed by mine.

"What dumpster did you steal that thing from?"

He smiles. "I actually stole it from a mail carrier years ago. It's a beater, but a good tune-up goes a long way." Pulling a bandana out of his pocket, he ties it around his forehead, looking up at me from beneath his lashes. "Are you going to stand there all day?"

"We're going into that?" I say, pointing toward the opening of the bike trail.

"The park is packed on Sundays, and I know how much you hate being shown up by little kids. I figured this would be a good alternative."

A map of the bike route is outlined on the trail sign. Its length and winding turns are ominously situated next to an animal crossing sign that depicts the possible run-in with a deer, snake, and/or squirrel.

"Do you happen to have a hatchet to protect us from rabid animals in your backpack?"

He laughs as he tightens the straps. "Don't worry. Your piercing voice is enough to scare them away."

I give him a dry look. "I'm not ready for this."

He rolls his eyes. "You've been riding a bike to work, in the city, weaving in and out of traffic without dying all week. You're ready."

"I've had a few close calls," I protest.

"And yet, you're still alive." When I make no move to mount my bike, he sighs. "This is a kiddie trail. It's mostly flat and wide enough to not have to worry about mowing anyone down."

Reluctantly, I swing my leg over the bike and kick the stand up. "If I die—"

"I'll sleep peacefully knowing I will never hear your voice again."

"Whatever. We both know you dream about me."

"And in my dreams, I successfully hide your body." He smiles and starts for the trailhead.

Deciding my chance of survival is better in numbers, I reluctantly follow. It's noticeably cooler under the protection of the canopy of trees, and the air reeks of pine and dirt. Other than the sound of our tires on the ground and a few birds, it's eerily quiet. Kip glances over his shoulder, giving me a quick smile. Goosebumps leap across my skin. I can't tell if it's because of how peaceful the trail is, or the way Kip's smile reaches his ears, causing the outer corners of his eyes to crinkle just the slightest bit. A breeze kicks up, eliciting another round of bumps, and I surmise it's definitely the nature.

We do end up passing a few hikers and fellow bikers, but for the majority of the ride the trail is empty. What Kip failed to mention is that the entire trail is on a slight incline. Kip makes a motion with his hand and points toward a hill in front of us. It doesn't look incredibly steep, but I know from attempting the small inclines in the city, this hill is going to be harder than it looks. Kip picks up speed, using his body for momentum. I follow his lead, pushing against the pedals with more force.

"Don't stop," Kip calls from ahead.

I don't even bother to look up as I push my legs to work against gravity, wheezing through my breaths. Before I realize it, I'm cresting the top and descending the opposite side, holding on for dear life as the pedals spin under my feet. I start to lose control of the bike, my front wheel shaking back and forth. I'm going too fast and Kip, who's already stopped at the bottom, yells for me to slow down.

It's a common blunder of mine to not think things through in times of panic. Pulling the brakes while descending at a forty-five-degree angle isn't one of my wisest decisions. But I only realize this after the bike catapults me over the handlebars and right into Kip. He circles an arm around my waste, catching me mid flight, and it throws us both to the ground as my bike flips over next to us.

I don't want to move, moaning when Kip pulls me up with him.

"That was fucking terrifying."

"In a good way," Kip says.

My mouth opens, ready to dish a sarcastic reply, but I decide against it. "It kind of was."

If a smile could hurt someone, it would be Kip's.

"Are you alright?" he asks, giving me a quick glance over.

"Fine."

We stand, dusting the dirt from ourselves. The trail ends on a lookout point on top of the hill. It takes a few blinks for my eyes to adjust to the sight, but after they do, I'm in complete awe. We've emerged onto a small plateau overlooking a sublet from the river.

"Worth risking your life for a view like this?"

91

"Absolutely. I had no idea this was so close to the city."

I've traveled the world, but there's nothing like discovering something amazing in your own backyard. We walk closer to the edge, but the minimal guardrail doesn't offer enough security for us to get too close. There's an overturned tree people use as seating, and I sit as Kip retrieves two water bottles from his backpack and hands me one.

"Thanks."

We both let our heart rates settle from the crash, enjoying the view. There's something to be said about a view like this. And yet, nothing at all.

Kip shifts his weight, situating himself against a fallen branch and using it as a makeshift backrest. A fine sheen of sweat covers his skin, making the cotton of his shirt cling to his biceps and chest. I have a vivid flash of Peter on top of me a few nights ago and how I used the image of Kip to get myself off. It was the first time I'd come having sex with Peter in a long time. I bet having the real thing would be infinitely better.

I can feel the blood rising in my cheeks and I force myself to redirect my thoughts. "Is it weird? Being out in the world after all this time?"

He nods once, quickly. "It's an adjustment. I wasn't very up-to-date on technological advancements as it was, but damn, things can change in four years." After a moment he realizes I'm still watching him, waiting for him to continue. "What? Were you looking for me to say something else?"

"There's not a right or wrong answer. I just want to hear something real, not something you've recited to Lilly a million times."

"I guess…" He takes a moment to gather his thoughts, twiddling a few straws of pine between his fingers. "I guess I miss feeling like I have a home."

"That is…the saddest thing I've heard all day."

He laughs, squinting against the sun as he looks at me. "You wanted honesty."

"You just told me that you don't feel comfortable anywhere you are. That's really fucking sad, Kip."

"Fine," he says, turning more towards me on the log. "Tell me something real about you."

I hold my arms out to my sides. "Ask me anything."

"Why did you ditch Lilly after the trial?"

My eyebrows shoot up, surprised by how quick his response was. "Been waiting for the right time to ask that question, haven't you?"

"It's a fair question."

Fair is subjective.

The trial revealed things about my father I was unprepared for. At first I was confused, trying to fill in the blanks. Between the media and Lilly's account of things, I wanted to hear it from his point of view. How did I not know my dad was a drug trafficker? How did I not know he's killed people?

…even my daughter has conditions.

The audio recording played during the trial revealed everything. My father hired a chop-shop to transport copious amounts of cocaine and weapons across state lines. Unbeknownst to him, he had accidentally hired my best friend, Lilly, to be the one to do it. Neither Lilly nor Kip were aware of the agreement between Taylor and my father. And they had no idea they were smack-dab in the middle of a federal investigation against my father.

. "I was angry for a long time."

"At Lilly?" There's no judgment or accusation in his question, only desire to understand.

Kip and Lilly ended up both taking plea deals, but Kip still had to testify. And at the time, it kind of pissed me off that she still showed up when they didn't need her. She was so stuck in life, lost, unsure of what she was going to do. All it did was remind me of myself.

It gives me courage to answer honestly. "At life, I think."

He nods in understanding. "I think we all were."

I recall Kip's passive demeanor as he took the stand as the trial progressed. I remember, even then, he didn't look mad that he was going to prison for something he didn't intentionally play a part in. If anyone had a right to be angry, it was him. And yet, he had this defiant look of indifference, as if he refused to let the circumstance win.

"How'd you find peace with everything?"

It takes him a second, but he eventually tears his gaze from mine. "I don't know if I have."

We fall into silence, letting the wind fill the lull in conversation. It's late in the day and the sun is already hanging low in the sky, maybe an hour away from turning the clouds pink. There's more wind up here, creating goose bumps along my bare shoulders, but the log we're sitting on is still warm from basking in the sun all day.

Up here, time seems to slow down. There's nowhere to be, nothing to see except for how beautiful the world is. Everything is so simple when you're able to look down at the world. It's almost like the fake, pretend world is down below. Down there, we're playing life. But up here?

This is real.

I look to Kip and am surprised to find him looking at me.

"Are you okay?" he asks, real concern reflecting in his eyes.

"Yeah. Why?"

"This is the longest you've ever gone without talking." He doesn't smile until I start laughing. "I'm serious. You looked really sad for a second."

"I love it up here," I say, breathing deep to fill my lungs with as much of the air as possible. Maybe if I breathe enough of it, I'll be light enough to fly.

"You do?"

I nod. "Yeah."

"This is what I want in life," he says. "Freedom to enjoy the things I love. Riding a bike, reading a book, eating a medium-rare steak. Life shouldn't be so complicated."

"How old were you when your mom left? Lilly never really talked about her." I didn't know I wanted to ask that question until the words had already left my mouth. Kip has so many moving parts to him, and I realize I want to understand how he ticks.

"That's because Lilly never really knew her. Our mom quit being present years before she left."

"When did she stop?"

"Being a good mom?" I nod when he finally looks at me. "I was still really young when my dad died, but I'd say it was right around then. She gradually fell into depression, quit trying so hard to get up every day, started drinking."

I ask the question I've been aiming for. "When did she stop being a parent and *you* started?"

He smiles contemptuously. "What's with the questions?"

"I want to know more about you," I answer truthfully. "We've known each other for a long time, but we don't really *know* each other."

I can feel more than see his resignation.

"When I was in third grade, I came home from school and found Lilly crying on the kitchen table. She was four, maybe five at the time, and the minute she saw me come through the door she leapt into my arms." He breathes out through his nose before continuing. "She was hungry, so I fixed her a Hot Pocket. I remember yelling down the hall toward my mom's room, asking why Lilly wasn't in school…if something was wrong."

This conversation seems too formal, like he's on a therapist's couch and I'm the doctor, taking notes and dissecting it, so I lie back on the log so he's doesn't feel pressured to look at me as he talks.

"I found her passed out on the bathroom floor, still in her sleep clothes from the night before. I remember being so mad, I yelled at her for leaving Lilly alone all day. She promised it wouldn't happen again." He waves a hand in the air with his words. "It progressively got worse from there."

"And by fifteen, you were stealing cars, working for a chop-shop to take care of your sister," I finish the story for him.

He smiles. "Basically."

"You're kind of a badass, you know that, right?"

He scoffs at my absurdity. "Duh."

We're smiling at each other, but we both really know Kip doesn't want anyone to think of him as a hero.

"Loving someone isn't a sacrifice, Kaley. It's a reward."

Something about the way he's looking at me makes me itchy.

"What about your parents," Kip says.

"What about them?"

"Were you close with them?"

I snort. "No. I always wanted a pony growing up, and they refused to get me one. And we were rich; they could afford a fucking pony."

"Why do you do that," he says, a tinge of anger lacing his voice.

I look at him out of the side of my eye, not wanting to raise my hackles quite yet. "Do what?"

"Turn everything into a joke."

I smile, but it feels forced. "Life is better laughing."

He makes a noncommittal noise in the back of his throat, turning his attention back to the scenery. "You're not funny."

"I think I'm hilarious."

Most of the hikers have left and it's just the two of us. We stay until the sky starts to lose the last few remnants of light. The ride back is much quicker than the ride up, but it's dark by the time we make it back to the truck. The crickets are the loudest I've ever heard them, canceling out the sound of the engine as Kip starts the truck.

Kip rotates his shoulder as he pulls out of the parking lot. "I'm out of shape," he says, picking up his water bottle.

"Or you just need to get laid," I say offhandedly.

He coughs through a swallow, arm braced against the steering wheel as he drives. "Normally I'd contest that, but you're probably right."

Shocked by his admission, I pretend like what I'm about to say isn't as monumental as it feels. "We should do it then."

He looks at me, slowly replacing the plastic lid on the water bottle. "Do what?"

I give him a look. "Don't play dumb, Kip."

"Me and you," he clarifies, using a spare finger to point between us, the water in the bottle sloshing in the process.

"Yeah."

Gaining his bearings, he pulls the bandana off of his forehead and lets it rest around his neck. "Not going to happen."

His easy dismissal perturbs me. "Why not?"

"It's not a good idea."

"We're two consenting adults. We can have sex if we want to."

"That's the thing. I don't want to."

I carefully observe the way he refuses to make eye contact. "Kip, you're pretty, but you're a bad liar."

He laughs, but it's quickly replaced with a deep breath.

God, even the way he breathes elicits a pounding desire within me.

He glances at me. "How would this work?"

"Well…" Confused by his question, I lift my hands to demonstrate. "I have a vagina, and presumably, you have a penis—"

"What I mean is…would this be a onetime deal?"

"Oh. It depends, I suppose."

"On?"

I smile. "How good it is."

His grip on the steering wheel is so tight, the worn leather beneath his fingers squeaks from the pressure. It's the only noise in the cab except for the rumble of the engine the entire way back to my apartment.

And it's a long freaking drive.

I spend the entire time trying to calm my racing heart. My teeth are clenched so tight they hurt, but I'm too afraid I'll fill the silence with mindless chatter if I let up. The last thing I need to do right now is push buttons. When we finally do park in front of my building, Kip is out of the truck, retrieving my bike before I can undo my seatbelt.

He says my name, eyes shifting from the bike and up to my face. "You're arguably the most beautiful woman most men would dream of being with."

I immediately know what his answer will be. "Kip, you don't have to sugar coat it."

He lets out a loud exhale, a small smile shining through. "You couldn't just let me do it my way, could you?"

"Absolutely not."

We smile, but if this is going to be a closed deal, there's something I need to do first.

When I take a step forward, his eyes follow the movement, holding perfectly still as I wrap my arms around his neck. I place my lips against his and he barely hesitates, if at all, and returns my kiss full force, humming a deep sound when my tongue meets his. He wraps his arm around my lower back, lifting me to my toes, pressing our bodies closer. The warmth from our overheated skin collides, and it's like falling into a bath, chills spreading across my skin. Maybe I'm not the only one who's been dazed since that kiss in the park.

And then it's over so quickly I'm sure I have whiplash.

He huffs. "God damn it, Kaley." He covers his mouth like a barrier.

"Sorry." But we both know I'm not in the least, and I can't hide my shit-eating grin.

He's angry, glaring, hands positioned low on his hips. I've seen this stance many times before, so I already know a lecture is coming.

I speak before he can start berating me. "Go home, jerk one out, and try not to think of me while you're doing it."

He blinks against my brashness and I smirk as I grab my bike and carry it up the stairs. I proved my point. I refuse to look down in his direction as I struggle with my lock, starting to rethink bringing the issue up to Tanya after all. Leaning the bike against the wall as I walk in, I let the door shut behind me, feeling the small, proud smile on my lips slowly dissolve when I'm alone in the apartment.

After a moment, I realize I never heard the latch of the door click in place. Turning around, I beg my heart to slow at the sight of Kip straddling the threshold. His facial expression mirrors his stance. He still isn't quite sure if he should stay or go.

"Why do you have to be so goddamn tempting?"

Where I was confident thirty seconds ago, I'm now wary. His confliction over whether or not he wants to be with me is almost enough to dismiss the entire idea. Almost.

"You make it sound like an insult."

Wavering for a moment, he finally makes a decision to step forward, letting the door close behind him. "You can't tell Lilly."

My heart jumps. This might happen. "She wouldn't care." My voice is already raspy at the thought.

"I care," he says. "She's my sister and you're her friend and it's weird to think she'll have inside information on my sex life."

"Any other stipulations?"

He runs a hand over his mouth, clearly stressed.

I close the remaining feet between us, looking up as I stand before him to meet his eyes. "You're seriously overthinking this."

He looks down at our hands and how I've intertwined our fingers. He releases them, trailing the back of his fingers up my forearm, up the underside of my bicep, barely grazing the side of my boob. The sensation fires through me as I watch. His touch is tentative, like he's forgotten what another person's skin feels like.

"I haven't done this…been with someone, in a long time."

That's stating the obvious. Unless he went through an experimental phase in prison, which I just don't see happening.

His hand reaches my neck, fingers trailing across my pulse points, and I fight the desire to touch him back. This needs to be his decision. "Even before prison, it had been a while."

Now I'm nervous. "How long?"

His lips thin before he answers. "Almost a year."

I breathe out. Okay. We're working with about five and a half years of celibacy. "That is a lot of pressure," I say, voicing my thoughts.

He cracks a small smile, finally looking up from his touch to my eyes. "I guarantee I'm the one under pressure."

I swallow, relishing the feel of his fingers over my throat. His eyes fixate on the movement, dilating at the same time.

"How so?"

His lips twist, a show of worry and humor. "Our kiss outside probably lasted longer than I'm going to."

I laugh. "Are you worried about the onetime-only deal?"

"I need at least two," he says, serious. I open my mouth to reply when he runs a thumb over my bottom lip, halting anything I was going to say. "Do you have protection?"

Walking backwards to my bedroom, I tow him along. "You should know me better than that."

I turn on a bedside lamp, pulling two condoms out of the nightstand and tossing them on the bed. Kip steps closer to me, but not close enough to touch. The air is thick as his breathing becomes audible in the small space.

His face is unreadable, almost a passive look in place. And I don't like it.

Reaching for the hem of my shirt, I pull the material over my head, letting it hit the floor. The air he sucks in is a telling breath. I unbutton my cut-offs and let them fall, stepping out of them without breaking eye contact. Finally, his eyes divert from mine as he follows my movements, reaching my feet and back up. When his eyes connect with mine again, there's no mistaking the blatant desire there as he gives in.

101

Cupping both sides of my jaw, he tilts my head back as he runs his hands to the nape of my neck, slowly pulling the rubber band from my hair. He wraps the strands around his wrist and pulls the hair over my shoulder. It's long, the length hitting his elbow from the lack of maintenance I've put into it. The tug forces my head back. It's domineering, slightly erotic, and the blood flowing through my limbs kicks into high gear.

Pulling his arm through the winding hair, he catches the last portion before watching it fall through his fingers.

I can feel the fan of his breath when he speaks. "You're so beautiful it hurts."

Those words are so beautiful it hurts.

I grasp the handkerchief still hanging around his neck. "Put your mouth on me," I say, diverting his mouth for better uses.

He doesn't delay, latching his mouth onto mine, delving into the kiss with everything inside him. At least, that's what it feels like as he pulls me against the pressure in his hiking shorts. Pulling the straps of my bra down, he follows the path with his lips until his head is bent at the perfect angle to pull my breast into his mouth.

This...

This is what I want.

I arch into him, finding the gap between his shirt and the waistband of his shorts, needing to feel something of him I haven't touched yet. His stomach tightens as I run my hand higher, bunching up the fabric with the movement.

He pulls away and I tilt forward, my body involuntarily trying to follow. We both are panting as he toes off his shoes and socks, reaching a hand across his back to remove his shirt. He picks one of the condoms up and locks it between his teeth, leaving it there as he unbuttons his shorts and pushes the material to the ground, ripping it open once his hands are free.

"We need to do this, like, right now."

102

I put my hands on his hips, trailing them inside his boxers, smiling when I feel him in my hand. "There's always round two."

Groaning, he wraps both of his arms around me, lifting me from the floor and placing me on my back. He rocks his hips into mine once, quickly, and his entire body jerks involuntarily at the sensation. He glides the condom on as I remove my underwear and he's between my legs within seconds. Pausing, we take a moment, breathing heavily. The way he's looking down at me is making me self-conscious.

I don't do self-conscious. I grip one of his hands and guide it between my legs.

He lets out a breath. "Kaley." Unsteady, he runs his fingers over me, exploring more for his benefit than for mine.

After a moment, I smile and tell him to quit teasing me. But it's gone the instant he pushes a finger in. Like his kisses, he gives, but takes away at the same time. I'm an instant gratification type of person, but there's something amazing about the way he draws it out. I push against his hand, and Kip responds, pushing back with the weight of his hips. An immediate buzzing sensation overflows within me and I find myself gripping his arm to the point of injury, chasing the in and out of his finger with my hips tilted up to meet the pressure of his hand.

"I can't remember the last time someone made me come with their hands." My chest rises and falls heavy between us as I catch my breath.

With a smug look, he glides himself inside me, dropping his weight onto his forearms once he's there. I lean up and kiss him, open to how good he feels. I can feel the slight tremble of the bed from his body shaking. Needing more, I rock my hips.

"Don't."

"I've got to," I say truthfully, arching into him.

He places a strong hand on my hip, holding me still. "Kaley," he reprimands. But it's a desperate, weak plea.

I dig deeper into the mattress, gaining leverage, and he groans at the sensation. "Move or so help me—"

My words cut off when he releases my hip, moving the grip of his hand to my thigh as he finally relents. And then he's *really* moving. And it's phenomenal. This isn't like his kisses or his fingers where there's give and take. And with every push in, rough sounds escape his lips. He sucks the hollow of my throat, my breasts, and back to my lips. His hands move just as quickly as his mouth, restless, finding new places to discover.

I'm not sure I'm breathing. I'm barely existing.

We've barely gotten started when he starts to lose coordination of his movements, and I feel the contraction of his body over mine. He locks onto my mouth, groaning around our labored breaths, body stilling as he finishes. But it doesn't relax him like I expect it to. Instead, he kisses me harder, putting more of his weight on me. He's on a mission, and I don't object. When he pulls out, it's only to reach for the other condom, resituating himself over me.

"There's no way you can go again."

"Trust me; I'm way more surprised than you are." A playful smile spreads on his lips, a hypnotic look in his eyes.

He kisses over my chest and down my stomach. I already know where he wants to go as he descends, lips grazing my belly button. I don't want him there, and I flip over onto my stomach.

He leans back on his knees. "Jesus Christ," he cusses. "You're beautiful in every way."

Wrapping an arm under my waist, he lifts my hips. This time he eases in slowly, completely at ease in this position.

"I can't believe I almost said no to this," he says, pushing in.

"Let this be a reminder."

He pulls out. "Of what?"

Looking over my shoulder, I watch him as he concentrates on where we're connected, a look of reverence.

"That I'm always right."

He looks up, meeting my eyes, and a smirk falls on his lips. "I'll give you this one time." Leaning over, he places my back against his front, pushing in deeper. "This time only."

His weight suddenly creates a lack of space and I curl my fingers into the bedding. Other than tiny adjustments, there's not any wiggle room in this position. I concentrate on feeling him, listening to his breathing, trying to keep up with my own. The smell of my sheets reminds me of where I am—in my bed, in my home, my comfort zone.

Abruptly, everything ceases, and I open my eyes to find that Kip's stopped moving. He pulls out, heaving my body onto his chest, positioning me over him as he lies back.

Placing his hands on top of mine, he says, "Look at me."

I hold on to the bandanna around his neck as I sink onto him, trying to ignore the way his eyes refuse to release mine. I grind down and palm my breasts, and he groans, eyes falling shut with the sensation.

This…

This is what I need.

eleven

"IF YOU TOUCH THE radio one more time, I'm going to make you walk."

"My ears are bleeding, Kip. They're bleeding. It's so painful."

Slapping the radio dial with the palm of his hand, he turns the radio off altogether. "You are the most dramatic person I've ever met."

"And you're so stuck in your ways, you can't see past your own dick. It's called compromising. I know, a totally foreign concept to you."

"It's my truck," he says, indignant.

"Maybe if I explain it, you'll have a better grasp of the idea. It's when two people both offer to make sacrifices to find a happy medium. For example, if we listen to my music on the way to our destination, you get to listen to your music on the way back."

He doesn't respond.

Huffing out a breath, I cross my arms, feeling more agitated with every second he refuses to bend. The cab of the truck is stifling hot even with the air conditioning working overtime. I adjust the vents to get a better angle so I don't have a bad case of boob sweat.

"Where are we going anyway?" Kip picked me up after work, but we're headed in the opposite direction of my apartment.

"I've lined up a realtor to look at some shops for buy or lease."

"Shut up," I exclaim. "Seriously?"

He fights his smile but loses out. It's hard to be mellow when someone is so excited for you. "I figured you're absolutely right. I've got the experience, so why not do something with it?"

"I'm sorry," I say, cupping my ear. "I couldn't hear you. Can you repeat that for me?"

"Kaley," he admonishes.

"That's twice in less than a week. Are you coming down with something? I've heard there's a late bout of the flu going around."

"I'm coming down with something, alright, but I don't think it's the flu," he says, eyes smiling. "And let the record show, the first time I admitted defeat, you had me in a compromising position."

"No, I'm pretty sure I was the one being compromised."

"Never." His reply is quick and surprisingly serious, shifting the conversation with just one word. "You have all the power when it comes to sex. You say when, you say where, and you say how."

For some reason his sincerity makes me feel guilty. Begrudgingly, I turn the radio back on, trying not to cringe through a fiddle solo.

Kip lifts an eyebrow in my direction.

"Surrendering," I explain.

He smiles, the one where the corners of his eyes crinkle with the movement. Reaching over, he turns the dial to the pop station I've been trying to set it on for the past fifteen minutes.

"What are you doing?"

"Compromising," he says.

"Now you want to give in? *Now*? No." I turn the dial back.

He gives me a look, flipping it back again.

"Stop."

"You stop," he says.

"I'm not arguing over this again."

"Good. Leave it."

Somehow leaving it on the station I originally wanted seems like I'm losing the fight, so I jam my hand on the dial and turn the radio off for good.

"Oh, we're back to this?"

"Yes," I say, refolding my arms.

"God, you're such a child," he says.

"*Me?*"

We park in front of a warehouse with a for lease sign on the side of it, but neither one of us makes a move to get out.

Kip yanks the key from the ignition and turns in my direction. "Yes, you. I've never met such an infuriating person in my life."

"You're not fucking cupcakes and pedicures either, Mr. I-think-the-sun-should-rise-and-fall-in-my-ass."

"It's my truck, so I should get to listen to the music I want."

"And I tried to compromise," I say, pointing at nothing in particular. "But you're so old and stuck in your ways that you refuse to budge."

He scoffs. "I'm thirty, not senile. You're just used to always getting everything you want."

I sputter through a response, so enraged by this point that I'm actually afraid for Kip's safety. "I do *not* always get what I want."

"Really? You don't?"

"No."

We have a stare-off, neither of us wanting to back down. Subconsciously, I know I'm irrationally angry at this point, but I can't stop it.

Kip, very reluctantly, lets his guard down first. "What are we even arguing about?"

I want to stomp my foot at his attempt to be rational because I'm not ready to give up yet.

"I don't know. You tell me."

He taps his thumb against his thigh, watching me, mulling something over. "If I tell you we can go get cupcakes and pedicures after we leave, will you drop it?"

I can't help it; a smile tugs at my lips. "What kind of cupcakes?"

He sees my resolve weakening, and maneuvers closer to me on the bench seat. "Vanilla?"

I shake my head, scrunching up my nose. "Too plain."

Running his palm up the outside of my thigh, he says, "Chocolate?"

"Too sweet."

His fingers reach the back of my shorts, fitting his palm underneath my right ass cheek. "Red velvet?"

"Too rich." I debate whether to make his pursuit easier by moving closer, or harder by pulling away. His fingers are entirely too close to where I want them to ignore.

Before I can officially decide, he has me under him with my back against the seat. "You're very hard to please."

I trail my hands up his chest, intertwining my fingers around the back of his neck. "You don't usually have this problem. I must have reached your level of tolerance today."

He looks from my eyes to my lips, nothing but desire on his face, which no doubt matches mine. "Maybe if you kissed me I'd be more patient."

He says it like he believes it.

We kiss, and any remnants of agitation dissipate with the touch of our lips. I've learned we're good at this. It seems that our sexual chemistry and annoyance for each other go hand-in-hand. Or maybe it's dick-in-vagina?

After we woke up naked in my bed after our night together, we argued about what Kip would tell Lilly about not coming home.

"Why don't you just tell her the truth," I say, sitting perched on the edge of the bed.

He takes a moment to look up from gathering his clothes like I've lost my mind. "We've been over this."

"You don't have to tell her it was me. Tell her you stayed the night with a friend."

"I'll figure it out on the way there."

"You're making this way more complicated than it has to be," I say, watching him bend over.

"Did you take my underwear," he says, shuffling the piles of clothes. "And where's my socks?"

"Yes, Kip. I horde dirty underwear and socks."

He rolls his eyes. "Then what happened to them?"

I throw up my hands, doing a half-assed job kicking clothes around on the ground to find them. "The boogey-man ate them."

"You're so helpful," he smarts, shaking out my clothes as well. "I don't see how you find anything in this fucking apartment."

Sighing, I get on my hands and knees, digging through the clothes and finding them underneath the bed. I drag them out and hold them up, an onslaught of remarks about how useless he is on my lips when I realize the compromising situation I've put myself in. Kneeling on the cold hardwood floor, only wearing panties, and eye level with Kip's dick.

Remembering the feel of his hands in my hair, the tensing of his body, still gives me chills when I think about it. There's not a more powerful feeling than making him lose all sense of restraint. I've encountered a lot of men, but I don't think I've ever desired to bring someone to their knees like I do with Kip. Which is odd, because no one can irritate me like him.

It must have been the best damn blowjob of his life, because he showed up at my apartment unannounced yesterday, and we argued about the value of a text message.

"You can't just show up unexpected, Kip. It's rude."

He stands on the other side of my doorway, forearm braced against the frame. "Because you're the face of propriety?"

"I'm busy."

"Really," he says, leaning forward, trying to peek inside my apartment. "Doing what?" His eyes land on what he caught me in the middle of, and he laughs. "Painting your nails? Sorry I caught you at such a bad time."

I huff, walking away from the door, knowing he's going to come in anyway. "All I'm asking for is a notice. What if I had someone over?"

He raises his eyebrows, shutting the door behind him. "Is that a possibility?"

Dropping onto the couch, I pick up the red bottle of polish and resume coating my toenails. "I know you're behind in the world, but one little text message wouldn't kill you."

I feel the couch cushion dip as he sits. I ignore him, chin braced on my bent knee, concentrating on steadying my hand. I was unprepared for the sinking feeling in my belly when I opened the door. My heart leaped into action, beating an erratic pace in my chest, an uneasiness making my stomach weak. It closely resembles the feeling I get whenever I find an eight-legged arachnid within ten feet of me. Except, I don't want to smoosh Kip under the heel of my shoe; I want to ride him like horse.

"How long are you going to pretend that you're not happy to see me?"

"Until you go away."

He smiles, rubbing his hands together as they rest between his knees. "Did your apartment get messier overnight?"

"I'm literally three seconds away from murdering you."

He laughs, something I'm hearing more and more of. "It's not like you could get away with it," he says.

"Oh, yeah. And why not?"

"I'm fairly positive you'd never get around to hiding my body. You don't make picking up after yourself a habit..."

"You have a weird fascination with how to conceal a murder that hasn't been committed yet."

He thinks on it a few moments, head cocked to the side in thought. "Huh," he sounds. "I read this weird novel about a lion and a lamb and I think it's really getting to me."

I hide my smile behind my hair. Placing his chin on my shoulder, he slides my hair out of the way to get a better view of my face.

"You know as well as I do that you're happy to see me." He places a small kiss to the underside of my ear. "Your heart rate betrays you."

I half sigh, half give in. It's hard to argue with the truth. "Can you at least promise to make an effort?"

Barely removing his lips from my skin, he says, "Yeah. Sure."

The fact we even made it this far today before pissing each other off and stripping naked is a freaking accomplishment.

We break for air.

"We need to stop," he says right before going in for another kiss.

"You stop."

"I need to be presentable, and this," he says, grabbing the front of his pants, "is not presentable."

"We can remedy that." To accentuate my point, I dip my hand into the waistband.

He groans, pulling my hand free and leaning back. "No." His face is comically stern as he gets himself together. "No," he repeats, firmer this time.

I roll my eyes and sit up. "Fine, but only because public indecency is a parole violation."

He quickly looks around the parking lot, checking to make sure it's empty. "I didn't even think about that."

"No one saw us, you're fine." I get out of the truck and I have to wait five entire minutes for him to emerge, looking slightly less flustered than I left him.

He reaches for my hand as we walk inside, and the feeling of his fingers intertwined with mine makes me smile. It's endearing in a very sweet way. The realtor is on his cell phone when we round the corner of the building. He looks up and gives us a once-over, smiling as he holds up a finger to indicate for us to wait a minute. Kip tugs me toward him, using his spare time to kiss me.

"It's too hot to be hanging on each other," I say, not making an effort to move him away.

His lips move a little higher along my throat, forcing me to tilt my head side with the motion. "It's not when the realtor I hired is checking you out."

Confused, I pull far enough away to look over Kip's shoulder at the guy in the suit. He's far more interested in his conversation, face tilted toward the ground as he talks. "You're imagining things. I'd know, trust me."

"He's interested," Kip assures.

"How do you know?"

"Because he's straight."

At that very moment, the realtor and I make eye contact. He looks familiar, but I can't place him.

"This is ridiculous," I say, detangling myself from Kip. "You're acting like we're together."

His face morphs into confusion. "Are we not? We're here," he says. "Together."

"You know what I mean." I push his shoulder, and he takes a step back, finally giving me breathing room. Somehow Kip makes me feel like a teenager, emotions all over the place.

"Sorry about that," the realtor says, holding out a hand for Kip to shake. "Brandon Benoit. Nice to meet you."

His name flips a switch and I suddenly remember where I know him from. *Bitty Brandon.* I feel the blood drain all the way to my feet as he reaches for my hand to shake next and I'm forced to make eye contact.

"Kaley."

His smile is so condescending, it takes a crucial amount of effort not to blurt out the actual size of his dick to smack it off of his face. Not that it matters. I still slept with him for money, regardless of dick size.

Ugh. *I hate myself.*

I've only run into someone outside of Hudson's once, and we both went out of our way to avoid each other. This is different and astronomically uncomfortable. I imagine I'd feel much more myself without Kip here, but he is, and I am, and Bitty Brandon is, and this entire situation is a big *nope.*

Kip clears his throat, knocking Brandon back into persona. "We're located outside of the warehouse district..."

His words fade as I come to the realization that this man has been inside me and I didn't even recognize him. The same way Kip touched me less than ten minutes ago. My gaze shifts from Brandon to Kip and back again, studying them side by side. It's very obvious Kip is vastly superior to Brandon. Kip may not have as much money as Brandon, but he's far more genuine. He's true to himself, no matter who or what he comes across. Unshakeable.

Shame creeps up my chest and into my throat, making my head pound from the pressure. The fact I've let Kip inside me after this man has been, makes a sick feeling crawl up my throat.

"Kaley?" Kip's voice catches me and I look up from a spot I have been absentmindedly staring at on the concrete. "You okay," he asks, concerned.

I force a smile. "It's really hot."

Brandon opens the door to the space, ushering us inside the building. "Let's get you inside then, where there's air conditioning."

Kip isn't buying it, but I determinedly avoid his gaze as I walk in. Unfortunately, Bitty Brandon's knowing smile is far too large to miss.

"I'm not immediately bombarded by the smell of cat piss, so that's a good sign," I say as I walk through the door.

So far the two previous rental spaces were a bust. One was in an iffy part of town and the other previously doubled as a bait and tackle shop. They both shared the same characteristic: the smell of urine.

"Can't argue with that," Kip says, following behind me.

"Told you the third time is the charm," Brandon says, turning on the lights.

Ostentatious would be a polite word used to describe Brandon, considering he refers to himself in third person. I've heard of salespeople using the technique because it helps pitch themselves to buyers, but it's counterproductive in my opinion.

One by one he flips the overhead lights on, revealing the space. It's a warehouse in the development district of downtown, mostly surrounded by construction sites and suppliers. It straddles the city line, close enough to downtown that it could draw in business.

"This is big," Kip says. "Can't be cheap."

"It is big, yes. But it's actually going into foreclosure soon. The owners are willing to sell at the pay-off price. It's especially nice since you're paying in cash."

The space is void of anything other than the concrete floor, metal walls, and the duct system rigged across the ceiling. There's a second floor that overlooks the shop with a staircase leading up to it on our right.

Brandon takes the lead. "This is a bonus area. It can be used as an office or storage space. It accounts for roughly six hundred extra square feet."

The loft is much cooler than the ground floor, the air ducts right over our heads. There's railing to protect anyone from falling fifteen to twenty feet to their death, and a tiny bathroom located against the back wall, partitioned off with two-by-fours and drywall.

"This could be an apartment."

Kip nods in agreement. "The bottom floor has enough square footage to add a storage room and a lobby." He spins in a circle, taking in the small loft. "I can divide this area into two parts, creating an office in the front and a small bedroom in the back."

Brandon nods in agreement. "This building has a lot of potential."

Kip looks to me, ignoring Brandon's selling point. He's pretty much overlooked Brandon's spiel, always referring back to me for my opinion. "What do you think?"

"Kip, I don't get why you keep asking me. I know nothing about auto shops."

"Do you think you could be okay staying here?"

"I think the real question is whether or not you're okay with it. This will be your home. It's somewhere you should feel comfortable no matter what."

He catches my reference. "I'm comfortable with you." He has his head tilted back, looking at the ceiling, body relaxed like he didn't just drop a serious truth bomb.

I guess I miss feeling like I have a home.

After a few beats too long of silence, Brandon suggests going over logistics, and they leave to go downstairs. I walk the distance of the loft, counting my footsteps to measure the length. The space can't be cheap. I haven't broached the subject of money with Kip. I know his father left money for him and Lilly, but I'm not sure how much.

Sex with Kip is good. No, that's not right. Sex with Kip is *intense*. It's exciting and new and all the fun things that I used to chase in high school and college. I forgot how strong the pull can be when I'm attracted to someone. He may be older, but from what I've gathered, sex has never been a priority for him. And yet, he has a way of making me feel like the inexperienced one. Sex for him is simple and primal, an urge he taps into, revealing a completely different side of his personality. I'm not ready to give him up, but I also don't want to lead him on.

My phone chimes and I pull it out of my back pocket. My finger hovers over the screen, hesitant. I'm fairly good at compartmentalizing my life, so I haven't given much thought to Peter, but his text brings him bubbling to the surface.

Going to be out of town for a few nights. Don't know when I'll be back. Do you need anything? —Peter

I switch apps on my phone, checking my bank account, gauging how far I can make it stretch. It's been slowly dwindling since Peter's been flaky lately, but I think I can make it another week or two if I count my tips. It'll give me more time to let whatever this is with Kip run its course. I reply and peer down at Kip.

He's standing with his hands on his hips as he listens to Brandon explain something, nodding at whatever he's saying. I smile at how serious his face is. I've known Kip for close to ten years and he's always carried himself with an air of severity, everything deserving of careful thought and consideration.

He looks up and catches me staring, a small smile playing on his lips. "What?"

Brandon stops talking, following Kip's direction, but I don't take my eyes off of Kip. "You must install a shower, non-negotiable."

A smile spreads across his face, enhancing the rough lines around his mouth. "What about a bathtub?"

I shrug. "I prefer showers."

This makes him happy. Kip signs some papers for Brandon to turn in a proposal to the buyer, and Kip should be expecting a phone call sometime within the next few days. Kip is outright smiling as we say our goodbyes, and it doesn't dissipate as we get into the truck.

"You're going to have to come up with a name," I say after we leave.

He nods. "One thing at a time. We don't even know if they'll accept my offer."

"It's a cash sell and over their payoff amount, Kip. They're going to take it. They'd be stupid not to."

He smiles because he knows I'm right, but ever the realist, he won't get his hopes up until it's set in stone.

We drive for a little while when he says, "Vanilla, chocolate, or red velvet?"

Caught off guard, I shake my head. "None. Bananas foster. Why?"

"Cupcakes," he answers as he points at a building and turns into the parking lot. I laugh as my eyes land on a bakery adorned with a large cupcake sign with an arrow pointing toward the door. He buys me a half-dozen of my favorite cupcakes and eats almost all of them as he waits for me to get my toes done at a nearby spa, and I reward him by using the remaining icing during foreplay.

twelve

"ONE HOUR," JANINE ENUNCIATES, holding up her index finger just in case I don't understand English or something. "If you're one minute late, I'm writing you up."

I hide my eye roll behind José, our fry cook. "I won't be late."

"Mm hmm," Janine murmurs.

José purses his lips. He isn't buying my shit either. I thank him for making me a last-minute lunch, blowing him a kiss as I leave. He doesn't find me the least bit entertaining and shakes his head in Janine's direction. I'm positive he's attempted to get me fired in multiple occasions, today probably being one of them.

I strap the to-go bag onto the rack Kip installed on the front of my bike after I complained about carrying my purse. I never thought I'd be this person. The person who rides a bike in the city. I was the last thing from envious when I'd watch people brave the cold of winter, rain of spring, and heat of summer to commute to and from work, biking through the streets. It didn't make sense. Not to mention the issue of the absolute chance of a hair catastrophe. No one escapes a bike ride with unscathed hair.

But here I am, pulling on a baseball cap to shield my eyes from the sun, more worried about my hair whipping into my eyes every time I have to look over my shoulder. I ride on the left side of the bike lane when passing parallel parking, cautious of running into a sudden door opening on the chance someone is exiting their car. Between drivers who think the bike lane is actually extra parking space, the occasional yappy dog, and construction, I've managed to become the epitome of every motorist's nightmare. I'll take up an entire driving lane if I have to.

Kip closed on the shop fairly quick. Cash sales apparently close faster than either of us realized, but Kip wasted zero time getting to working on fixing the space up. So much so, we've barely seen each other. This past week made me catch on to the fact Kip is the main instigator in our…friendship. Without him dropping by unannounced or forcing me along with his plans, we don't see each other. I'm used to being alone, but Kip makes alone a whole lot less interesting.

There's a barrage of vehicles parked in front of the building and a plumber holds the door for me as I push my bike inside. I have a better understanding as to why he's been so MIA. The amount of work he's already done is remarkable. Bay doors have been installed on the wall facing the street, and the front is framed to separate the lobby from the work area. In the loft, workers are putting up sheetrock, creating a definable apartment.

Spotting Kip, I heft my bike over the heads of some guys eating lunch on the concrete floor. There's a car lifted up off the ground amid the disarray, new tools scattered across the floor beneath it. I silently observe as Kip removes the last tire and stands. His overalls are undone, gathered around his waist, leaving his white undershirt marred with grease. He has a tire in each hand when he makes eye contact with me, and he smiles, dropping the weight in his hands.

"What are you doing here," he says, wiping his hands on his shirt before kissing me.

I make a yakking noise and wipe my mouth. "You taste like dead seaweed and salt."

He smiles, eyes crinkling. "Sweat, babe. It's sweat."

Kip's term of endearment catches me off guard. He's not the type to use nicknames lightly, let alone something affectionate.

"I brought you lunch," I say, untying the bag of food from the bike and holding it up.

"Thank Jesus." He snatches the bag from my hand, opening it and peering inside. "I'm so hungry, I was about to eat my left arm." Unraveling the club sandwich, he takes a humungous bite.

"You already have a customer?"

His eyes follow mine to the car. "Lilly had a friend who needed her rotors replaced, so I'm just doing a small side job for her." He looks up at the loft. "Want to take a look at the apartment?"

I take his outstretched hand as we navigate through the workers. "This is happening so fast," I say.

"I need to have income coming in at some point, and it's going to take a while to get everything up and ready, so why wait?"

We ascend the steps and Kip takes a step back when we reach the landing, allowing me the room to look around. The front of the loft is already sectioned off so the apartment isn't visible from the stairs. There's a small door to the left that leads to an open floor plan. There's a more definable area showcasing where the living room and kitchen will be, and the back wall is getting framed to extend the bathroom a few feet. It's lacking all of the details, but I can already find Kip in it. It's where he'll finally feel at home.

I smile. "This looks great, Kip."

"It's a rough start, but it has potential," he says. Taking the last bite of his lunch, he tosses the wrap into a garbage can, retrieving a beer from the refrigerator.

"You have an entire case of beer but no food, and you're starving?"

He takes a long drag of the bottle, leaning his hip against the door. "Got to stay hydrated," he says. "Do you want one?"

"No thanks. I still have to finish my shift. Plus, I hate beer."

He gives me a confused look. "You love beer."

I slowly shake my head. "No, I don't."

"But," he trails off, trying to put pieces together. "You always drank all of my beer."

My eyes widen when I figure out what he's talking about. And then I laugh. And laugh. And *laugh*.

"What the hell are you laughing at?" He's smiling but still absolutely perplexed by my laughter.

"I have a confession to make," I say, finally getting the chance to reveal something I've been holding on to for years. "Remember how mad you'd get when you came home and had no beer?"

He nods his head slightly, wondering what I'm getting at.

"I never actually drank them."

"You didn't?"

I shake my head.

"So…what did you do with them?"

I suck air through my teeth, letting the anticipation build. "I poured them out."

For a moment, he doesn't move, or blink, or even breathe for that matter. "You poured them out," he reiterates, making sure he heard me right. "My beer?"

"Yup."

He blinks. And blinks again.

"For years, I came home to find all my beer gone, and you were just pouring them out?"

I nod, unable to stop my smile.

He finishes the beer in his hand and slams it down on the counter. "I worked an extra hour almost every day so I could afford that shitty six-pack of beer, and all the while, you were fucking *pouring them out*." He's genuinely irked by the revelation.

"The way you keep repeating it is actually starting to make me feel a little guilty."

"I—why would you do that?"

"You kept telling Lilly how bad of an influence I was, and it kind of got under my skin…a little."

"You were a bad influence," he affirms, throwing his arms in the air. "You kept drinking all of my beer!"

"I really didn't know it would be such a big deal." The whine in my voice makes me feel like a child who got caught eating cookies before dinner. *But I couldn't help myself.*

He shakes his head. "Unbelievable."

This is the Kip I remember. The Kip with control issues and zero patience.

He side-eyes my reaction. "Why are you smiling?"

"You're doing that thing," I explain. "Where you try so hard not to smile but can't help it."

He looks me straight in the face and says, "I'm not smiling."

"Not with your mouth—no—but with your eyes. You secretly think I'm hilarious."

He tries so hard to keep his face neutral, but ultimately, eventually, a smile creeps through. I lift my arms above my head in triumphant celebration.

"Come here," he demands, pulling me to his chest, a look of admiration and reproach at the same time. He leans his back against the fridge, positioning my body between his legs. I try to ignore all of the eyes in the room, but I catch a few workers glancing in our direction. They watched Kip and I go from arguing to cuddling in a span of minutes, and by the expression on their faces, it's weirder from an outsider's perspective.

Kip catches on to my mood because he asks the workers to take a break. He waits for them all to leave before he says, "What are you thinking?"

"I think it's perfect for you."

His smile cuts to the side, eyebrows furrowed. "That was strategically sardonic."

"Not at all," I assure him. "This is where you're meant to be."

"Then why does it sound like you're telling me something I don't want to hear?"

I run my hands over his hair, starting at his temples and continuing down the back of his neck. I can barely catch the length of it between my fingers. "Are you going to let your hair grow long again?" I say, changing the subject

He closes his eyes. "Mm, depends."

"On?"

"Whether or not you stop scratching my head."

I laugh and graze the hair at the base of his neck.

"Do you want me to grow it out?"

I shrug. "I like it short. Or long. It doesn't really matter to me."

His hands ravel around my waist, dipping toward the curve of my back, sinking into the waistband of my shorts. "How long do you have before you have to be at work?"

"My break is an hour, but I need to leave in time to ride back."

He palms my backside, smiling as I scratch the hair around his temples. "I can give you a lift back. It's the least I can do since you brought me lunch."

"That's right," I say. "I saved you from starvation."

He smiles, teeth blaringly white against the deep russet of his lips, and opens his eyes. They lock onto something behind me, and Kip hurries to remove his hands, putting distance between us as he stands straight.

"Andie."

A petite brunette looks hesitantly between us as she walks around the room divider. God knows how long she's been standing there, watching us. By the look on her face, she's more apprehensive than voyeuristic.

"Sorry if I'm intruding," she says, making brief eye contact with me before looking back to Kip.

Kip steps around me, putting even more space between us. "No, you're fine. I thought you weren't coming by until after your late class was over."

"It was canceled last minute. Since I was already on campus, I figured I'd come straight here." She holds up a paper bag with the name *Chuck's* across the front of it. "And I figured I could bring you lunch. I noticed you didn't have any groceries last night."

She's bringing him lunch? And she was here last night?

She makes eye contact with me again, this time longer, and I can see the proverbial wheels spinning. She wasn't expecting me. At least, not expecting to find Kip reaching second base with someone.

"Okay, well," Kip says, rubbing his hands together. If I'm not mistaken, Andie being here makes him nervous. And I *definitely* don't like it. "It won't take me long to put the rotors on. Forty-five minutes, hour and a half, tops."

"If it's not a problem."

"None at all," he says. "If you could meet me downstairs, I'll be down in a minute."

"Oh, yeah. No problem." She smiles and turns away.

No faster does he turn around than the words leave my mouth. "She was here last night?"

"She came and dropped off the car with Lilly."

I give him a look. "And brought you lunch from your favorite burger place?"

He cocks his head to the side, observing my body language. "You know my favorite restaurant?"

Remembering Lilly mentioning wanting to set Kip up with one of her friends, I narrow my eyes at him. "Isn't she a little young for you?"

"She's only a year younger than you," he says without missing a beat.

I scoff. "That's younger than your little sister, for Christ's sake."

Slowly, a smile spreads across his face, an overconfident gleam in his eyes. I scrunch up my face, confused by his sudden change in demeanor. And then it clicks.

I slam the heel of my hand to my forehead. *No.*

"No?"

"Did I say that out loud?"

Kip nods animatedly. "Yes. It's okay," he says. "We don't have to talk about it."

I would wither and die where I stand before I'd ever admit I'm jealous. "I'm guessing this means you can't give me a ride back to work?"

He laughs at my attempt to change the subject. "If I don't, will you be distracted by thoughts of Andie and me alone?"

My answer is rapid fire, automatic. "No."

"Good," he says, pulling away and smacking my ass. "Means you'll be safe."

I scowl at him, rubbing my backside, coming to a stop when I find Lilly and Justin standing at the mouth of the stairs. A young boy stands between them and Justin is giving Kip the biggest shit-eating grin I've ever seen.

"Hello." The boy smiles, cheeks deepening in color every millisecond he keeps eye contact with me.

"Who is he," I ask, pointing to the kid.

"This," Justin says, placing a hand on the boy's shoulder in a playful manner, "Is Cal. He lives in the townhouse to the right of us."

"All you need to know is that I'm pretty much a badass."

My mouth falls open in shock and Lilly rolls her eyes to the ceiling in silent prayer.

Justin's smile only grows. "He's eleven and still sleeps in Ninja Turtle pajamas."

"Hey," Cal protests, a scowl marring his boyish features. "Raphael is also a badass."

Lilly smacks him in the back of the head. "Stop cussing or I'll let Mr. Wilson send you to your room next time."

Cal scowls, but it's short lived. Kip and I make eye contact, completely confused and blindsided by the direction of their arrival.

Lilly gives Kip a pleading look. "Can you assign him something to do?"

"Can I get an explanation as to why I'm being assigned babysitting duties?"

Cal's scowl returns at Kip's insinuation he needs to be babysat.

Justin answers for her. "Lilly thinks it's her job to intercede all of Mr. Wilson's parenting decisions regarding Cal's punishments."

"He's so unreasonable though," Cal whines, and Lilly gives Justin a cocksure smile.

"Is he, though?" Justin says, face compressed sarcastically as he looks at Cal. "Is he really?"

"Look," Kip interrupts. "I don't care what he did, just keep me out of it. I'm trying to start a business and the last thing I need is figuring out what to do with a kid."

"I'm almost twelve," Cal protests.

Justin gives Kip a look, and I think they both silently agree they think Cal is a little too cocky for his own good. "Fine," Kip concedes. "He can clean up after the workers."

"Thank you so much," Lilly says, relieved by Kip's agreement. "Besides, it's not like you have anything better to do. She smiles, but there's a level of thinly veiled aggression under her words, and I struggle to find the meaning of them.

"Nothing at all," he replies sarcastically.

She shakes Cal's shoulder, trying to give him her most supportive smile, only receiving a bored expression in return. "I'm going to go say hey to Andie really quick and then we can go."

Justin watches Lilly reach the bottom of the stairs before turning his attention back to us. With his hands in his pockets, he tilts on the balls of his feet. "So…we'd be happy to give you a ride if you need one."

"Thanks, but I think I'll just ride back," I say.

"Are you sure?" he asks. "I wouldn't want you to be distracted."

Well fuck.

thirteen

KIP'S BEEN SLEEPING FOR almost fifteen hours and I'm starting to wonder if he's been drugged. He came over after working on the shop yesterday and passed out the second his head hit the couch cushions. It's been three weeks since the paperwork has been finalized on the space, and Kip spends every waking minute working to fix it up. His main priority is getting the loft set up for him to move in since Lilly and Justin plan on making a move to the city in a few weeks. Lilly offered the townhouse to Kip, but he wants to be closer to the shop. An egotistical side of me likes to think it's because he wants to be closer to me, too.

He's lying on his back, mouth hanging slightly open as soft snores fill the air. I'd turn him over like I did multiple times during the night, push him onto his side in an effort to alleviate the noise, but I'm actually starting to find them comforting. It reminds me that he's here.

I run a fingertip over the high curve of his shoulder, down his bicep, and onto his forearm. I hadn't pegged him to be such a heavy sleeper, but he doesn't even stir as I continue my exploration of his skin. It's rough, marked with tiny indentions and scars, the kind that come with doing manual labor for a living—a few wire-thin lines across his forehead that are barely perceivable while he's sleeping, but I know will show up the moment his eyes open. I'm tempted to wake him so I can watch the way his features come to life like they do when he smiles.

Heavy knocking reverberates through the apartment and I jerk upright in bed. The only people who come to my apartment are Peter and Kip. Considering one of them is in my bed, the likelihood is that the other must be at my door.

Panic.

Nearly falling over, I shove my legs into sleep pants, catching myself on the corner of the nightstand as I struggle to pull a shirt on correctly. Double-checking that Kip's still sleeping, I shut the bedroom door behind me and jog to the front door. I let out a breath of relief when I look through the peephole, because—Jesus Christ—that was almost really, really bad.

"Hey," I greet Lilly. "It's barely breakfast."

"I know, I'm sorry. I had an interview super early this morning, and since I was right around the corner, I figured it wouldn't hurt to stop by."

Hurt? No. Freak me the fuck out? Yes. "No, yeah. Come in."

She drops an oversized messenger bag on my counter. "You haven't happened to talk to Kip lately, have you?"

"Yesterday. Why?" Technically, I'm not lying.

She shakes her head, shrugging the question off. "Just wondering. Do you have anything to eat? I didn't have time to grab breakfast this morning."

I scrunch my nose and shake my head. "I don't really have much of anything. The Broken Egg is a few blocks away if you want to go grab something together."

"Yeah, that sounds good."

A distinct sound resonates from my bedroom, and she gives me a quizzical look. "Is that...snoring?"

I clamp my lips together and shake my head back and forth. She looks down the hall towards my bedroom and back to me, and I see the pieces fall into place as she comes to the right conclusion. She's already halfway down the hallway before I can stop her. She hits the door with the palm of her hand, pushing the flimsy material open to revealing Kip lying on his back once again.

His snores are possibly the cutest signs of exhaustion I've ever heard.

Lilly stands there, taking in Kip's naked torso peeking out from underneath the sheets and his pile of work clothes outside the bathroom door.

Trying to keep my voice low, I whisper, "He asked me not to tell you."

She doesn't acknowledge me as she bulldozes past me. I'm helpless to do anything but follow her, simply a spectator to her wrath as I watch her storm down the hallway and into the kitchen. Flinging the refrigerator open, she finds her target.

"Lilly," I say cautiously, trying to talk some reason into her. "At least you know where he's been."

But I know I can't stop what's about to happen. Lilly is fiery and there's no stopping her once she sets her mind to it. Poised over Kip, she squirts mustard straight into his open mouth. Both of my hands fly to my face as I watch Kip sit up, coughing through wet breaths, eyes wide with shock. He begins gagging once he registers the taste of mustard, leaping from the bed, naked as the day he was born as he runs into the bathroom.

"Lilly!" He spits into the sink between words. "What. The. Actual. Fuck. Is wrong with you?"

My eyes meet hers and I can see the tiny bit of fear mixed into her ire. She's still pissed, but wise enough to be scared. Even she knows she might have pushed him too far. Kip emerges, holding a towel over his crotch as he wipes the last remnants of mustard from his mouth with his hand. If Lilly wasn't in the room, and Kip wasn't so distractingly angry, I'd find this way more appealing.

"You and Justin may pull this shit with each other, pranks and fuck knows what else, but *I* am off limits."

I'm proud of Lilly as she holds her ground. "And my friend isn't?"

I mentally fist pump Lilly, beyond ecstatic she's not wilting under her brother's stare like she used to. For most of the time I've known Lilly, she's always bowed to her brother's command. But then I look at Kip, and I might actually be more scared for Lilly than she is. They stare at each other, both refusing to back down.

"Okay," I say, redirecting their focus. "How about we let Kip get dressed, and then we'll convene in the living room after you both take a moment to calm down?"

Neither one of them argues with my logic, and Lilly averts her eyes like she's suddenly embarrassed by the situation. She shoots me a glare on her way out and I manage to hold in my smile until the door shuts behind her.

"It's not funny," Kip says, sitting on the edge of the bed with towel still draped over his lap.

I hold up my fingers in a pinch. "It's a little funny."

He runs his hands over his face. "I shouldn't have stayed."

I'm not expecting the punch-to-the-gut feeling that comes with his words. It's not even like we had sex. He only came over to sleep. It's weird. *Right?*

I walk to the bathroom and begin cleaning up the remnants of mustard. The springs from the bed squeak as Kip stands, but I'm not expecting the feel of his arms as they wrap around my middle. "Your apartment is closer than Lilly's. It made more sense to crash here." His eyes meet mine in the mirror, steady when he says, "And I wanted to."

I sigh, giving him a small smile. "You have a serious snoring problem."

He knows I'm deflecting, but he doesn't push. Releasing me from his hold, he places a soft kiss to my shoulder before leaving to get dressed.

Kip and Lilly are on completely different wavelengths when it comes to communicating, so I know by letting them talk it out first it'll be more beneficial for all of us. They've always been super close, relying on each other more than they probably should. Siblings are supposed to grow up, start different lives apart from each other, focus on their own paths. But Kip and Lilly's lives are still incredibly interwoven, neither of them making a decision without careful consideration of the other. No doubt it's because of their upbringing. It's not unexpected considering they've only ever had each other—them against the world—but I thought the last four years Kip spent in prison would diminish it a little. Apparently not; the table just flipped.

If being an only child taught me anything, it's that I only have myself to rely on. It makes life tremendously easier the sooner people learn that.

Turning the shower on, I check under the sink for a towel and cuss when I find it empty. I pad down the hall toward the laundry room, stopping when I hear the tail end of Lilly's sentence.

"…of herself."

Kip replies, "She's capable of more than you think."

"She doesn't have the ability to form real attachments, Kip. Look around you."

There's silence while I assume Kip looks around.

"Money, clothes, people," she says, punctuating each word to drive her point home. "There's not a single thing she couldn't live without."

"And that's a bad thing because...what? She's too independent for you?"

It's a thinly veiled insult and Lilly knows it. She's struggled with finding her own voice, learning to depend on herself, and Kip hit the nail on the head.

"I'm not saying she's a bad person. She's not." Her voice is strained, agitated because he's not really listening to what she's saying. "I'm just looking out for you."

"That's why I didn't want you to know," he says.

"I'm not trying to tell you what to do—"

"No, you're not." He leaves no more room for argument.

I make eye contact with Kip as I walk into his view toward the laundry room. The slight widening of his eyes reveals more than their conversation did. Lilly notices and follows his gaze. My tight-lipped smile is strained, but I grab a towel from the dryer and head back to the bathroom without addressing either of them.

The bathroom is hazy and steam billows out from the shower when I pull back the curtain. It's suffocating, but in a way that makes me feel like I can breathe. The humid air fills my lungs and it purges the ickiness in my chest. I stay in the shower for a while, letting the warm water soothe the coldness of Lilly's words. The look on Kip's face, as if I had caught him confessing something, replays in my mind. I hadn't thought what they were discussing was that significant, but apparently it was to him.

I find Kip reading something on his phone when I enter the kitchen. His head snaps up when he hears me open the fridge. I pour a glass of milk and sit opposite him, pulling his plate of toast towards me. He doesn't stop me.

"She'll mind her own business from now on," he says.

I shrug. "Lilly knows me. She's seen me at my lowest and lower," I say, biting off a chunk of bread. "I don't blame her for worrying."

His eyes divert over my shoulder, distracted by a news report playing on TV. "It was a one-dimensional conversation."

"Kip, it's fine." I smile to prove my point.

He refocuses on me, eyebrows drawing together. "Why do you do that?"

My chewing slows as I try to understand his question. "Do what?"

"Pretend like nothing bothers you."

"Because it doesn't. It's not like what she said isn't true."

"So you agree? You're incapable of loving someone other than yourself? That's what you're saying?" He holds my stare, challenging me to lie, unbelieving of the truth.

I missed more of the conversation than I thought. "Do you?"

He doesn't fall for my reverse tactic. "Don't try to turn this into something it's not. Do you believe you're incapable of love?"

"That's a different question from the one you just asked me."

"How?"

"Is the question whether or not I can love in general, or whether or not I can only love myself? Which one is it?"

"Stop playing these games with me, Kaley. Do you think I don't know you better than that?"

"I'm simply asking for clarification."

"I want to hear what you think is the truth."

I give him an arbitrary list. "I love freshly painted toenails, fresh green tea, a bottle of sauvignon blanc." Kip's stare hardens and it encourages me to keep going. "You already know I love cupcakes—"

Irritated, he slaps the counter. "I'm constantly letting you in, being honest with you whenever you ask me something personal. And yet, you can't give me the same fucking consideration."

His anger drives something in me to repel. I want to push him further and I'm not sure why. "I love Lilly, and Lance, and even you, all in different ways."

He's reaching the end of his patience. "Give me something real, Kaley," he says, slow and precise.

Fine. Forcing myself to curb the desire to see just how far I can push him, I tell him something I've never told anyone. "If I can love a man as vile as my father, then I should be able to love anyone."

The harshness of his stare slowly rescinds, and I watch his pupils jump back and forth across my face. I drop my gaze to the remaining bits of toast scattered across the plate in front of me, finding it easier than facing his scrutiny head on.

When I can't take it any longer, I look up. "Happy?"

He begins shaking his head long before he speaks. "No."

fourteen

PETER TEXTED ME THIS morning to let me know he's back in town and looking forward to seeing me tonight. His message was like a reality slap to the face because I already agreed to spend the night with Kip earlier in the week. He was being super vague when he asked me to meet him at the shop, not letting me in on what he had planned.

I spent the better half of the day analyzing my bank account while getting ready, unsure who I was actually getting ready for until about thirty minutes ago when I replied to Peter's text to cancel. Not to mention attempting to sort through my feelings as to why I'm so eager to turn down a significant amount of money for Kip in the first place.

I'm running extremely low on funds, but I can't seem to find it in me to care when I have Kip to distract me. I even splurged on a new dress, not caring that the purchase slipped my bank account closer to zero than I've let it get in a long time. I admire the way it fits, running my hands down the material as I inspect it from different angles in the mirror. There's no way Kip won't love it. It's easy to forget my problems when Kip feels bigger than all of them.

He supersedes all of my worries and replaces them with his serious smiles.

I'm slipping on my shoes when there's a knock at my door. Confused, I check my text messages to make sure Kip didn't mention picking me up. I had sent him a picture of my new dress and he replied with a suggestion to pair it with cowboy boots. My middle finger emoji earned me a kissy face in return, but there's nothing about picking me up. Not that he would give me a heads-up before coming over, anyway. I'm way more used to him showing up unannounced than I ever thought I'd be.

I should've known before I opened the door that the knocks didn't land heavy enough to be Kip's. "Peter."

He slowly takes in my appearance, face locked tight as his eyes scan from my head to my feet and back again. "You look real sick, Kaley."

He's pissed. Shoving past me, he knocks the door into the wall, leaving a hole where the doorknob punctures the sheetrock. I've never been scared of Peter. Apprehensive? Yes. But never scared for my safety.

He turns abruptly, backing me towards the door. "Want to clarify some things for me?"

"Sure, Peter. What would you like to know?"

He doesn't miss the defensiveness in my voice. "You're seeing someone else?"

Hesitantly, I nod.

"Is it serious?"

I shake my head. I don't know why it feels like I'm a liar. Maybe it's because I've begun noticing how truly awful I am at it.

Peter doesn't believe me either, and his face shows his resignation. "I've heard the rumors," he says. "I figured you were trying to fill the gaps in pay since I've been so busy lately."

"At first," I agree. "But this is different. This isn't about money."

He sneers. "When is it ever not about the money?"

I can't argue with his point. I say I'm sorry, because I don't know what else to say.

He folds his hands, holding his index fingers against his mouth as he thinks. "You're sure you want to do this?"

He acts like I have a choice. I nod, because he's looking for an answer.

He mimics the motion, stopping when he speaks. "What if I say no?"

My eyebrows hit my hairline, unbelieving of what I'm hearing. "No, I can't see him? You don't own me."

"No," he says, shaking his head. "What if I said you can't break us."

"Peter, there isn't an *us*. There hasn't been for a long time."

"Everything I've done for you means…nothing," he says, flippantly waving his hand in the air.

"I am appreciative," I say, meaning it. I don't know where I would be without him. "But it doesn't mean I'm indebted to you for the rest of my life. I get a decision to leave."

"So you can have sex with other men for money, but you can't have sex with me, someone who actually gives a shit about you?"

"I haven't slept with anyone else in a while. I just…can't anymore." And I mean it in every sense of the way. Thinking about someone other than Kip touching me makes me ill in the truest sense of the word.

For some reason Peter softens, reminding me of why I gave in to his pursuits in the first place. He kisses me, and even though it doesn't feel right, it doesn't exactly feel wrong either. It feels like goodbye, and I think we both need it a little bit.

It's not until his mouth leaves mine and reaches my neck that I feel like he's pushing for more. "One last time," he says.

I shake my head. "Peter, I can't."

He doesn't listen as he lifts me onto the counter, pushing my legs apart, situating himself between them. "One last time," he repeats, emptying his pockets. "I brought you something." Keys, wallet, balled-up gas receipt…an envelope.

My heart stops.

I can't take my eyes off the envelope, and Peter doesn't take his eyes off of me as he removes his wedding band, setting it on the counter next to my thigh.

"It should be enough cash to last you until the end of the year. I brought it thinking it would make you feel better since you weren't feeling well."

A slow anger burns in my chest, but it's directed at myself, not Peter. I know I can't turn it down. I should. It would be the first time I've ever refused his money, and it would also be the first time I've ever been selfish enough to do so. It's easier to pretend like the money doesn't matter when I'm with Kip. But now it's right there in front of me.

I don't know when I started using Kip to drown my worries, but reality just came crashing back down.

Peter says my name.

Answering in the only way I can, I slowly pull his tie free of his collar, fearing if I open my mouth I'll say something incredibly self-serving. I keep my eyes trained on the actions of my fingers as I unbutton his shirt. I don't feel connected to my body, like they're not my fingers slipping each button through each slot. It can't be my fingers. My fingers should be hailing a cab, paying the driver, and knocking on the door to Kip's shop in less than thirty minutes. There's no way *my* fingers are undressing Peter.

He slides his hands up my thighs, nudging the fabric of my dress up as well. My new dress. My new and oh-so-soft dress. My throat dries up when his fingers reach between the fabric of my panties, pulling them down my legs until they hit the ground.

I'm too here. Present. In the moment.

He removes his belt and unzips his pants in hurried movements. I catch a glimpse of his penis as he pulls it over the top of his pants and I look away. I don't want to look at him.

I can't do this.

I force the thought from my mind and plant my mouth on Peter's, throwing myself into the act. He groans in approval, pulling me from the counter and forcing me over the arm of the couch. I nearly choke on air when I feel him between my legs, finding my opening.

I can't do this.

Suddenly, he's pushing in, and it's more real than it was mere moments before. This is already happening.

I can't do this.

I repeat myself, but this time out loud. Peter freezes his movements but doesn't withdraw from me.

"I can't do this," I declare for a second time, finally gaining enough sense to pull away.

Except Peter won't let me. The grip on my waist tightens, refusing to let me go. "Kaley," he says my name in warning. "You owe me this."

My hands sink farther into the couch cushion and my throat burns from the onset of tears. "I can't."

I don't need to look at him to know he's seething. But instead of retreating, he begins moving again. I try to stand upright, but he places an arm across my back, forcing my face to replace my hands on the couch as he continues to work himself in and out of me.

"Please don't make me do this." My voice dissolves into silence when I conclude he's not going to stop what we started. I should have said no and turned down the money. I should be meeting Kip.

Relaxing into the couch, I watch the clock next to the door tick away the minutes. With each pass of the second hand, this gets closer to being over. Each tick I can hear over the repeated thrusts, slowly and steadily letting me know time is passing.

When it finally is over, I barely hear him redress, and am surprised when I feel his lips meet the top of my head. He doesn't speak. He doesn't need to. He lets his money do it as he places the envelope in front of me on the coffee table.

And then I finally allow myself to cry.

I cry for so long, my head swims when I finally stand. I take off my dress, stumbling down the hall and into the shower, where I cry some more. I'm not even sure as to why I'm crying. I just have this overwhelming sense of loss. I manage to bathe and wash the makeup from my face before the water turns cold.

Wrapping the towel tighter around my body, I avoid my image in the reflective surface of the mirror when I get out. I don't know why I have an urge to brush my teeth, but I do. Then I rinse my mouth out with mouthwash twice, feeling like it didn't do its job the first time. My phone sounds from the bedroom and I already know who it is before I look at the name on the screen. I sit cross-legged and wait for the ringing to stop, noting the three calls I missed while in the shower.

I was supposed to be at Kip's over an hour ago. I know I need to say something, anything. Any excuse is better than nothing. Mrs. Cecile's apartment caught on fire, sudden case of the chicken pox, my cat died. Anything other than radio silence. But every time I prepare myself to answer, it physically hurts when I imagine his voice coming through the phone.

I go back and forth, undecided on whether I want to tell him what happened or ignore that anything happened at all. In all actuality, Kip and I aren't officially together. The only explanation I owe him is why I didn't show up tonight, but it doesn't necessarily need to be the truth.

I don't know how long I stay like that, but of course life has a way of making me face my consequences head-on.

Kip's voice travels through the apartment as he calls my name. It's mere seconds before he spots me from the hallway, eyes wide when they land on mine. "What the hell? Why haven't you been answering your phone?" he snaps. His eyes take in my appearance, concern overriding his anger. "Have you been crying?"

My mouth opens, but nothing comes out. There are too many thoughts and too many wrong ways to say them.

He kneels next to me on the bed, cupping my chin as he forces me to look at him. "Tell me what happened."

His eyes are apprehensive, like he already knows that whatever happened was bad and it was probably my fault. My eyes well with tears because I know I can't lie to him. He deserves the truth.

Standing with my back to him, I open the top drawer of my dresser. "Let me get dressed then we can talk."

It takes a few minutes, but I finally hear the bed shift as he stands, leaving the bedroom door open as he walks into the living room. My hands shake as I force my limbs into a pair of sleep pants and a T-shirt. I pinch myself hard enough to force my thoughts to settle, needing something to halt the sporadic jumping of my heart. I find Kip leaning against the kitchen counter, and I stop short when I spot the lacy fabric in his left hand. My brand new dress is draped across the stool. I hadn't thought to pick up from where I took it off.

"Kaley, *please* give me a logical explanation." He holds up the pair of underwear, maintaining eye contact as he dangles the fabric from his fingers, dropping them onto the counter between us. As if the underwear isn't incriminating enough, the metal ting of a metal ring hits the counter. "Anything. Anything that would make sense," he pleads.

Peter's never left a tie or sock, let alone his wedding band. I would have never thought to double-check for it.

"Kaley—"

As if my life can't get any worse, knocking interrupts the moment. I start for the door, but Kip holds up a hand, halting my movements.

"I'll get it."

I say his name, but he doesn't stop as he covers the distance to the door. He doesn't bother to check the peephole before he swings the door open, revealing Peter on the other side.

"Hey, I'm sorry. I forgot my—" Peter looks up from adjusting his cufflinks, the words dying on his lips when he comes face to face with Kip. Neither of them speaks as they take in each other's appearance.

Once again, I find myself comparing two very different men I've been with, one considerably superior to the other. Kip's body language screams hostility and Peter doesn't miss the subtle way Kip angles his body in front of mine.

"Kaley," Peter says, pointedly ignoring Kip's presence. "I left something. Can you grab it for me?"

Kip doesn't give me a chance to reply before his fist connects with Peter's face. I rush to put myself between the two of them. Taken off guard, Peter stumbles back a step and wipes blood from the cut on his lip. Kip reaches back and snatches the ring from the counter and flings it at Peter's chest where he scrambles to catch it. Then Kip promptly slams the door in his face.

Finally gaining the courage, I meet Kip's eyes, and I'm taken back by what I find. There's not anger, or even the shame I feel, but disappointment. It's what I expected least, and way worse than anything I could have imagined.

He huffs out a breath, shaking his head at his own thoughts, and then runs a hand down his face. There's a level of hurt in his features that I have trouble comprehending.

"Who is he?" he says, voice tenuous.

"Peter was one of my dad's defense attorneys. He gave me this apartment to live in after all of our property was seized."

"In exchange for…what? Sex?"

Suddenly, standing feels extremely tiresome, and I sit on the edge of the coffee table. "It's complicated."

Kip's eyes land on the envelope on the coffee table the same time mine does, and he snatches it before I can. Not that I could stop him anyway. He sifts through the bills, mouth moving as he silently counts, tossing it back down when he gets to a point when he's seen enough.

"Really fucking complicated," he spits out, finally showing a glimpse of anger. "How many times?"

"This was the only time since…you and I," I say, pointing between us.

He swallows, forcing his words out. "Are there more?"

I want to lie so bad, but I know he won't miss a beat if I do. "I haven't in a while, but I work a few nights a week as an escort at an exclusive bar downtown."

"This explains so much," he says, voice losing its momentum. "The way you keep your eyes open when we're having sex. The way you focus on something else, anything else…but me."

Biting my lip, I stare at the ceiling as I take in the information. He can attempt to psychoanalyze this all he wants, but he can't. I have sex with men for money. That's it. It's a choice. A choice I've continued to make over and over again.

My eyes burn when I blink, and I force them in his direction. "What did you think we were, Kip? Together?"

He lets out a deep breath through his nose, unbelieving of my lack of remorse. He speaks behind the fist he has against his mouth, almost like he doesn't want to say what he's about to. "I thought you were falling in love with me."

The silence does nothing to muffle the sound of my heartbeat pounding in my ears. A wave of nausea hits me and I vaguely contemplate puking right where I am. I stare at him, dumbfounded, trying to piece together when or how he came to that conclusion.

The way he's looking at me, equal parts hurt and confusion disguised as anger, tells me everything I need to know.

He never asked permission to fall in love with me because he knew I'd never give it.

My voice is shallow, a sense of hopelessness taking over. "It's not what I'm capable of, remember?"

He shakes his head. "I don't believe that."

"You can't or you won't?"

"I know you feel something for me, even if you don't want to admit it."

I hate his self-assuredness, like he knows me better than I do. "Are you sure you're not just projecting your feelings onto me?"

He clenches his jaw. "That would make you feel better, wouldn't it? If this was all one sided and I imagined everything. Then maybe fucking someone else wouldn't hurt quite as much."

Even though I pushed him, his spiteful words penetrate something inside me. "Just leave." Not wanting to give him a chance to throw any more stones, I stand, shoving him. "I said leave," I yell louder this time.

Reluctantly, he staggers a step towards the door. "You can tell yourself whatever you need so this doesn't break you," he says, voice steady. "But we both know you're a bad liar and you can't lie to yourself forever."

My body quakes with barely contained rage, and I want him out before he sees it break. I open the door and stare at a blank space on the wall until he finally steps through the opening. His hand shoots out, stopping me right before I shut the door all of the way. My eyes meet his through the gap.

"I wish you could see yourself through my eyes." With that, he releases his hold of the door, letting it close as he walks away.

fifteen

I PLACE TWO BOTTLES of wine on the counter and drop the exact change next to them. The store cashier looks at me in shame and I raise an eyebrow in her direction, challenging her to say something. It's seven in the morning and I just walked a mile and a half to get here. The last thing I need is her judgment. Never mind it's my fifth trip in three days.

She rings me up, albeit begrudgingly, and I shove the bottles into my oversized purse as I walk out. I feel a hand shoot out to steady me as I trip over the curb in front of the store, and I thank the person without looking up.

I'm treading water. At least, that's what it feels like. Every breath I take feels like it suffocates me a little more and I can do nothing to stop it. My lungs burn and my head swims, and I'm sure I'll go down at any moment. There aren't enough showers or tubs of ice cream to medicate it.

The stigma surrounding heartbreak is a ginormous fucking joke. I don't want a movie marathon or frozen yogurt. Not unless it's a slasher movie where the girl gets revenge on all the men she hates in her life and the yogurt is infused with wine. I hear they make that now. I'm sure it's expensive.

Peter's given me two weeks to find a new apartment and I've already wasted an entire weekend and sixty-seven dollars and some odd change I could have spent looking for one.

Oh my God. I stop mid-step, looking up from the dirty sidewalk in disbelief. I've turned into *that* girl. The one who mopes around and ignores her life because of a boy. I've witnessed them throughout my life and I always thought they were being overdramatic. I mean, no one is worth screwing your life up for. But here I am, wasting away the days and secretly hoping Kip will walk through my door without calling because he knows I can't stand it. I even left my door unlocked on the off chance he came by while I went on a booze run.

I pick up my step, annoyed with myself. I'm going to go home and begin packing and call Janine because I'm sure I'm going to be suspended for no-showing yesterday. And then I'm going to take a shower, because my hair seriously needs it.

I'm trudging up the stairs when the door to my apartment opens. My heart jumps in my throat as I freeze where I stand, waiting for whoever is leaving my apartment to come into view. My eyes land on Lance's bright blond hair and it's like I suddenly remember I can't breathe again, and I want to reach out and beg him to fix it.

"Hey. What are you doing?"

I meet him at the top of the stairs. "I went to grab a few necessities," I say, walking past him and into the apartment.

Lance walks in behind me and shuts the door. I should be more embarrassed than I am about the state of my apartment, but I can't find it in me to care.

"You do realize you left your door unlocked, don't you?"

Emptying my purse, I set the wine bottles on the counter and begin looking for the wine opener I had last seen around midnight. "Yeah, don't worry. I won't do it again."

I know I need to start pulling myself together, but I can barely stand to look Lance in the eyes without crumbling. *One more day*, I tell myself. I'm drawing the line after today then tomorrow I'll make myself be a functioning member of society.

Lance gives me a look, leaning his body over the counter to see what I'm digging for through the kitchen drawers. "Are you looking for the wine opener right behind you?"

I stop and pivot in place, feeling a small smile of relief form on my lips when I spot it. "Yes," I say, snatching it like it might try to hide from me again.

"You do realize it's barely breakfast," he says, a confused smile tugging at the corners of his lips.

The cork pops out and I do a small celebratory arm lift before shoving the wine opener in my bra. Maybe I'm not doing as bad as I think, considering I'm actually wearing one. "Want a drink?" I ask, holding the bottle up.

"Uh, no," he says. "Not much of a wine drinker. Or an eight a.m. drinker."

Sneering at him, I take a healthy sip of the liquid and almost immediately, the pressure in my chest seems to lessen. "Why are you here again?"

"Maybe I'll come back later when you're sober and…showered."

"Lance, if there ever was a day you should be nice to me in fear I might legit murder you, today is that day." I finish the glass and pour another.

He eyes me, and I think he actually might be a little scared. "Let's move into the living room."

A real soothing buzz begins to take over and I nod animatedly. "Where it's comfier."

"Yeah." He nods. "And farther away from all the sharp objects."

I fall back into the couch and giggle, definitely feeling lighter. "You're back from work quick this time," I say. "I feel like you just left."

He sits down and smiles. "Wow. I can really tell you missed me."

I roll my eyes. "What's up?"

He rubs his hands on his thighs, and even in my intoxicated state, I can tell he's nervous. "I have some news I thought you'd like to know."

"Okay?" Lance is very rarely serious, at least with me, so his nervousness is off-putting. "You're kind of freaking me out."

He lets out a small laugh and it works well to soothe me. "No one's died. I mean, not yet anyway. Mrs. Cecile is apparently immortal." She must have caught him coming in. "Are you still working at Hudson's?"

Dumbstruck, I stare at him a full ten seconds before I find it in me to speak. "How'd you know I work at Hudson's?"

"Come on, Kaley. I'm self-involved, not stupid."

I rub my forehead and take another drink of wine, staving off the headache threatening to ensue. Lance and I maintained a friendship with…partial benefits when I crashed at his place during the trial. We slept together randomly, but for the most part, Lance was gone more than he was home. I suppose it makes sense he'd do some investigating when I moved out.

I finish my second glass of wine, sufficiently satisfied with my level of drunkenness. "How come you never told me you knew?"

He shrugs. "You obviously didn't want me to know." There's not an ounce of callousness in his tone and I can tell by the look on his face he doesn't judge me. He's more upset I hid it.

"It's not exactly something I go around telling people." I pretend I'm waving to someone I've just met. "Hi, nice to meet you? You're a rocket scientist? Oh, I'm a waitress who doubles as an escort a few times a week. Nothing glamorous."

"If anyone knows the struggle of revealing their career choice to people, it's me. But we've been friends a long time, Kaley. You know I would never judge you."

"Okay, so I work at Hudson's. What about it?"

He lifts his arm and drapes it over the back of the couch. "The Attorney General is ruffling a few feathers. He's been digging around the place. Some people think he's going to try and take it down."

I huff out a laugh, which quickly turns into a yawn. "Is he new? Only a fucking idiot would try to take down the co-op."

Lance's yawn follows mine. "He *is* new. Just entered office a month ago."

I shake my head. "He's asking for trouble."

"He's trying to hold the people in power accountable. Hudson's is the government's best and worst kept secret."

The way he says the last part makes me feel like there's more to the story. I sit up and look at him. "Is there something you're not telling me?"

"What? No." When I don't back down, he sighs. "People are starting to talk. Supposedly, the Attorney General has hired a private investigator to keep tabs on the place, so obviously you're one of them."

I raise my eyebrows. "Am I being followed?"

He starts laughing. "Of course you'd jump to the most extreme conclusion. I'm just saying, be careful."

"Oh, great," I say sarcastically. "How long are we going to pretend like the government doesn't know what my porn history looks like?"

"In that case, we're both screwed. I hope whoever is in charge with keeping track of my online habits is really into girl-on-girl action."

"You do realize you're a pig, right?"

He snorts like a pig in reply.

I shake my head, smiling. "But, just so you know, I quit working there a few weeks ago."

He's intrigued. "Seriously?"

I nod and regret it, the walls around me tipping sideways with every movement.

"Can I ask why the sudden change?"

I want to blame it on Peter, and I want to blame it on Landry, but the truth is, I haven't really put the effort in to work extra nights since Kip. "Have you ever been in love? How do you know?"

Caught off guard, he asks, "Like, what's does it *feel* like?"

"Yeah."

He shrugs, looking just as confused as I am. "I don't think there's a definite answer for that. I think it's different for everybody."

"Okay, what's it like for you?"

He gives me a small smile. "Why are you asking such weird questions? You're not normally so sentimental when you're drunk."

I groan, flopping back into the couch. "Because I think I was in love, and now I don't know how to not be."

"Wait," he says, turning slightly in my direction. "Who are you in love with? When did this happen? Do I know him? Is he someone you met at Hudson's?"

I hold a hand in the air to stop him. "We're not together anymore, so it doesn't matter. I just want to be able to breathe again."

Lance furrows his brows, almost alarmed by my confession. "It matters to me," he says, placing a hand on his chest.

I lift one shoulder in question "Why?"

"Because I care," he says, hand still splayed across his chest. "You've never, not once, shown any kind of interest in having a relationship before. This guy must be a big deal if you're serious about him."

"Trust me, it surprises me more than it does you." He huffs out an irritated breath. "What are you so upset about?"

He looks away, his face losing the harshness of his irritation before looking back, this time softer. "You know, for the longest time I thought I'd be the one you'd finally get serious with."

Wait…*what?*

Laughing at my facial expression, he nods. "Yeah. I thought we're so much alike, why not be together? Not at that time, of course. Later in life when we would both be ready to settle down."

"How long ago did you come up with that crazy idea?"

"Not long after we met, actually. Even though I was undercover, I knew we were basically the same person."

Almost too afraid to ask, I say, "You didn't really think it was a possibility, did you?"

A small smile forms on his lips. "Nah, then I would remember how awful a sleeper you are, and how many times you woke me up in the middle of the night by kicking me in the nuts."

His words are meant to lighten the mood, but I can't find it in me to laugh. Maybe it's the alcohol, or maybe it's the truth, but I'm fairly positive Lance never quit thinking we'd end up together. My stomach twists at the thought of hurting Lance in the way I'm hurting now, but I also know what he feels for me isn't real. If getting my heart broken has taught me anything, it's that real love is painful.

"You don't need to reproduce anyway."

He laughs. "Says the girl who smells like ramen noodles and toenail clippings."

"Lance, that's seriously gross."

"Don't have to tell me twice."

Assuming he might be a little serious, I stand. "Fine, I'll go take a shower. When I get out, want to grab some breakfast?"

"Yeah," he says, smiling. "As long as you're sober enough to be seen with."

I don't bother to roll my eyes, too afraid of the consequences it'll have in my drunken state of mind.

"Don't forget, the government sees what you're doing, even behind closed doors," he calls as I walk down the hallway.

"I need new friends," I mutter to myself.

I manage to wash my hair and most of the important parts of my body, and I'm actually quite proud of myself by the time I get out. A few slips made me really question whether or not I needed assistance. Getting dressed is challenging, but I do feel immensely better clean and dry. The burning in my chest is still there, but it's tamable. For now.

"Do you want to try The Broken Egg on the corner?" I call towards the living room.

When I don't get a reply, I march down the hallway to find the apartment empty. I peek out of the window and I watch as Lance gets into his car without saying goodbye. His confession lingers in the back of my mind and I idly wonder if he's running. Because that's what it looks like. Maybe Lance and I are a lot alike, but I'm not sure if I want to be.

I lie in bed for over an hour after he leaves, staring at the ceiling as I will my mind to sober up. What I'm thinking about doing has to be a side effect of the alcohol. I need to get up and do what I should have done from the beginning. I force myself to ignore the bliss that comes with ignoring life and the guilt pushes me up and out of bed. Tucking my hair under a baseball cap, I stumble down the stairs with my bike and prepare what I'm going to say.

When I arrive thirty minutes later, I've yet to come up with a sound excuse, but I manage to make my legs walk up the steps of the large grey building. A police officer opens the door for me, smiling politely as I enter. There's a receptionist stationed at a desk to the right as I enter, and she asks how she can help me.

"I'm here to see Cody Landry."

She types on her keyboard vigorously. "Was he expecting you?" she asks.

"No, but tell him Kaley Monroe is here to see him."

"He's in a meeting. You can have a seat and wait if you like."

I lean on the desk, forcing her to look up from her computer screen. "I'm not going to wait. If he finds out I left here because you wouldn't notify him of my presence, he's going to be livid."

She cocks a brow at me, condescending. "Do you know how many people come in here and threaten me with that?"

I shrug, uncaring. "Do you want to take the chance this time might actually be legit?"

She shakes her head, sighs, and picks up the phone. "I'll let his assistant know you're here, but I'm not making any promises." She speaks into the receiver, repeating my name and my insistence to see Landry. There's a long pause before she hangs up, looking at me in mild surprise. "He'll see you. Go through the double doors, all the way down the hall, and his office will be the last on the right."

"Thanks," I say, already heading in that direction.

The halls are stark white and windowless, adding to my anxiety. I've never been claustrophobic, but the lack of escape options is off-putting. I knock and Landry's voice ushers me through. A thin, modelesque woman is straightening her skirt as Landry redoes his belt buckle, both flushed from physical exertion.

"Sorry to interrupt," I say, saccharine.

Landry's smile is all but sweet. "It's not a problem as long as you tell me what I've been waiting to hear. Lacey, can you call Todd and tell him I'll be late for lunch?"

Nodding, she click-clacks past me in her heels, closing the door behind her. Landry smoothes his tie against his chest with a palm as he sits on the edge of his desk. I place my hands on the back of the leather seats placed in front of his desk, keeping a sizable barrier between us.

"I'm not doing it," I say, meeting his gaze head-on.

He doesn't react, at least, not outwardly. "You're not going to do what?"

"You know what."

Shifting, he uncrosses his arms, grabbing the lip of the desk at his sides. "We had a deal."

"No," I argue. "You backed me into a corner and I was forced to agree. But I'm not doing it. I won't."

He smiles. "I've been in this business a long time, and I've never met a person who doesn't care about their self-preservation like you."

"If you out me as an escort, I'll expose everything."

His eyes flare wide, revealing the ire hiding behind his clam exterior. "You're threatening the wrong person."

Or the right one, depending on the way you look at it. "It's not a threat unless you make it one. Leave us alone and you won't have any problems. I won't ever speak of you or mention anything we've discussed ever again."

"No one would believe you. You're nothing but a girl who sucks rich men's dicks for a living."

"The daughter of John Monroe, the man who organized the largest trafficking ring in the history of the state, would be of enough notoriety to start raising questions. One mention of your name, and the FBI and DEA would be breathing down your neck."

"If you knew this all along, what made you wait until now to back out?"

I shrug. "It doesn't matter. I changed my mind? I no longer need the money? Whatever the reason, it's of no consequence to you."

Sucking on his teeth, he picks up a paperweight shaped as an apple from his desk, tossing it between his hands. "If you won't do it, you know you'll have to pay."

I shift on my feet, aching to appear unaffected. "How much?"

He holds up the marble apple, eyeing me over it. "How much do you think this paper weight costs?"

I shake my head and shrug. "I don't know. Twenty bucks?"

"Two thousand dollars." My face must show my surprise, because he smiles. "Extravagant, I know. Technically, it's just a rock carved into the shape of a fruit—nothing special. So why would I be willing to pay so much for something so insignificant?" When I don't answer, he continues. "Because I wanted to. Something is only worth what you're willing to pay for it. I saw this paperweight and thought it'd look perfect on my desk, so I bought it."

Inside my head, I start an imaginary slow clap. *Cool story, bro.*

He places the apple down. "Tell me, Kaley, what do you think your life is worth?"

I smack my lips, contemplative. "No more than…one, maybe two hundred dollars."

He lets out a laugh, truly finding my answer hilarious. "You're funny."

"It's about time someone acknowledges I am."

His smile dims and there's an edge of anger dancing behind his eyes. "Unfortunately for you, I find your life way more valuable. I was thinking closer to one, maybe one hundred and fifty thousand dollars."

I choke on my own spit, slapping a hand against my chest. "I'm sorry. Repeat that for me."

"You heard me," he says, standing. "I'll be generous and knock it down to one, but not a penny less."

"Are you on short supply of paperweights?" I say, truly confounded as to where he thinks I'll get this type of money.

This time he doesn't laugh. "I'm serious, Kaley. Probably more than you realize," he `says, eyeing me.

"Landry, I barely have a hundred dollars in my bank account."

"Last I checked, your boyfriend does."

I shake my head. "I'm no longer seeing Peter."

He shakes his head. "We both know I'm not talking about him."

My stomach drops. "How do you know about Kip?"

Buttoning his coat, he walks past me and towards the door. "He assaulted the most powerful defense attorney in the city. Word gets around." He opens the door, obviously excusing me. "You've got two weeks to bring me the money."

I want to argue, but I know it's useless. I'm halfway down the hall when I hear him call my name.

"Just because I'm letting you walk away right now, doesn't mean you've gotten away with threatening me."

I swallow, glancing over my shoulder at him. He's leaning against the doorjamb, face hard. "When should I expect my punishment?"

He shrugs. "Depends on whether or not I feel like you're making headway on our agreement."

The ride home is filled with doubt and anxiety that I'm making the wrong decision. There's no way I can come up with that much money. My mind wanders back to Hudson's, but I can't even entertain the idea of going back to that—the meaningless men and cheap sex. If I focus on it too long, unease settles in my belly and it makes me think things about myself I'm not sure I want to. Walking in on Landry with his secretary made me sick, and I wasn't even participating.

And Kip. I could never do that to Kip, no matter the consequences.

sixteen

GAINING THE COURAGE, I finally knock and fight the urge to puke on the doorstep. Maybe the alcohol isn't all the way out of my system. It's been twenty-four hours since I've had a drink, but it was a *lot* of alcohol. I'm fairly certain I've puked over less.

God, *what am I doing?*

I messaged Kip two days ago and he never replied. I had managed to wait over twenty-four hours before calling him, assuming he needed to warm up to the idea of speaking to me, but he never answered. This morning, I woke up petrified that I may never see him ever again, and the thought alone was enough to propel me to find him.

I glance over my shoulder, feeling like I'm being watched. I'm probably just being paranoid. Fricking A, I feel like I've been waiting forever. What if he's ignoring me? His truck is in the driveway, so I'm pretty sure he's here. It was less nerve racking facing Landry.

I knock again and I hear him yell he's coming a second before I see him through the foggy windowpane. Through the window, I see him falter a step, pausing before he finally turns the knob and opens the door.

"Hey," I say, slightly out of breath.

He stands with a hand braced against the doorway, the other still holding on to the door. He's in jeans and a T-shirt, but his hair still looks messy from when he woke up this morning. His face is guarded and it does nothing but remind me of the colossal fuck-up that I am. There's a chance I might not kiss that face again, and I can't think of a single thing more terrifying.

He finally replies. "Hey." Shuffling his weight onto the other foot, he scratches the back of his head. "Is everything okay?"

I almost laugh out loud at his questions. *Can't you see I'm drowning?* I am the furthest thing from okay.

"I'd like you to come with me somewhere." That didn't come out right. "I mean, I want to show you something…to give me a chance to explain."

His pupils jump back and forth between mine, looking for something, but I'm not sure as to what. Coming to some sort of conclusion, he grabs his keys from the hook by the door. "Let me grab my wallet."

My heart kicks into high gear, but I manage a semblance of a nod.

He reemerges with slightly styled hair, like he ran his fingers through it a few times to tame it. "Where to?" he says, opening the driver-side door of his truck.

We get in and I say, "A neighborhood on the West Bank. I'll direct you once we're closer."

There's a beat of tense silence before he nods, and it almost looked like he wanted to say something but decided not to. I want to push, but I know I don't have the right to do that. Not after everything that's happened. We ride toward the interstate in silence, and I never would have thought I'd miss country music so much.

"I tried to call you," I say.

He shifts, glances at me, then shifts again. "I broke my phone."

I don't ask how he broke it. We don't talk the entire hour drive. As much as it slowly eats away at my soul to have so many unresolved feelings between us, I know it has to be on his terms. Kip needs to feel like he has control of this situation, and I'm willing to give it to him. No matter how much it kills me.

"Here," I direct him, pointing to the blue ramshackle house on the left.

There's a smattering of kids' toys out front and a rusty swing set under the lone oak tree. The grass is slightly overgrown and the flowerbeds have been neglected for so long they've turned into dry dirt beds. A kid comes barreling out the front door, causing the screen to smack into the side of the house as she runs towards the playset. Another kid follows, making the same smacking sound with the screen door, and a woman yells from inside.

Kip looks away from the kids playing. "Whose house is this?"

I point at a young boy sitting on the other side of the tree, almost imperceptible from our standpoint with a book in his hand. "That's my brother—Jackson."

"Brother?" he says, eyes squinting to get a better view. "I thought you were an only child."

"I thought I was, too, until Peter disclosed his birth certificate to me after the trial. Apparently my dad had an affair and did a damn good job hiding it. Jackson is my half-brother."

"Does he know you're his sister?"

I shrug. "I don't know. I'm not sure what his mom has told him about our dad or my family."

"You haven't contacted him?" he says, eyes traveling from my brother back to me. In this light, the blue of his eyes looks iridescent. I study them, urging myself to remember what they look like in case I never get to see them like this again.

I shake my head. "It doesn't feel right."

"What do you mean?"

My eyes land on the figure of a woman standing behind the screen door. She has a hand on her hip and she uses the other to shield her eyes from the fading sun. "Paula, Jackson's mom, used to teach elementary school before she had Jackson. It was barely enough to pay the bills then, and it definitely didn't cut it once Jackson was born."

"Your dad didn't help?"

Paula opens the screen door and calls for the kids to go inside for dinner. Jackson doesn't stir, completely absorbed in his book. Paula calls for him a few times before giving up and walking down the steps and across the yard to get his attention. He snaps his head up when she's within a few feet of him, and Paula's smile can even be seen from where we're at, amused by Jackson's reaction. He bookmarks his page and stands, and Kip gets his first, full view of him.

I shake my head. "Jackson has cystic fibrosis."

Kip looks back towards the house, watching as Jackson and Paula walk up the stairs of the porch. Jackson is nine, but his stature looks that of a kid much younger. His arms and legs are noticeably thin under the weight of his clothes. He can pass as a normal, healthy seven-year-old, but he's actually an ever-sick nine-year-old.

"Whenever Peter told me about them, Paula was close to losing the house. She quit teaching when Jackson was diagnosed so she could stay home and care for him, and now she babysits whenever she can to make ends meet."

It takes him a moment, but understanding registers on Kip's face and I look away, too afraid to see what he's thinking. "Does she know the money comes from you?"

I shake my head. "No. I'm sure she knows it's from somewhere on my father's side."

He says my name, but I don't look at him, eyes still trained on the house.

"I was sixteen when he was born. It was the year I received a pearl-white BMW with white leather stitching. It was exactly what I wanted, everything detailed, even down to the size of the cup holders." I laugh at how ridiculous it sounds, how incredibly entitled I was. I believed I had earned that car. "And all the while, my baby brother was in and out of the hospital because the doctors couldn't figure out why he wasn't progressing like a normal newborn. And to make matters worse, my dad acted like he didn't exist."

"Kaley, that isn't your fault. You can't blame yourself for something you knew nothing about."

"Maybe not," I say, half shrugging. "But if I'm being honest, I'm not sure I would have done anything about it anyway."

"Why do you think that?"

"All I cared about was the new make-up palette that was out or who I was going to homecoming with. I overlooked all of the signs my father was a disgusting human because it benefitted me to stay ignorant."

"You were a teenager. You cared about normal things a teenage girl cares about. It wasn't your responsibility to check and make sure your dad was doing things morally apprehensible."

"But I didn't even care to look," I say, finally meeting his eyes. "I didn't care about anyone, or anything, but myself."

He shakes his head slightly, like he can't quite believe the words coming out of my mouth. A part of me feels good that he thinks so highly of me, but the other, self-aware part of me knows it's only false.

Deciding the argument is futile, he directs the conversation elsewhere. "So why haven't you contacted him yet?"

"What would I say? Our dad only took care of one of us, but I want to be your sister now that he's gone, is that okay?"

He gives me an incredulous look. "You didn't consider the possibility he might just be excited to have a sister in the first place?"

"On the slight chance he would be accepting, I'd have to go through Paula first. I can't just waltz in and demand a relationship with my brother I didn't know about until four years ago."

He eyes me, speculative. "Are you sure it's not the added fear she might not let you, so you keep your distance to protect yourself from rejection?"

"Slow your roll," I say, holding up a hand. "You're putting words in my mouth."

"You don't have to say the words to make them true. If there's one thing I can fault you for, it's not giving your brother the chance to gain someone else to root for him. I know it's hard for you to understand as an only child, but having someone to rely on sometimes makes all the difference."

I find comfort in his presence. Every now and then, I'll unconsciously find myself leaning towards him or about to grab his hand, and my breath will catch when I remember I'm not allowed to do those things anymore.

Guilt is a nasty thing. It doesn't care about forgiveness or rationale. It slithers in to remind me of all the bad things I've done, and worse, of all the good things I *could* have done, but didn't. He doesn't force me to see his side, and I'm grateful as I instruct Kip to wait until nightfall.

"I'll be right back," I tell him, opening the door.

"Wait," he says, grabbing my arm to stop me. "Where are you going?"

I'm hesitant to show him because I don't want him to think I'm only doing this for his benefit. Knowing he's not going to let me go until I tell him, I retrieve the envelope from my purse. "I'm going to slip this in the mailbox."

His eyes move from the white envelope and back to me. "I'll go," he says.

"No, it's okay—"

"Kaley, this isn't the neighborhood to be walking around with this much cash on you. I'll do it."

For a split second I debate mentioning his control issues, but force myself not to for the sake of keeping the peace. "Fine."

He instructs me to lock the doors as he gets out. There's something in him that feels, and that something is better than nothing. It makes me want to push him, purposefully disagree with everything he says, to see exactly how deep those feelings run. But I also know Kip will reveal what he wants and it has to be his choice.

I'm just starting to get worried and I scream when he knocks on the driver window. I hear his chuckle through the glass and I scowl at him as I lean over to unlock the door.

"Did I scare you?"

"Ha ha, so funny," I mock, snapping my seatbelt on.

He laughs harder as he starts the ignition and drives away. He doesn't turn the headlights on until we're a decent distance from the house. Even though he disagrees with my decision to stay out of Jackson's life, he goes out of his way to help me keep my secret.

Holy shit, *I'm in love with Kip*.

It's the first time the thought hasn't set panic to my insides.

"What are you smiling at?" Kip says, glancing from the road, to me, and back again. His face is a mixture of concern and amusement, eyes hiding a smile he refuses to show.

I choose my next words very carefully. "I can't imagine anyone but you touching me."

Quickly, the happiness in his eyes dissipates altogether and he focuses on driving again. "Then why'd you let him?"

His words hurt in a different way than I've ever hurt before. "I couldn't figure out why it made me sick, at first. Not until we were already…there," I say, trying to find an easy way to put it. "Then I couldn't stop it."

Kip's head snaps in my direction. "What do you *mean* you couldn't stop it?"

Shit. "It's not what you're thinking."

"Then tell me what I'm thinking," he says, his tone harsh but a tad doubtful as well.

"I allowed it to get to a point of no return, Kip. No matter what, I allowed him to go there."

My body slams forward in my seat and I brace a hand against the glove compartment as Kip pulls to the side of the interstate. "He forced you to have sex with him?"

"Kip, no. I told you it wasn't like that."

"So you're saying you wanted to have sex with him and it was completely consensual the *entire* time?"

My mouth goes completely dry as I replay the night in my head. It's kind of blurry, but I can recall bits and pieces. I've spent days trying to avoid overanalyzing it, but now I'm having difficulties remembering it at all.

"I-I don't…"

Kip's voice washes over me, much more calm than before. "Take a deep breath." I do as he says. "Take your time and tell me what happened."

Focusing on the moment, I let the most vivid aspect come back to me. The feel of the threads of the couch under my palms, the smell of his cologne, the weight of Peter's forearm on the curve of my back, and the sound of the clock ticking.

"I couldn't go through with it," I say, hating how small my voice sounds. "I told him I wanted to stop, but he didn't."

"It's okay," Kip says, wrapping a hand around my neck and bringing my head to his chest. At some point he had scooted closer to me on the seat. "It wasn't your fault."

It's weird how he keeps saying that like he truly believes it. I don't know how he can't see how wrong he is.

"Kip, I'm so sorry."

I don't have to specify for what, because he already knows. He doesn't reply as he holds me, and I let him because I'm too selfish to stop it. It takes a while for the tension to leave his body, letting go of his bout of anger. Finally, he releases me and makes me look at him. "That first day at Lilly's, when you showed up with a bruise on your face, was that him?"

I had forgotten about that bruise since it faded so long ago. I shake my head. "No."

"It was someone else?"

I hate that I can't lie to him. "Yes."

He takes a deep breath. He must be able to tell that I don't want to discuss it because after a moment, he says, "We aren't as different as you think."

"Yeah? How's that?"

He licks his lips, eyes moving between mine, and I can tell he's about to reveal something that he's never told me before. "I had a year-long affair with a married woman when I was seventeen."

The surprise must read all over my face because he smiles, and it loosens the rein around my chest.

"I was stealing her BMW because I knew the parts would resell really high. She caught me, and instead of calling the cops, she invited me inside."

"You had sex with her so she wouldn't report you?"

He nods, a touch of embarrassment touching his cheeks. "It's how I lost my virginity."

"And you kept sleeping with her for a year because…?"

Glancing away, he shrugs nonchalantly. "I wanted to."

I huff out a small breath of laughter. "I suppose we are a lot alike."

He smiles but becomes serious again. "I don't think you should stay in your apartment."

"I only have a week left before I have to leave, so I won't be there much longer. I've been looking at other places."

It doesn't seem to pacify him, but he eventually nods, if a little reluctantly. "We should get going," he says, slowly starting to pull away. He holds my eyes as he moves to his side of the truck and starts the ignition. We drive the rest of the way in silence and I don't mind it this time. Emotions I can't pinpoint squeeze my chest as we park in front of my apartment.

"Thanks again for coming with me," I say, prolonging getting out of the truck.

He nods. "Thank you for sharing it with me. Your brother and everything," he clarifies, but doesn't detail what everything means. It's my turn to nod, and I open the door to get out when his voice stops me again. "Give me some time to think, okay?"

I nearly fall to my knees in relief and I vaguely note how unhealthy it is for me to feel like my life is do-or-die without him, but it's uncontrollable.

"Okay," I say, trying hard not to show how much hope he's just given me.

seventeen

"KALEY, WAKE UP."

My eyes snap open and I jerk upright in bed, head-butting Kip in the forehead.

"Fuck," he cusses, holding a palm to his head.

"Ow." I fall back, holding my head in my hands. "Why are you standing over me like a creeper while I sleep?"

"I was trying not to freak you out."

"Good job," I say sarcastically.

He rubs the spot on his forehead once more before dropping his hand. "Pack whatever you need for tonight and tomorrow. We'll come back for your stuff in the morning."

I lean on an elbow and switch on the bedside lamp. "What time is it?"

"A little after midnight."

"Kip, it's the middle of the night."

"I know, I just told you what time it is."

I laugh. "So let me sleep. I'm fine."

He glares at me. "You're not fine. I broke into your apartment with a flathead screwdriver and you didn't even wake up. It's not safe for you to be here."

We stare at each other a few seconds and it takes every ounce of willpower not to smile and give myself away. Showing up in the middle of the night is revealing his true feelings and just how much he cares. He knows it. If I make it a big deal, he might second-guess his decision. I need to act like everything is normal.

Rolling my eyes, I fall back into bed and pull the cover tighter around my chin. "I'm not going anywhere but back to sleep."

In one swoop, the blanket is stripped from my body and I scream at the cool air against my exposed skin. "Have you lost your mind?" I yell, reaching but failing to get the cover from him.

"Maybe," he says, eyes trailing over my body.

It's then I realize how exposed I actually am. A tank top and sleep shorts don't cover much.

"It's nothing you haven't seen before," I say, yanking the covers from his grasp. "Now go away."

Once I'm covered, it's like he snaps to. Kip may be different from any man I've met, but he's still a man. "I'm not leaving you here," he says.

"Fine," I say, peeling the edge of the covers back. "Sleep here, but I'm not going anywhere."

He hesitates. "Kaley…"

Too tired to argue, I scoot to the other side of the bed and flip over, putting my back toward him. "Turn out the light when you make up your mind." He doesn't reply and it's silent for so long, I start to wonder if he will actually leave.

When his side of the bed dips, I can't stop my smile. I listen as he kicks off his shoes. There's another moment of silence and I imagine him debating how much of his clothing he'll shed. Kip normally sleeps in his underwear, sometimes nude after we would have sex, so I know jeans a t-shirt will be the furthest things from comfortable for him.

"Just get undressed already. I'm not going to touch you."

I hear his sigh, followed by him standing and undressing. Listening intently, I calculate which item of clothing he's working on. First his shirt, then the button and zipper of his pants, and I hear the way the material glides down his legs as he takes them off one pant leg at a time. Warmth spreads throughout my body and I realize just the sound of him getting undressed turns me on.

I'm so screwed.

Turning off the lamp, he gets in bed. He repositions the pillow I vacated, sliding down enough to get under the covers. There's a few minutes of him fidgeting before he finally stills. The quiet is so loud it makes my ears ring. Apparently, I'm listening too hard.

He speaks, his voice a deep, soft whisper. "Relax."

I hadn't noticed, but my body is strung tight. Having him so close, with so much touchable skin and surrounded by his smell, is setting every fiber of my being on fire. I count to ten in my head and hope I can dispel the tension. It doesn't work.

"Are you mad at me for breaking into your apartment?"

I let out a burst of laughter, turning over so I can see him. It's dark, but my sight adjusts to the dark enough to make out his features. "No. I should be, but I'm not." Matter of fact, it makes me all too happy.

I hear him swallow before he speaks. "I couldn't sleep."

"Are you still having nightmares about mustard?"

It's his turn to laugh, and his teeth reflect the only light in the darkness. "You're never going to let me live that down, are you?"

I smile. "Never."

His teeth disappear and I know whatever he's about to say will be much more serious. I'm just not expecting what it is. "Do you think you can love me?"

It's like someone reaches inside my chest and squeezes my heart until the point of bursting. Then all at once, it releases, pumping furiously.

I've said the words in my head. I've come to accept the fact I do. But saying them out loud to the person who has the ability to walk away at any moment is a completely different story. Especially because I've created a shit-storm any person in their right mind would run from, let alone walk away at a leisurely pace. If I don't, I ruin the possibility he might stay. I'll hang on to that slim possibility, simply because the alternative is the scariest scenario I can imagine.

"I already do."

I don't know what I expect him to do or say, but doing nothing is not it. He doesn't move or speak or even breathe, and I wait in stilted silence for an acknowledgment I'm not alone in this. It gets to a point I can't take it anymore, and I move my body closer to him by a few inches, needing to feel something from him but unsure how to make him do it.

"Say something," I plead. There's no way he can miss the absolute vulnerability in my voice.

Clearing his throat, he says, "I just love you so much right now."

All the air leaves me and we remove the remaining distance between us. The moment his lips meet mine, I quit drowning. I've never felt more alive than I do right now, and I never want to let it go. He holds my face still as he uses his mouth to claim me. This isn't a negotiation. There isn't a chance to back out. If I love him, which I do, I don't get an option to break us. He tells me all of this with his mouth.

He breaks away but doesn't let go, his eyes imploring mine. "Tell me you love me."

This time, I say it without hesitation. "I love you."

I've barely said the words when he's kissing me again, pressing me firmly to him as his hands move from my face to my back. Breathing has never felt this effortless. I run my hands over the muscles of his stomach and up his chest, loving the way his skin feels beneath my touch.

"Kaley," he moans against my mouth.

I dip my hand farther south. "Kip."

He reaches down, stopping it before it descends any lower. "Wait a second," he says, his breath harsh against my lips.

"There's always a round two, remember?"

Kissing the top of my hand, he pulls away, and I don't like the distance. "Not tonight." He uses his spare hand to smooth the hair from my face.

I swallow back the feeling of rejection. "Is there a reason why?"

"I want our next time to be different than here, in this apartment, where so many bad things have happened."

Where Peter has touched me.

"You want a fresh start," I say.

"Yeah," he says, seemingly relieved I understand. "I promise, I want to…badly. But I also want it to be in my bed, under my roof." *On his terms.*

Kip is a very proud man, and I've wounded his pride and it's already asking a lot of him to stay here with me tonight. I hadn't quite realized the sacrifice he was making to stay with me. It only makes me love him more.

"Do you think you can forgive me?" I don't want to say Peter's name, too afraid it'll change the mood of our conversation.

"I know sex is purely physical. You can have sex with someone and it mean nothing to you. I've been there." He snuggles into the pillow more, tugging me to his side.

My body sinks farther into his side. It's nearly impossible to describe the relief. "How do you know you won't wake up one day and resent me for it?"

"Because I know you didn't want to," he says softly. "I'm going to be honest and say it still hurts a little, but I get why you felt like you had to. Not only for Jackson, but for yourself. He literally owns your life. It's hard to say no to someone who holds that kind of power over your head. Trust me, I get it."

"I wouldn't blame you if you couldn't, you know?"

He sighs, eyes trained on the ceiling. "Kaley, I chose to forgive you the moment I left your apartment that night. You've never experienced anything like us before. I don't fault you for being relationship illiterate, especially in the messed up situation you were in." He runs his fingers in tiny circles on my forearm draped across his chest as he thinks. "When did you begin a relationship with him?"

"After the trial," I say. "At the time, I had mentioned to him that I needed a new place and job."

His fingers still. "He propositioned you?"

"It wasn't exactly like that," I say, trying to organize my memories. "We flirted a lot. I mean, I flirted with everyone a lot, so I hadn't thought anything of it. That was, until he invited me on a trip to Europe as an assistant."

Kip's makes a sound of disbelief, somewhere between a cough and grunt, and I laugh. "It's obvious now, but at the time I thought he was being sincere. We did end up sleeping together, but the money didn't show up until a few months later when I found out about Paula and how close she was to losing her house."

"He offered to help you," he says, putting the pieces together.

"Yes. But now I see it for what it was…just a way for him to gain leverage over me."

I can tell he doesn't want to ask whatever he's about to, but needs to. "And the bar? Downtown?"

"Peter started skipping out on the nights we were supposed to meet up, and that also meant I didn't get the money for Jackson. It was an easy alternative."

Breathing deep, Kip resumes making tiny circles on my arm and I know he's done asking questions for the time being. There's probably a million more he's sorting through, but for both of our sakes, he's asked enough for tonight. He pulls my hand to his mouth again and I'm grateful for the small gesture. Everything Kip does is methodical, especially in regards to my feelings. He's gentle with me in the most powerful of ways.

I tell him I love him, and for the first time, he tells me, "I love you too."

eighteen

WAKING UP WAS STARTLINGLY wondrous this morning. The first few seconds came at me fast, making me wake with a start. Kip's body was warm against my back with his legs intertwined with mine and my hand still in his over my belly. I relished in the moment, unmoving for close to thirty minutes before he woke up. It was the best way to start the day.

Kip, unfortunately, is a coffee drinker. So the first business of the day was to go get coffee and packing supplies. Kip before coffee is energetic, Kip after coffee is downright demanding.

"Okay, I'll start in the kitchen because it'll be the most complicated to pack and you can attempt to tackle your closet and bedroom."

"That's not fair," I say. "You picked the room I use the least."

He laughs. "Do you want to switch?"

I think about a box of unmentionables hidden in a shoebox under my bed and shake my head. "No."

We spend the day in separate parts of the apartment. Occasionally, he'll come ask if I want to keep something or donate it. We pass each other as we deposit the boxes by the door or when we need to trade tape or newspaper, and I live for those moments. He pretends he's focused on whatever he's packing up, but I feel the way his body changes when I'm nearby, the way his eyes follow me when he thinks I'm not looking.

"Hey, Kaley?"

"Yeah?" I say, looking up from organizing shoes according to style on my bed.

He points at a stack of newspapers on my dresser. "Can you hand me a few of those?"

"Oh, yeah. Sure." I reach over and hand him some.

"Thanks."

I can't stop the involuntary smile that takes over my face as he leaves. Just being around him makes me giddy. It's almost like I can finally enjoy being in love.

He peeks his head back in and I hurry to cover my smile. "Do you have the scissors?"

I shake my head. "I haven't seen them."

He doesn't move for a split second, a hint of a smile in his eyes as he takes in my predicament. "I love you." he says, and then leaves before I can even comprehend what just happened.

We said it to each other last night, but saying it in the light of day where there's nothing to hide behind is another. My smile only grows as I stare down at the mountain of shoes around me.

"Kaley?"

My head snaps up at the sound of Kip's voice, and embarrassment floods my cheeks at being caught smiling like a dumbass at nothing *again*.

"Stop coming in here," I yell, throwing a group of newspaper at his face.

He ducks just in time for the bulk of the newspaper to hit the door, looking up at me like I've lost my mind. "What did I do?"

"You know," I say, pointing a finger at him.

His smile is Cheshire. "I have no idea what you're talking about." Slowly, as if afraid, he leans in my direction.

I hold his stare as I force air in and out of my lungs. "What are you doing?"

He stops, lingering over me, holding my stare. "Getting a roll of tape."

It takes a moment for his words to finally register. "What?"

He pulls away, holding up a roll of packing tape from the dresser behind me. "I didn't want you to throw it at me."

A grin spreads across his face as he steps away, tossing the tape in the air and catching it as he leaves. I drop my head and groan into my hands. His chuckle echoes down the hallway.

Together we clear the apartment faster than I ever could have by myself. My bedroom is empty except for the furniture that came with the apartment, and the bathroom is the last thing for me to do. I check Kip's progress of the kitchen and living room and find he already has the majority of the items put away already. He's on his knees with his back to me as he inspects my DVD collection as he packs them.

"How's it coming?"

He turns at the sound of my voice. "I'm honestly a little concerned for your mental stability." I give him a questioning look and he holds up a DVD. "All of your movies are fucking creepy."

I bust out laughing, and by the look on his face, it only adds to his concern. "I went on a drunk scary movie spree."

He tosses the DVDs in his hand into the box and closes it up, placing it on top of all the other boxes. Standing, we both take in the pile of all my things stacked by the door.

"Thank you for helping me," I say. "Now I just need to find a place to move them to."

He makes a face like it's obvious. "My place."

I give him a dumb look. "Kip, I'm not moving in with you."

Holding his hands palm side up, he says, "I never asked you to."

"So we're just moving all of my stuff to your place and I'll stay there until further notice?"

"Look, I'm not looking forward to having to pick up after you either, but you don't have a lot of options right now."

It's my turn to hold my hands up, because we both damn well know he's been cleaning my apartment every time he comes over. "I'm not moving in with you, Kip."

He nods, cocking his head to the side. "Okay."

"Okay?"

He shrugs. "Okay." Opening the apartment door, he picks up two boxes and walks outside.

"Where are you going?"

"I'm putting my new stuff in my truck."

Following him, I read the hand-drawn label on the side of the boxes. "So you need a DVD collection you're too chicken shit to watch and tiny ceramic elephant figurines?"

"My girlfriend has issues, but this is the weird shit she likes, so I'm trying to show her how invested I am in our relationship. It's new, but I have high hopes." We reach his truck and he stops by the tailgate. Nodding his head in the truck's direction, he says, "Can I get a little help?"

I look at the tailgate and back to him. "You're kidding, right?"

"I can stand here all day." Clenching my teeth, I pull the handle and let the tailgate drop with a loud bang. "Easy," he says, placing the boxes down. "She's a classic."

I fold my arms across my chest. "This is happening whether I want it to or not."

He stares at me blankly. "Nothing's happening." Then he turns around and walks back up the stairs.

I'm so infuriated, my hands shake as I follow behind him. "I am tired of you dictating everything I do."

My words do their job and he stops mid-step, pivoting towards me at the top of the stairs, face contorted in disbelief. "What did you say?"

"You're taking away my right to choose," I say, but this time calmer.

His voice shakes from his own thinly veiled anger. "I am nothing like him."

He doesn't have to say who for me to know who he's talking about. My head snaps back. "I never said you were."

"You insinuated it. I have never forced you to do anything, and I sure as hell haven't used you for my own benefit."

"No," I say, regret already setting in. "I promise that's not how I meant it. You are vastly different from any man I've ever met, let alone been with. I know you're nothing like him."

He takes a deep breath and runs a hand over his mouth, finding a sense of calm he didn't have seconds before. "I'm not trying to make you feel like your feelings don't matter. They absolutely do. But there isn't anything else for you to choose from right now. Later, if you decide you want something else, you will be able to do so. I'm just trying to buy you time."

It is the most logical option. "I don't ever want you to feel like I'm using you."

His gaze softens. "You're not. Didn't you like waking up with me this morning?"

"Of course, but we're moving so fast."

He cups my chin in his hand. "We're moving at whatever speed life gives us."

Mrs. Cecile's door opens right as Kip leans in to kiss me and I drop my head onto his shoulder with a groan.

"You're moving today?" she asks, staring at us through the gap in her door.

I lift my head and lay it against Kip's shoulder. "I am."

"Well," she says. "I'm sad to see you go."

I give her an incredulous look.

Before I can reply, she says, "But I'll be ecstatic to finally get some real sleep. Hopefully my new neighbors don't practice gymnastics at night." She begins to close her door before she realizes she has something else to say. "Or argue as much as you two do." Then she slams the door.

Kip and I bust out laughing.

We get everything packed into the back of his truck and I leave the place I've called home for the last four years. I'm sadder than I thought I'd be, but Kip seems to understand why I wanted to do one final walkthrough to make sure I didn't leave anything. Tanya says she'll miss hearing about my life when I turn in the keys, but assures me Mrs. Cecile gives everyone just as much crap as she does me, which kind of makes me sad. I thought I was especially annoying.

Kip and I don't speak until I notice we're headed in the wrong direction. "Where are we going?"

"We've gone over this already. My place."

"But your place…oh," I say, drawing out the sound. "We're going to the shop."

He smiles, a touch nervous by my reaction. "Is that okay?"

"Yeah," I say, matching his smile. "I didn't know it was finished."

"The space needs some work, but the apartment is done. Actually, I was finishing packing at Lilly's when you showed up the other day."

When we arrive, I read the large sign hanging up in front of the building. Smiling, I look over at Kip. "Beater's?"

Almost like he forgot what he named his own shop, it takes him a moment to figure out what I'm talking about. "I couldn't come up with a name. I don't know if it's a good name from a marketing standpoint, but hopefully my work will speak for itself."

He turns around back and parks in the alley, right beside a brand new staircase that leads to what I assume is the door to the apartment.

"I didn't think you'd want to have to walk through the shop every time you came over," he explains, reading my thoughts.

Kip unlocks the door and holds it open for me to go in first. The space is small even for a studio apartment, but it doesn't feel crowded. The railing overlooking the shop is closed in, and the bedroom is built up on a platform, separating the space from the living room and kitchen. The furniture is simple, a couch with a TV mounted, and the small kitchen has all new, streamlined appliances.

All of the details recede to nothing when my eyes land on the kitchenette set by the foot of the bed. The table is set with dishes and silverware on top of a white tablecloth. I walk over to it, fingering the wilting petals of the flowers in a vase in the middle of the table. This is why Kip had wanted me to come over.

It's like I tripped back into the water and I'm fearful of going under again, my breath suddenly fighting for space.

Kip wraps his arms around my middle, pulling me into his chest. Running his lips up the outside of my throat, he creates goose bumps all along my arms and chest. "Why don't you take a shower and I'll unpack all of the boxes."

"It's my weird shit. The least I can do is help."

He places a kiss on the curve of my neck. "Let me do this for you," he says.

"Stop trying to make me feel better."

I can feel more than see his smile. "You're overthinking. Don't worry about the table. I'll burn it if that's what you want me to do."

He's at a loss for how to move past this as much as I am, because burning furniture is not going to fix it. I smile. "You know what I've never done? Gone camping."

"Really?" he says. "Even I've gone camping, and I missed out on a lot of childhood rites of passage."

"Thanks for rubbing it in," I say jokingly.

"Primitive camping is permitted on the hills," he suggests.

"Oh, I don't know. They have all those signs about animals and snakes and possibly dying from falling off a cliff."

"This is getting way off track," he says, spinning me around. "Go take a shower."

"All my soap and shampoo is in the truck"

"Do you not think I have soap?"

I scrunch up my nose. "Two-in-one shampoo doesn't substitute as soap."

"I have even better," he says, grinning where it reaches his eyes. "Three-in-one with body wash."

nineteen

I SHUFFLE THE PAN from one hand to the other, wondering how the hell my life has turned into this. I'm bringing a homemade pan of banana pudding to Lilly's housewarming party, not as her friend, but as Kip's date. I have to be in an alternate universe. "Does Lilly know?"

Kip takes the pan from me, easily shifting the bottle of pinot under his arm, and shuts the truck door as I get out. "She knows something happened between us, but doesn't know what or why. Not for a lack of trying, either."

I smile. "Figures."

We head up the stone walk toward the wooden front door. The house is a deep red brick, situated on a cul-de-sac in the back of the neighborhood. It's not like the mansions I used to live in, but it's not exactly cheap either. Lilly must have gotten a good job.

"She'll forget about it," he says dismissively.

I'm not so sure. "Is she still mad? You know, about us?"

He pauses, turning around to look at me. "She was never mad at you."

I snort. "Have you forgotten the mustard?"

He shudders, but I pretend I didn't see it. "She has underlying hurt that I kept it from her. It's easier for her to direct it at you instead of dealing with me about it. There's a part of her that doesn't want to ruffle my feathers."

"I can't say I blame her."

"What does that mean?"

"Well, you're kind of overbearing."

He frowns. "No I'm not."

I make a face. "You've always been a tad controlling."

"You would have never learned how to ride a bike if I hadn't pushed you," he says, a challenge in his words.

"Riding a bike isn't vital to my existence, Kip. It's not like you instilled life-altering knowledge."

I ignore his cocksure smile and push the doorbell. Everything about this night has me on edge, but I can't quite put my finger on why.

"Stop worrying," Kip says, nudging me with his free elbow. "She'll be happy to see you."

My eyes widen. "She doesn't know I'm coming?"

He has the audacity to look guilty. "I was going to mention it…"

"Kip," I say through my teeth.

The door opens at the most opportune time and Justin appears, coming to a standstill in the open doorway. "Oh, this is going to be good," he says, smiling like my arrival is the best thing he's seen all day.

Kip glares at Justin, shoving the pan of pudding at him until he's forced to take it. "Everything will be fine."

Justin doesn't look so sure, but he smiles at me as we enter. "Who made the pudding?"

I give him a look. "Who do you think?"

"I've missed Kip's cooking since we moved."

Justin leads us through the foyer and into a beautiful chef's kitchen with dark cabinets and granite countertops. Lilly and a guy I don't recognize linger by the bar, and Lilly does a piss-poor job of concealing her surprise at seeing me. Last she heard, Kip and I weren't together.

Kip goes in for a hug, ignoring her reaction. "The house is impressive, Lil. But don't you think it's a little…much?"

She pats him on the back. "I never want to move again, so I wanted something we could grow into."

"Hi," I say, making for the most awkward eye contact ever.

"Hey," she says, weary.

"The house is really amazing, Lilly."

She manages a smile. "Thanks."

The guy swivels on the bar stool in our direction, effectively breaking the tension as he gives me a once-over, holding a hand out for me to shake. "Nice to meet you," he drawls, a gleam in his eyes.

"Who's this?" Kip asks Lilly, pointing a finger in the guy's direction.

Justin sets everything down on the counter and smacks Jacob's hand out from between us. "This is my little brother, Jacob. He hits on anything with a vagina, take no offense."

He's cute, maybe a few years younger than me, with wavy dark hair and equally dark eyes. He looks like a puppy. He smiles, pretending to be sheepish, and it's not hard to imagine a lot of girls falling for it.

Jacob picks up an already poured shot and hands it to Kip. "Your girl is seriously gorgeous."

Kip is unsure how to react as he takes the shot from his hand. "Let's refrain from talking about her like she's not here, yeah?"

Jacob's eyes narrow the tiniest bit as he pours more shots. "No problem." He hands me a glass of clear liquid. "You're gorgeous," he says, winking at me.

Kip looks like he wants to say something, but even he can't get mad at Jacob's boyishness. He and Justin make eye contact, and all Justin can manage is a shrug. Almost an *I told you so.*

"There's beer and wine in the fridge if you're thirsty," she says, picking up her own glass of wine. "Everyone is already outside. The food is on the grill, but it should be ready in a few minutes."

We all congregate on the back patio. Lights are strung overhead and around the in-ground pool. A few people lounge around an outdoor table next to the grill, and I feel my first real smile break through at the sight of Lance drinking a beer as he checks the meat.

He makes eye contact with me and smiles, wrapping me in a hug. "I didn't know you were coming," he says.

"I can't believe you're still on break. When do you go back to work?"

"The chief is giving me some time off."

"I bet you don't even know what to do with yourself," I say, hitting him on the arm.

His smile wanes a little and it's then I realize his eyes have landed on Kip. Kip wraps an arm around my waist as he shakes Lance's hand, and I physically watch Lance figure out that Kip is the person I was talking about the other morning he was at my apartment.

"Hey, Lance. How's it been going?" Kip says.

It takes a moment, but Lance returns the greeting. "Doing good. How about you? Justin told me you opened your own shop?"

Kip feels the tension, but he can't figure out exactly why it's there as they discuss muscle cars and the logistics of working for yourself. I excuse myself to greet the rest of the guests. Cal is here with his grandfather, Mr. Wilson, and I hear him warning a petulant Cal away from the dessert table. Justin brought a few buddies from work, and they're all super nice. I laugh as they sneak a drinking game out from under Mr. Wilson's nose.

It's when my eyes land on the two girls at the end of the table I freeze. Andie and another girl are sipping their drinks, smiling as they discuss something quietly, and dread fills me. Pulling on my big-girl panties, I make my way over to them.

Andie looks up first and smiles. "Hi, I remember you. Kaley, right?"

I nod, but before I can talk, her friend butts in. "How do you know Lance?"

"We were friends in college," I answer.

"Oh, so you two are close?"

I shrug, unsure how to answer that question myself. "I guess."

She leans in, prompting me to follow her lead. "Is he single?"

I smile as understanding dawns. All three of us glance in Lance's direction and watch as he chugs the beer in his hand, flipping a steak with his free hand as Kip stands awkwardly next to him, also downing his own beer.

"He is."

She and Andie trade excited glances, and I take the moment to excuse myself, feeling good about my solid effort at being friendly. Lance announces the food is ready, and Lilly brings out a platter to put the steaks and potatoes on as the rest of us move inside. The dining room is open to the patio, making the space casual and open for entertaining. I wait for Kip by the door, locking eyes with Lance as he walks past. If I'm not mistaken, an imperceptibly quick flash of hurt shows through, and my heart catches. My gaze lands on Kip, and I know he saw what I did, too.

When we take our seats, I slide my hand into his under the table, and I take a breath of relief as he interlocks our fingers. We eat with our folded hands on his thigh, even though it's beyond difficult to cut steak with only one hand, but neither of us moves to undo them.

"When do you open?" Jones, Justin's friend from work, asks Kip.

Kip takes a moment to sip his beer. "I don't have a set date yet."

"That's really cool though. Starting your business and all that jazz. I've been thinking about starting my own private security team for years, but I don't have the balls to do it."

Justin takes a bite of steak, looking at Jones. "You never told me that."

"Yeah, I mean, it's kind of a pipe dream."

Kip holds his beer between his fingers, shaking his head. "It's gut wrenching, for sure. I'm not even sure I would have done it if Kaley hadn't pushed me."

Lilly's head swivels in my direction for the first real time since we sat down. "Really?"

All eyes are on me, and I fight the urge to hide under the table. "I, uh, had mentioned it, but Kip took the initiative. He's been working really hard to get everything up and running so quickly."

Jacob pipes in. "And what do you do, Kaley?"

Lance snickers behind his beer, drawing everyone's attention to him. "What doesn't she do?"

Kip's hand tightens in mine, and I can feel heat traveling to my cheeks. Justin's head snaps in Lance's direction, and it's obvious he knows what Lance is referring to, only adding to my silent humiliation. Lance pointedly avoids Justin's stare as he drinks more beer. It's then I realize the haze of red glazing them, and it sets alarms off inside my head. Things are about to go bad fast.

Lilly leans forward. "What does that mean?" she says, short. It's almost…protective?

"It means," he says, cocky. "She gets around."

I swallow my emotions, too many of them to keep track of.

Kip glares at Lance. "I think you should leave."

He meets Kip's stare, but there's no heat behind his eyes. They're empty, and it makes me sad to think I did that to them. "I think I'll leave when I want to, and I haven't finished my dinner." Lance stabs his untouched steak, sawing it in half.

Mr. Wilson stands, motioning for Cal to stand with him. "Lilly, thank you for the dinner, but we're going to head out."

"No," I say, standing. "We'll leave. I'm obviously the problem here."

Lance holds his hands out, palms up. "What problem? There's no problem. Sit, eat, be merry."

Kip urges me back into my seat, and I'm silently begging him not to engage him. Not here, not in front of everybody, and not in front of Lilly. She deserves this party and everything she's built for it, and the last thing I want to do is ruin it for her.

"This is my sister's house, and therefore my home, so I have authority to kick you out."

Lance scrunches up his face. "I'm not leaving."

Justin drops his head in his hands. "Lance, don't do this."

He gives Justin an incredulous look. "You're taking her side?"

No one stops Mr. Wilson and Cal from leaving this time, but Lilly hurriedly grabs the pan of banana pudding Kip and I brought to give to them as they leave. Jones looks like he's prepared to break up a fight, Jacob looks embarrassed for asking me a simple question, and Andie and her friend watch like we're a spectator sport.

"I'm taking my soon-to-be wife's side, and you're picking the wrong fight if you think she's going to go against Kip's word."

Lance's face contorts in disgust. "How would she feel if she knew her brother's girlfriend is a prostitute?"

Lilly's mouth falls open and Kip jerks from the table. Justin, Jones, and I all stand, ready to stop anything from happening. Kip is eerily calm as he looks at Lance. "You have ten seconds to leave."

"Or what?" Lance draws. "You're going to assault a federal agent? I'm sure your parole officer would love that."

"Lance," Justin says. "You're drunk. Go home, get some sleep, and feel like shit in the morning, but there's no need to make it worse by getting your face beat in."

There's a moment of silence before Andie speaks. "I'll drive him. Lolene can take my car."

Everyone waits for Lance's reply, sighing in relief as he willingly stands. He stumbles over the chair, but manages to catch himself before falling. Digging in his pockets, he finds his keys and hands them over to Andie. He stops by the fridge on his way out, retrieving a few more beers. He makes eye contact with me, and I know I need to speak with him before he leaves.

"Kaley," Kip says, grabbing my hand to stop me.

I squeeze his hand in mine. "I'll be right back."

Reluctantly, he lets me go, and I keep my head ducked as I leave the room. I find Lance leaning against his car, watching me approach like a petulant child. The way he outed me to everyone stops me from consoling him. Andie and Lolene wait by the front door, giving us space to talk.

"How could you do that to me?"

He clenches his jaw, but I can see the hurt wavering behind his anger.

"That wasn't fair, Lance. Not to our friendship, not to Kip or Lilly, and not to me. If you had something to say to me, you should have said it to me in private." I blink back tears at the realization my only friend thinks so poorly of me.

"Kaley," he says, softening.

I shake my head, stopping his words. "I never knew you had feelings for me. You can't blame me for being with someone else because you never spoke up."

He drops his arms, running his hands over his face. He takes a moment, wavering when he looks up at me. "It wouldn't have mattered. You've never looked at me like you look at him."

"You don't know that."

"I do," he nods. "I didn't believe it until I saw it, but you love him."

My heart hurts for him, because I do love Lance, just not like I do Kip. He's right, because I've never needed Lance like I do Kip. Kip has the ability to make breathing easier and harder all at the same time—it's borderline addicting.

He drinks leisurely from the open bottle in his hand. "You know where I'll be if you need me."

And because we both know our friendship will never be the same, I hug him quickly before he opens the passenger side door without looking back at me. When I walk back into the house, I find everyone has migrated to the kitchen.

"How do you know everything before I do?" Lilly says to Justin.

Justin releases a breath before replying. "It's not my place to tell you her business."

Kip is leaning against the bar, beer in his hands when he sees me enter. He stands and I make my way towards him, fitting into his side.

Lilly doesn't waste time jumping to questions. "How long have you been working as…" she says, waving a hand in the air as she looks for the best description. "…an escort?"

"On and off for the past few years," I reply honestly.

"Does this have anything to do with your and Kip's falling out not that long ago?"

I shift uncomfortably and Kip answers for me. "Kaley hasn't worked at Hudson's since we've been together." They've clearly covered the basics while I was outside.

Lilly's eyes narrow, and I can tell I'm not going to like what she says next. "And you trust her?"

Kip nods once, not an ounce of hesitation. "Yes."

Justin looks at Lilly and they do the weird communication thing they do where they talk without words. It was weird years ago, and it's even weirder now.

Jacob slaps a hand on the granite counter top. "Well you shouldn't," he says, cocky grin in place. "At least, not while I'm around."

Kip looks at Justin, unbelieving. "How old is he?"

Justin barely rolls his eyes, smacking his brother on the back of the head. "Old enough to know better."

"But too young to give a fuck," Jacob tacks on.

Lilly can no longer hold back her smile, and Jacob beams at us in a *my job here is done* way. I'm pretty sure all of us are grateful for Jacob's immaturity at this point.

twenty

I LIE WITH MY head hanging outside the tent, eyes turned up towards the sky while I watch the limbs of the trees sway high above. It's really fucking hot, and I have no idea how Kip maintains his energy in this type of heat. Even way up here on the hill, the wind does very little to deter the scorching summer sun.

Kip settles down next to me, leaning over and blocking my view. "You're humming," he says between heavy breaths through his nose. Sweat drips from his hair and onto my cheek, his bandana doing little to stop it.

"So? People hum all the time."

He smiles. "To country music," he clarifies.

The song playing on the portable radio finally registers and I scowl. "Now it's going to be stuck in my head all day."

"Just admit you like my music."

I shake my head, indignant. "Nope."

"If nope means yes, you are correct."

The truth is, some songs have grown on me. Plus, I got a good look at Sam Hunt on TV the other night, and I can't really argue against the sight of him singing about back roads and bogs.

"Are you done?" I say, changing the subject.

He balances a forearm over his knee, looking at the campsite he put up…by himself. "For now. I'll gather some wood before the sun goes down so we can have a fire tonight."

"Explain to me why we're camping at the end of summer again."

We biked up the hill to a secluded camp spot behind the trees. Primitive camping is permitted, but the sign "strongly recommends" early spring and late fall as prime camping seasons. Kip dismissed the warning of bears.

"There's a cold front coming in tonight, so it's going to be drastically cooler tomorrow," he says. "And because it's fun and you've never been."

Sitting up, I kiss him. "I can think of a lot of fun things to do at home, in the air conditioning, pretty much anywhere else."

He smiles against my lips, but pulls back, retrieving a few twigs and leaves from my hair for me. "This gives us a chance to scope out the advanced bike trail before we attempt to navigate it on two wheels." Smiling, he stands abruptly. "Do you want to go exploring?"

I squint against the sun. "And possibly have a run-in with a brown bear? No thanks."

He rolls his eyes and reaches down, pulling me up entirely too easily with one arm.

"Fine," I say, wiping dirt from my backside. "I'm up."

"That's my girl."

He uncaps a water bottle and hands it to me, like calling me his girl is totally normal. He takes the lead, shouldering his book sack, which holds water and other nameless supplies he carries around. We follow the trail, sticking close to where the woods are less dense. I spend more time admiring him than the scenery, but he doesn't complain, just smiles when he catches me. He likes it.

"Tell me something you want to do before you die," he says, picking up twigs for a fire later.

I hand him an especially dry stick, wiping my palms on my shorts after I check for bugs, and ignore his knowing smile as he resituates the stack in his hands. "You go first," I say.

"Mhm," he sounds. "I'd love to have a family. You know, the whole married with kids spiel."

"How many kids?"

He shrugs. "I don't know. However many my wife is willing to give me."

I smile, loving the way he has the all-American dream mapped out in his head. "Raising Lilly didn't scare you enough?"

He smiles. "You would think so, but she came out alright, I suppose."

"A little klepto, but that's only a minor flaw."

Laughing, he picks up another stick. "Your turn."

I contemplate my answer. "I don't really have any life goals. I guess my dream for the future would be to live near the beach. I'd lay in a hammock, drink mimosas, and read books all day."

"So you don't want a family...or a job for that matter?"

I smile. "Sometimes I miss school."

"Really?" he says, surprised.

"Yeah. I mean, I did well in school and it kept me organized. It challenged me to do something, gave me a purpose to get up in the mornings, I guess."

"Why don't you go back?"

"Money, mostly. I don't have a clue what I want to major in and no resources to waste time trying to figure it out."

"There's other stuff we can look into, like financial aid and grants."

We. As long as he keeps saying *we*, I'll do anything he asks.

I wink at him as I pass him on the trail. "Maybe one day." Neither one of us mentions our conflicting life goals.

Every now and then he'll stop and pick a dandelion for me to make a wish on, and we find a natural spring to drink from next to some limestone rocks. It's roughly the size of a small fishing pond, with water pouring down into the pool from the side of the hillside. The water is clear with a tint of green, and feels amazing against our overheated skin as we take turns pouring it over our hair and necklines.

"This is so pretty," I say, wringing out my hair.

A family arrives nearby, waving as they approach. Kip and I return their greeting, smiling at the two young boys in swim trunks, too eager to wait for their mother's command to put on sunscreen.

"I've been meaning to ask you something."

Kip looks up from refilling our water bottles with the running water. "About?"

I know I need to tread carefully. Kip's shop is his baby and I don't want him to feel like I'm telling him what to do with it. "Shoot me down if you don't like it."

He waits for me to continue. "Okay?"

"I've been thinking about the shop opening, and maybe it'd be a good idea to throw a party. Like a grand opening."

He recaps the bottles and shoves them in his backpack as he stands. "For a maintenance shop?" he says, unsure.

"Well, yeah. There's a lot of up-and-coming business around you and we could invite them to set up tables with their information. It would give everyone a chance to network and market themselves. And there would be door prizes and an open bar to draw people in," I say, rushing my words, too anxious to talk slower.

"That doesn't sound too bad."

I pause. "Really?"

He shrugs. "Yeah, why not?"

Smiling, I kiss him square on the mouth. "Thank you," I say, skipping ahead.

He smiles, a tad confused as his eyes follow me. "Why are you thanking me?"

"For taking me seriously," I say. "For being big enough to take what I suggest into consideration and trusting me to have your business's best interest in mind."

"Kaley, you're overthinking it."

I roll my eyes, standing with my hands on my hips. "Kill my mood all you want, but I'm happy I get to organize a party."

He shakes his head but kisses me on the forehead. "We can sort out everything later."

We eventually make our way back to the campsite and Kip gets a fire started just in time for twilight. It's not nearly as bad as I thought it would be, the temperature dropping along with the sun. He even managed to sneak ingredients to make s'mores without the chocolate melting all day. What is way worse than I had expected is the sounds emanating from the trees. Animals, so many of them, scurrying and yowling, some noises I've never heard before in my life.

Kip smirks as he shoves a burnt marshmallow into his mouth. Lord, help me. I want to be that marshmallow.

"It's not funny," I whine, whipping my head in the direction of a hoot owl.

He laughs. I give him my best intimidating look, but his smile remains in place. "Come here." He motions for me to come closer to his position next to the fire. He leans against our rolled up sleeping bags we probably won't need, cradling my head in the crook of his arm as our gazes turn to the stars.

"I love you," I say, liking the way the words fall from my lips.

If possible, I feel his body relax further, arm tightening around my hip. I say it when I feel it, when I can't think of anything else, when my mind refuses to let go of the words—still amazed by their meaning—I say it. Liberally, openly, and knowingly. It helps me breathe.

Every time feels better than the first.

I don't think Kip predicted how sappy I am. Hell, I didn't either. Now I feel like every emotion is felt tenfold. When I'm angry, I'm fucking furious. And when I'm happy, I'm nearly ecstatic. Sadness is the hardest to release, almost drowning me at night as I lie awake by myself. Opening up makes every single feeling magnified. I'm trying to navigate it, but sometimes it feels like too much. I'm doing the best I can.

I turn over, placing my chin against my hand splayed on his chest. His eyes are hooded, looking down at me in affection. It's one of those intense moments I have to tame, afraid of how out of control it'll get. Time and time again, I find myself clenching my jaw out of fear of what will come out of my mouth. I no longer want to fill the void of silence, I want to trap it.

Leaning up, I press my lips against his. I slip my tongue into his mouth, relishing the taste of him, different from every man I've ever been with. With the arm he has wrapped around my hips, he presses my body closer to his. Our kiss deepens and I place my leg over his waist so I'm straddling him, putting him right where I want him. The grip he has on the side of my throat tightens, and I feel his need between us. I moan into his open mouth.

He releases me from the kiss, breathing heavily as he puts space between us, and I immediately resent the look on his face.

He's done this, multiple times already, stopping us from progressing past kissing.

"We can't," he says softly, brushing stray hairs away from my face.

I swallow the hurt and pull myself off of him, too embarrassed to look at him. He leans on his elbow so he can see my face.

"I can only be turned down so many times, Kip, before it starts to feel like rejection."

He clicks his tongue in admonishment. "You know it's not like that."

But it *is* like that. I don't need anyone in my life dictating what they think is good for me. I know what is and isn't good for me. Kip's insistence that he knows what's better for me than I do for myself makes me see red.

"But that's what it feels like," I remind him. "It doesn't matter how honorable your intentions are, it hurts."

"Kaley, we skipped the dating aspect of a relationship and jumped right to the intimacy. We need a foundation for our house to stand on when everything else falls through. We can't replace words with actions."

"I am using words," I say bitterly. "Don't you hear me saying all the words? So many fucking words."

He smiles. "I love you," he says. "And I'm proud of you. But you've replaced all emotional connections with sex, and you can't do that to us." He pauses to rub his fingertips over my lips. "To me."

And just like that, my anger dissipates, leaving a feeling of melancholy. Guilt is already setting in. I hate how utterly exhausting emotions are.

"I want this to work," I say bleakly.

Kip tilts my face toward him so I'm forced to look at him. "We are working. We're together, and here, and both refusing to let go of each other. That's enough. For now," he tacks on.

I breathe out, shaking my head in the process. "Is this as scary for you as it is for me?"

"It's terrifying," he says, smiling.

He kisses me, slowly, languidly, showing me we don't need more than we have in this moment. For now, it's enough.

I'm smiling at him when his eyes seem to cloud over, growing in size as they focus on something near my head.

Fear paralyzes me as I fight to keep my breathing under control. "What is it? What's by my head, Kip?"

He grabs a nearby shoe and holds it over my head. "Don't move," he says, eyes trained on whatever is near me.

I close my eyes tightly. "Get it away, get it away, get it away," I repeat.

I'm panicking, two seconds away from full freak-out mode, when Kip's slams the shoe down on the ground beside my face. Sitting up, I shriek at the sight of the largest, smooshed spider I have ever seen in my life. "Oh my god, it was two centimeters away from eating my face."

Kip's laughter makes me smile, even in my terrified state. "You're scared of something this big," he says, holding up his thumb and forefinger an inch away from each other.

"It can kill me," I protest.

He smiles, managing to pull me down on top of him by one arm. "Highly doubtful. It might have lived in your hair for a couple of days though." My eyes widen as I ponder the very real possibility there's actual spiders in my hair and he laughs again, running his fingers through the strands. "I'm kidding."

Once I'm certain I'm not harboring spiders, we talk about our pasts and futures, our dreams and the possibilities they might not come true, and our greatest fears. We talk until we fall asleep where we lie, with my head tucked under his chin and his arms around me. When I start to feel the cold seep in, I wake to find myself alone. The embers of the fire barely give any light, but the full moon provides enough to spot Kip sitting with his back to me, feet dangling from the ravine.

He tilts his head back, taking a drink from the beer in his hands. He stays like that for a while, looking out at the dark expanse of the trees and water below, occasionally taking a swig of his beer. The ravine isn't any more than twenty feet, but it's enough to do major bodily harm, even enough to kill. My worry grows as I ponder how much he's actually had to drink while I've been asleep.

He doesn't hear me as I approach, and his head snaps up when I run my hand through his hair. "Are you trying to kill me?"

He doesn't reply, grasping my hand in his as he tugs me down to his level. "I'm just enjoying the peace and quiet."

I tug my legs out from under me and sit next to him, wrapping both my arms around him for security. It's not as scary at night, but I know it's only because I can't see the ground. "You couldn't do that by the campsite?"

He drinks the last of his beer. "I used to come out here a lot as a teenager."

"This spot?"

"Yeah. I drank my first beer here. Me and Taylor," he says, reaching for another bottle next to him.

Taylor was Kip's best friend before they both went to prison. Taylor's dad took Kip in when he was a teenager, taught him how to steal cars for money. Once Taylor's dad died, they continued running the business together. From my understanding, Lilly and

Kip considered Taylor family. That was, until he underhandedly convinced them to work for my dad.

"Have you spoken to him since everything?"

"I wrote him a letter while we were serving time, but he never responded. I heard he's out though."

"You think he's still mad about getting busted?"

He shrugs. "Who knows. He always was a loose cannon. Even as teenagers, he would do the dumbest shit. I was constantly bailing him out of trouble."

I smile, hearing the fondness in his voice. "So you're saying he was the fun one while you were the stick in the mud."

He smiles. "Yeah. I'm kind of angry at him for knowingly putting Lilly in danger. I'm not even sure what I would say to him if I saw him."

I lay my head on his shoulder. "Maybe it's a good thing you haven't."

He looks down and wraps an arm around my shoulders. "Are you cold?"

"I'm freezing," I say, shivering.

Standing, he helps me to my feet, and only then do I catch the slight wobble of his balance. My heart skips a beat and I wait until we're a healthy distance away before I scold him. "You're *drunk*?"

He smiles lazily. "I am."

His laissez-fair attitude pisses me off. "You could have died!" I yell.

Attempting to sit down, he loses his balance halfway through and lands on his butt. "But I didn't, and I faced my irrational fear of heights."

I'm so angry, I want to throw him off the cliff myself. "What are you trying to prove to yourself, huh? You're not invincible."

"That," he drawls, pointing at me. "I am not."

He reaches for another beer and I snatch it away from him. "I don't even remember packing this much beer."

He laughs. "That's because I packed it, duh." Reaching for the back of my knee, he tugs me down onto his lap. "I'm sorry I scared you," he says, snuggling into my chest.

I push his head back, making his bleary eyes align with mine. "You do realize you haven't faced anything, right? Being drunk automatically makes all brave efforts null and void."

His face falls. "Really?"

I can't help but smile at his child-like disappointment, even though I know it's only the alcohol swimming in his belly. "Yup. You're going to have to redo it again, except sober."

He drops his forehead to my collar. "Ah, man."

I laugh, holding his head to my chest, combing my hands through his hair. "Why did you feel like you had to face them tonight?" I say.

He speaks into my shirt. "I've watched you face your fears and it makes me want to do the same."

Confused, I say, "What fears have I faced?"

"Loving me."

He shuts down any rebuttal I was prepared to give, leaving me speechless. He kisses me through the fabric of my shirt.

"You *are* freezing," he says, rubbing his hands up and down my arms. "Let's get the fire going."

"I'll get it," I say, standing. "Don't do anything stupid."

I pack more dry leaves and logs onto the fire and unravel the sleeping bags, shivering as I lay it out beside Kip and get in. Before climbing inside the covers with me, he strips his shirt so he can warm me up, pulling me into his chest. He doesn't complain when I use his feet to thaw my frozen ones.

"Kip," I say, voice eerily loud in the night.

"Mm," he sounds, close to falling asleep.

"Loving you isn't the scary part."

He pulls me closer, breathing into the mess of hair on top of my head. "I know."

I'm terrified of hurting him, and he's still willing to take the chance on us anyway. I wonder how long we can pretend this is going to work.

twenty-one

I'VE NEVER LOVED A door as much in my life as I do this one. I sigh in relief as the lock easily gives and I immediately drop the bags I'm holding, exhausted from carrying them from the party store six blocks away. Tonight is the night of the opening and it's to no one's surprise that I'm picking up last-minute supplies.

"Hey." Kip comes up behind me, kissing me on the cheek.

"Hey, okay, so they didn't have the red cups, but the clear should look fine with the—" I come to a standstill when I turn around.

"Lilly and Andie came over early to help set up."

I narrow my eyes at him. He at least has the decency to look contrite. Lilly, on the other hand, looks like the cat who ate the canary. Andie looks so cute in her tea-length dress that I could kill a puppy.

"Where's Justin?"

"He went to pick up Cal. He's punished again, so I offered to let him tear tickets at the door." The kid has surprisingly grown on Kip despite being super annoying.

"Let me guess, caught stealing again?"

Kip gives Lilly a look. "I don't know. Lilly won't tell me."

Andie takes a small step between them, breaking up their argument before it gets started. "What do you need us to do?"

"Look, Andie," I say, shooting it to her straight. "You seem like a nice girl. But I'm not. I don't know what Lilly's been feeding you, but Kip's not available."

It takes a split second, but Lilly busts out laughing and Kip hides his smile behind a hand.

Andie's eyes are wide. "You think Lilly's trying to set us up?" she says, wiggling a finger between her and Kip.

Confused, my eyes shift between all three of them. "Isn't she?"

And Lilly's laughter grows.

"No. I'm shadowing him as a project for my business management class. No offense, but Kip isn't my type. I like my guys to be a little…younger."

Lilly's condescending look tells me everything I need to know.

"I'm so sorry for the confusion," she says. "I'll…just leave you two to…yeah." She leaves and I pin Kip with a stare.

He gives me a cocky smile. "You let me believe Lilly was trying to set you up with her."

"You believed what you wanted to."

I hate it when he's right. "But you didn't say otherwise."

"And miss witnessing you panic over being jealous? Never."

Lilly retrieves some of the supplies and passes by us on her way out, a satisfied smile on her face. "You've always set your own traps."

"You enjoy this way too much."

She doesn't deny it.

Groaning, I reject Kip's attempt to wrap his arms around me. "Go away so I can get ready."

"I have to shave," he says, following me to the bathroom.

I slam the door in his face. "Too bad."

By the time I finish getting dressed and make it down stairs, Kip is dressed, shaved, and already greeting people coming in through the door. Half the shop is partitioned off with drapes, leaving the front open for the party. Local businesses are set up around the perimeter of the room, and people are already taking advantage of the bartender centered in the middle.

Kip is shaking hands with a middle-aged couple coming in when I place a hand on his shoulder. He smiles at my arrival, eyes lingering on my dress a moment too long. It's *the* dress. At first, I couldn't stomach the sight of it. Everything about it made me sick, from the color, to the fabric and smell. I was going to throw it away when I found it packing, but something stopped me. Something resistant. This dress was meant for Kip, and I'm going to wear it for him.

I hold my breath as I wait for him to speak.

He smiles only through his eyes. "You're so beautiful."

Relief floods my lungs because *he gets it.*

"I'm sorry," Kip says, turning his attention back to the couple he's all but forgotten about. "This is Marty and Julie. They own Royal Flush Plumbing next door. Marty, Julie, this is Kaley. She organized tonight's event."

"Thank you for coming," I greet them.

"Good job on marketing," Marty says, shaking my hand. "You reeled me in the minute I heard there was going to be an open bar."

We all laugh and his wife rolls her eyes. "He failed to mention our daughter, Anna, is manning a table for us. She's a huge car fanatic."

At the mention of their daughter, Kip points in the direction of a girl talking animatedly with Lilly. "They've been talking nonstop for forty-five minutes."

I laugh, remembering all the times I had to endure Lilly rambling about torque and valves. Marty and Julie excuse themselves to exploit the free alcohol. Kip continues to greet people as they enter and I stand with Cal to the side, handing people their tickets. He blushes when I compliment him on his tie.

He manages to break free of his hosting duties, whispering in my ear as he guides me to the bar. "You're making it very difficult to concentrate."

"You're welcome?" I say.

"This dress," he says, pulling the fabric at the small of my back.

Suddenly unsure I might have misread his reaction earlier, I have to ask, "Is it okay?"

His smile pulls up to one side. "It's perfect. The color suits you." He flattens his hand over the material covering my backside as he positions me against the bar. He orders a glass of wine. "It's so soft. What's it made of?"

"Challis."

He hands me the glass of wine. "Never heard of it."

"I bought it for you."

His thumb strokes the curve of my hip. "I love it."

A gagging sound breaks us apart. "This is way grosser than I imagined it would be," Lilly says.

Kip wipes a hand across his mouth to hide his smile. "Can I help you with something?"

"Actually, I was hoping I could talk with Kaley for a minute."

They both look to me. "Yeah, sure," I say, finishing off the remainder of my drink.

Kip motions for the bartender again. "Can I get a refill?"

"I'll take a glass as well," Lilly says, leaning next to me.

Kip shakes his head. "I'm not going to get through the night without drinking." He kisses me on the cheek before departing, shooting Lilly a warning as he passes by her.

Lilly smirks at his retreating back. "He's so cute in love."

I'm slightly taken back by her open observation, but can't help but agree. "He is, isn't he?"

We watch as he peruses the tables, a surprisingly personable host. "He's happy," she says.

I don't know what to say in reply, so I nod and drink more wine. When in doubt, drink all the wine. It can literally do no wrong.

"I'm not going to apologize for wanting to protect my brother."

"I would never expect less and I told Kip the same."

"He's an amazing person and he deserves someone just as amazing."

I swallow, nodding. "I agree."

"But I can't argue with his happiness. As long as he's happy, I'm happy."

"I appreciate that."

We sip our wine in silence and pretend this isn't the most awkward conversation we've ever had.

"So…where's Justin?"

"Outside, pretending he had a phone call to take but really smoking."

"You sound like you disapprove."

"Nah," she says, making a face into her glass. "It's his vice, he can have it. I'm more aggravated by the fact he tries to hide it after all these years."

"He didn't used to. When did it start to become a secret?"

"He tried quitting a couple of years ago when I was in 2L, but he never truly gave it up."

I nod like I understand, but I don't really. I wasn't there to get a play-by-play of her relationship like I should have been. Not that Lilly would've been particularly open, but I would have a better understanding as to what happened in her second semester of law school that made her boyfriend want to quit smoking.

Lilly sighs loudly. "This is dumb. We've never had a problem with our friendship before."

"I'm sorry for kind of dropping off the face of the Earth."

She smiles. "It's okay. Really. I'm not mad. I was, for the sake of honesty, but not anymore. And I'm okay with Kip and you, you know, together. It's still hard for me to wrap my head around, but I'll get there."

I pretend to pretty-cry. "Does this mean we're best friends again?"

She nods, swallowing a sip of wine. "I think so."

"Cool," I say, clinking my glass against hers.

Drinking the last swallow of my drink, I spot Kip looking at us across the room. He's not listening to the conversation he's supposed to be participating in, his eyes locked on mine. There's a heat in them I haven't seen in the weeks since everything happened with Peter. I've been beyond sexually frustrated, but I don't think I accurately predicted how much tension could build over time.

"Oh my God. I can't." Lilly turns and walks away. "I just can't."

I smile, and when I look back at Kip, he's engrossed in the person talking to him. I make my way outside, wanting to know if Lilly's suspicions are true. It doesn't take me long, as I follow the trail of cigarette smoke around the side of the building.

Justin's head snaps up and I smile. "Don't worry. It's just me."

He releases a cloud of smoke. "I've tried so many times to quit."

"Can I bum one?"

He digs in his pocket, producing a pack and holding it open for me to pull a cigarette free. "I didn't know you smoked."

I shrug, taking the lighter from his outstretched hand. I inhale one good time, coughing once as I exhale. "I haven't had one in years, but I've dropped enough bad habits lately I figured I could pick up an old one."

"There's a good turnout tonight. Good job."

"It's the free booze."

He smiles, taking one last drag. "I better get inside and keep an eye on Cal. God knows what he's pilfered already."

"No wonder why you can't quit smoking. You've got two authentic kleptomaniacs to keep in line."

He shakes his head, sighing a dramatized breath. "Someone should give me a medal."

Exhaling, I smile. "Not all habits are worth breaking."

I eventually make my way back inside and turn down the air because it begins to get stuffy with the amount of people crammed in the space. Cal helps me draw tickets for the prizes, and I'm pleased with the donations from the participating businesses, as are the winners. Marty and Julie stay late to help pick up once people start piling out, and Kip breaks his rule of unprofessionalism and drinks a Jack and Coke with Marty before the night is over, tinting his cheeks the perfect shade of pink. His normal six-pack of beer doesn't hold a candle to a double of Jack.

Justin is walking Cal out the door, the last two to leave, when Kip places a hand on Cal's chest. Kip holds his hand out, palm up in front of him.

"What?" Cal says, staring at Kip's hand innocently.

"You know what. Give it to me."

He grumbles, removing a silver bottle opener from his pocket into Kip's palm.

"What do you even need this for?" Kip says, shaking it.

"I don't know. I could use it as a bookmark?"

"I'm cutting a portion of your wages for stealing."

Cal doesn't argue, slouching as he leaves. Justin shakes his head in disbelief. "It's getting worse."

"I'm working on it. Your fiancé doesn't help. Tell Lilly to quit coddling him."

Justin's smile grows as he shakes his head. "You're not getting me murdered today, tell her yourself."

Kip doesn't argue, but doesn't look happy about it, locking the door behind them.

"Tonight went well," I say, using his arm for balance as I slip off my heels, moaning in relief. "You were great."

Kip's fingers brush mine as he takes the shoes from my hand and the sensation makes me look up at him. The fire in his eyes has returned, but now it's intensified without other people present. He cups my cheek and bends the few-inch difference in our height to kiss me. My mouth opens of its own accord, and he takes full advantage.

We've done a lot of kissing these past few weeks. A *lot*. But none of them were like this. This kiss would have been too dangerous to tempt.

I say his name, not sure if it's a question or a plea. I'm nervous in a way I've never been with him.

His eyes implore mine. "Let me show you how different it can be."

My shaky breath is my reply.

I let him lead me up the stairs. I'm expecting him to take me to the bed, but am shocked when he stops at the couch. Dropping back into the cushions, he slowly releases my hand and kicks off his shoes and socks. There's something sexy about a man dressed with bare feet.

"Take off your dress." It's not a demand or a question, just words put together for my benefit.

I reach for the hem, fidgeting with the material. This is so different from all of our other times. I know how sex with Kip can push me to a limit I'm not sure of. It's not about taking off my clothes, because I've never been shy about being naked around people. I have a nice body—genetics have been good to me—but I'm suddenly struck with a sense of…fear.

"I'm scared," I admit out loud.

He shakes his head, face calm. "Don't be. You know me. You know I won't ever hurt you."

"It's not that. It's…" I say, trying to find the right words. "Irrational."

He sits up, framing my outer thighs with his hands. "Is it though?" He doesn't bother to wait for an answer as he bunches the fabric of my dress up to my waist, holding it in one hand, exposing my underwear. "Technically, you know the mechanics," he says, trailing his mouth at the juncture of my thigh. "You're highly experienced in the act of having sex."

He cups his spare hand between my legs, putting the exact amount of pressure to make me squirm, and I place a hand on his shoulder for balance.

"But you don't know what it's like to love someone you're doing it with." He moves the fabric of my underwear aside and pushes a finger in. "To know the person you're with will do just about anything to get you there first."

The movement of his hand combined with the huskiness of his voice makes the ground beneath me tilt, and I think it's my own form of vertigo. The two measly glasses of wine I had couldn't possibly be enough to make the world tilt on its axis like this.

Unexpectedly, he retreats, taking his hand with him, and he looks up at me from his relaxed position on the couch. "Now undress so I can show you."

With unsteady hands, I pull the material up over my head and toss it to him. He catches it, tossing it over the arm of the couch, a look of reverence in his eyes. His chest rises and falls marginally more quickly, but it's noticeable in the quiet of the shop.

"You know you're beautiful. You don't need me to tell you something you already know," he says. "What you don't know, is how I can never stop thinking about touching you. All the time, all day, even when you're not near. But I also know you don't care for being overly affectionate, so I limit myself to three true touches an hour."

I feel like I can and can't breathe all at once. Drowning and floating. Living and dying. I slide the lacy underwear off and toss it to him as well. "Keep going."

He holds the underwear in his fist, smiling behind it. "You don't know how much I get turned on when we argue. I can't think of anything I want to do more than fuck some sense into you."

The words are naughty, but his expression behind them shows nothing but admiration. A part of me wants to close my eyes so I can focus on his words and the way he says them without being distracted by the way he's looking at me. It's conflicting in the best way.

"Kip, I need you to touch me."

"If you insist," he says, placing both hands behind each thigh, making me straddle his lap.

He lets me take his shirt off, pressing his bare chest against mine, his head tilted back as he kisses me. I run my fingers up the stubble of his throat, over his chin, tracing the outline of our mouths. I need more. He grinds into me, not caring about the layer of clothes he still has on.

"Bed," I demand against his lips.

"Be patient," he says, cupping my breast.

"Are you trying to start an argument with me on purpose?"

He smiles, placing his mouth on the same breast he's holding, and I no longer care about the bed.

"You're right. Here's fine." Without removing his mouth, he picks me up and carries me to the bed. "Oh, now you're just being ridiculous."

It's like my words land on deaf ears as he switches to the other breast. I run my hands through his hair, aching to get closer. Just when I don't think I can take any more, he begins making his way south. I've never liked it when someone goes down on me. There's something intimate about it, something vulnerable that I could never get past. But he doesn't stop between my legs like I'm expecting him to. He stands and removes his clothes, then kneels on the foot of the bed, staring down at me as he holds my ankle in his hand.

"You don't know how I've watched you. Even years ago, I knew you were worthwhile." He places a kiss on the inside on my ankle, and says, "One."

I'm confused as he moves on to the inside of my knee.

Kissing that spot as well, his eyes meet mine as he says, "Two."

It's when he reaches for my hand I begin to understand as I watch him place another kiss to the spot between my index and middle finger.

"Three."

He's counting my freckles.

He reaches my collarbone, this time placing an open-mouth kiss to my most prominent birthmark. "Four." Flipping me over, he places his lips to the underside of my right ass cheek. "Five." And finally, making his way back up, he kisses the underside of my ear. "Six," he says, breath warm against my neck.

It's a freckle I hadn't known about.

He stretches his body over mine, and I can feel his arousal between us. He tugs my hair to one side, kissing me as he presses his hips into my backside. "You don't know what it feels like to have complete control of the situation and still relax enough to enjoy it."

Reaching between my legs, he dips a couple of fingers in, pulling back to tease in just the right spot before pushing back in. I lean back into his hand, loving his more than my own. And that's really saying something.

Then, slowly, I feel him guide himself inside me and I moan into the bedding. He grinds one time, making us both moan at the sensation, before retreating. His breath is hot at my ear, his chest against my back, and he takes the hands I'm using to grip the sheets and pins them over my head with one of his. The other, he leverages under my waist, creating the most agonizing angle.

"Thank you for allowing me the chance to feel you," he says, right before pushing back in.

Each thrust feels better than the last. With every in and out, Kip's breaths and sounds echo through me. I have no control in this position as his body moves over mine. My hands are pinned, and when he pushes my legs together, bracketing them with his, I'm completely at his will. It elicits a brand new sensation and I squirm, overwhelmed by it and unsure how I feel about not being able to move.

"You can say stop at any point," he says, pulling out and easing back in. "But you won't, because you know I'll get you there."

And he's right. He has my body strung beneath his from head to toe. Every time he pushes in, I feel a renewed flush flood my veins. It's almost too much. It feels so good it *hurts*. Even if I wanted to say stop, I couldn't. I come, harder than I honestly, truly ever believe I have before.

"That's my girl," he says, reverent.

He pulls out and flips me over, and it's then I realize I'm crying. The wetness of my cheeks are cold against the air. But Kip knows what I need and doesn't stop, entering me as he kisses me like I'm everything he's ever wanted.

I'm pretty sure he's mine.

twenty-two

I JERK AWAKE, HEART pounding from a fear I can't place.

Kip stirs next to me, eyes bleary as he opens them. "Are you okay?"

I quickly take inventory of my body, deducing that I'm fine. "I think it was a bad dream."

He wraps an arm around me as I lie back down. "You don't remember it?"

Shaking my head, I say, "No. Not really. It's more like a feeling."

"Night terror," he says, concerned. "Have you had them before?"

I shake my head. He tucks me into his side, brushing his fingers through my hair until I fall back to sleep.

twenty-three

"DO YOU HAVE A…" I attempt to read Kip's handwriting and guess, "Front set of semi-micro phallic brake pads?"

The man on the phone laughs. "Do you mean semi-metallic?"

I squint at the sloppy letters. "I think so."

"It has to be semi-metallic. Let me check." I hear his fingers jumping across a keyboard as he checks their database. "We do have them in stock."

"Great. I'll be there in fifteen to pick them up."

I hang up and peek my head over the railing at Kip working below. His head is tilted back as he gulps water from a bottle. Since Janine fired me for taking a self-appointed weekend off, I've been working as Kip's secretary. At first, I refused. Kip in everyday life has control issues, so I expected Kip in work mode to be ten times worse, but he somehow finds a balance that works.

"They have them in stock. I'm going to run and pick them up. I'll be back in a few."

"Thank you. I think I left the keys in the ignition."

I give him a look. "Did stealing cars not teach you anything? It's only four blocks, so I'm going to take the bike. It'd be the same amount of time considering I'd have to search for a parking spot anyway."

"Okay, babe. It's rush hour, so be careful."

I roll my eyes. "It's not any more dangerous than making me bike up a sheer cliff."

"At least you know what to avoid on the bike trail. You can't avoid moving vehicles."

"Say that to my elbows."

"Love you," he says, smiling at my insolence.

I can't help but smile back. "Love you, too."

Shrugging on a light jacket, I pull it over my hat as I mount my bike. The temperature has started dropping considerably at night, and the wind shear is no joke. I wave at Julie through the window of the shop next door and she waves back. Marty and Julie have been super amazing for business. Marty is a car fanatic and apparently has tons of car fanatic friends who he sends Kip's way. It's a bonus that Kip prefers to work on rebuilt muscle cars. He's been super busy, working long days, but Kip doesn't complain. He's happy to be doing what he loves and actually breaking even.

I'm pedaling across the next intersection when a guy on a motorcycle cuts from traffic, nearly killing me as he swerves into the bike lane. I have to ditch my bike, barely escaping death as I stumble over my feet. I cuss and give him the middle finger even though I know it's useless. I flip my bike over and notice the front rim is bent from where I hit the curb. An SUV stops beside me and something about it makes me uneasy. I'm already taking steps away from it when the back door opens and a man makes eye contact with me as he gets out. I try to scream, but he covers my mouth, wrapping both arms around me as I kick, and shoves me into the back seat before anyone can hear me.

I kick any and everything I can make contact with, bowing my body away from the hands trying to tame me. The hand covering my mouth muffles my attempts to scream. I bite down and taste blood, and it makes me want to vomit, but I don't let up.

"Fucking bitch," the man yells, pulling his hand from my mouth.

I spit, trying not to swallow the liquid. There are three men, but I can barely see past the rush of adrenaline screaming for me to get free.

"Stop resisting. This is just a warning."

Yeah, okay.

Two hands manage to get hold of my forearms, and I know it's the first step to losing this fight. There's no way I'll be able to use my upper body as long as he has control of my arms, and by the look of his stature, I'm not going to be able to break free.

"Landry," the man says, halting my movements. "What do you want me to do with her?"

My head is in the lap of the man I bit as his hands hold down my arms beside my head. Another man finally traps my legs beneath him by sitting on them, and I'm officially rendered useless.

It's then I notice Landry sitting opposite us, watching everything unfold with a devilish smile on his lips. "You're not going anywhere, so you might as well conserve your energy."

"Why are you kidnapping me?"

He adjusts his suit, leaning forward with his elbows on his knees. "I never understood that term. You're an adult. Shouldn't it be called adultnapping?"

I jerk my arms from the man holding them and he lets me go. "Are you trying to be cute? If you're going to abduct me, at least pretend to be serious about it."

His smile grows. "You're too cheeky for your own good. My presence alone should be enough to scare you. This guy?" he says, pointing a finger at the guy on the left of me. "He's made men bigger, more powerful than you piss their pants."

"Sounds like you're sexist."

"This Guy" smiles but doesn't look away from the door. "Not many women get caught up in this business. Besides, I like to make women wet in an entirely different way."

I gag. "I bet it took you all night to come up with that one."

Landry redirects the conversation back to him. "Have you made any progress on the deal we made?"

"God, can you stop calling it a deal? It implies that I have a say when I so obviously don't."

"Fine," he says. "Have you made any progress in securing the money that's going to save your ass? Better?"

Unfortunately, no. "I've looked into it."

He looks at me, dubious. "You've…looked into what?"

I shrug. "It."

"That's not very reassuring, Kaley."

"It's not? I was so sure it would pacify you."

He smiles big. "If you hadn't already screwed me out of business—literally—I might actually consider taking you on a real date."

"I didn't know I wasn't allowed to work at Hudson's. If I had known you only allowed escorts who worked for your company to solicit men, I obviously wouldn't have done it."

"But you did. If you wouldn't have requested payment after we slept together, we wouldn't be in this position."

"Maybe if you were a better lay I wouldn't have charged you."

My insolence must have pushed him too far, because he motions to "That Guy" and before I know it, there's nothing I can do to protect myself from the back of his hand hitting my face. The blow knocks me to the floor of the SUV, way harder than I had predicted it would be, and a low throb engulfs the side of my face.

I blink to rid my eyesight of the blurring. "I thought you said this was going to be a warning."

Landry comes into view, leaning over to get a better look at me. "This is considered a warning," he says, using a finger to push a few strands of my hair back. "I told you the night I approached you with this offer that things could go very bad for you if you didn't cooperate. This is just a taste of it."

"You don't want to do this," I say, hoping I find a redeeming quality inside him.

"This is strictly business. If I let you get away with working business out from under me, other girls will think they can do it too."

I sit up and ignore the way the world tilts on its side. "What more do you want from me?" I say, hating the pleading in my voice.

Landry folds his hands in front of him, placing them against his stomach. "You can always come and work for me." My silence is enough of an answer. "Kip won't let you?"

"He doesn't even know. I haven't told him anything."

"You created this mess, Kaley." He looks down at me, repentant. "At least now you know I'm an equal opportunity employer."

I let out a snort. "So noble of you."

Landry laughs. "I have to say, your attitude is a nice change from the normal gang bangers we deal with."

"Thanks for the compliment. I'll be sure to leave a review with your HR department."

He smiles and I can't think of anything I hate more. "I was skeptical when he told me, but I'd have to say your father was right, you are *very* feisty for such a pretty girl."

Oh, yeah. *My father*.

"That Guy" kneels on the floorboard next to me, and something inside me wants him to hit me. I'm angry and disappointed in myself. I just want to feel something other than uselessness.

"The only way you could make a girl wet was if you threw a million dollars into the nearest body of water."

He smirks as he pulls on a pair of leather gloves. "You'd be the first to jump in."

"You should do what you do best," I say, smirking right back.

"And what's that," he says, leaning over me. It's intimate in a strange way, and I hate that the other men are witnessing it. If I'm going to face off my attacker, I at least want to do it with dignity. Landry's presence is especially looming as he watches.

"Stand on your tippy-toes and suck Landry's dick."

It's in this millisecond of a moment that I know I'm seriously convoluted and completely fucked up. As I watch him rear his hand back, I feel victorious and I keep my chin jutted out, defiant. I want this and it sickens me.

twenty-four

PRESSING AGAINST THE SWOLLEN area of her lip, she doesn't flinch from the pain. She does it again, but harder this time. The reflection looking back at Kaley in the mirror doesn't show a hint of pain as she digs her finger into the skin. Blood trickles from the cut and the metallic liquid coats her tongue. She holds her hands under the faucet and splashes the water on her face, taking a moment to watch the blood rush to the drain.

The door to the apartment opens and Kaley is amazed by the lack of response from her heart. When Landry finally dropped her off at the apartment, it was close to midnight and the apartment was empty. She felt guilty for not immediately calling Kip, knowing he was probably looking for her, but there's a part of her that was hoping he'd be gone a little longer.

"Justin's on his way."

Out of the corner of her eye, she sees Kip and Lilly enter the living room and Kip spins in a circle, running his hands through his hair. "And he called Lance?"

Lilly nods. "He left a message but hasn't been able to get in touch with him."

Kip sighs, looking up from the ground, and he and Kaley make eye contact through the gap in the bathroom door. "Kaley?" He closes the distance to the bathroom in two short strides and pushes the door in with his hand. "Oh my god." His eyes widen in horror, landing on the mess of her face. "Kaley, what happened? Oh my God." His hands shake as he searches for a place to put them, settling on her upper arms. "Oh my God," he repeats. "We need to get you to a hospital."

She pulls away from him, but he doesn't acknowledge her desire for space. "What hurts the most?"

Lilly squeezes her way into view and her gasp is loud against the bathroom walls. "I'll call 9-1-1."

"No," Kaley stops her, placing a hand over her movements. "No police."

Everyone takes a moment to let Kaley's words sink in. Kip gives her an incredulous look. "What are you talking about? You need a hospital."

"I'm fine. Just...no police. They can't help."

"Kaley," he says, trying for calm. "You're scaring me."

She takes a deep breath, trying to be understanding of his panic but not finding it within her. "I just want to take a shower and go to bed."

Wiping a hand across his mouth, he keeps it there, forcing himself to keep it shut.

Lilly places a hand on his arm. "Kip, she's in shock."

It takes him a moment, but he releases the tension in his jaw. "Okay," he says, voice much calmer. "We can take a shower."

"By myself, Kip. I want to take a shower by myself."

His emotions flitter across his face too fast for Kaley to keep up, barely registering one before another masks it. "I'm not going anywhere. I don't know if you have a concussion or some type of head injury. The last thing I'm doing is leaving you alone."

Kaley reins in her annoyance. "All I'm asking for is a few minutes."

He's already shaking his head, torn by her irrational behavior.

Since the pleading doesn't work, Kaley changes tactics. "This isn't a negotiation. I'm telling you to leave."

"Kaley, it's not going to happen." He looks her up and down, coming to some sort of a conclusion. "What are you hiding from me?"

When she doesn't reply, he reaches for the hem of her shirt and she slaps his hand away. "Don't touch me."

His head snaps back in surprise, hurt mixed with disbelief, and it fuels his suspicions. Snatching the material between his hands at her collar, he stretches the hem at her throat, tearing the material apart.

"Kip," she yells, trying to stop him.

But he's on a mission and ignores her failing attempts to stop him as he rips the shirt in half. The image of Kaley's body sends his back against the door, a whole new level of shock forcing him backwards. Bruises cover half of Kaley's chest and abdomen, the marks ranging in size with no rhyme or reason to their position.

She snaps, humiliation marring her cheeks. "Are you happy?"

He swallows, unable to look away from her marred body. "Did they—did they touch…"

She turns away from him, not wanting to hear the rest of his sentence to dispute the question. Shouldering out of the now ruined T-shirt, she turns on the showerhead and steps under the cold water. The bathroom door opens and closes, signaling Kip's departure. She stands in the shower for so long, the water runs from hot to cold, and her body starts to protest. Sliding to the floor, she lets her head rest against the tiles, sighing in relief as she closes her eyes against the spray of water. Her muscles appreciate the break.

Her body jerks awake before her eyes do, and it takes her a moment to blink against the light, figuring out where she is.

"You're fucking freezing," Kip says, cradling her to his chest.

She doesn't fight it simply because she's too tired to. Her body shakes uncontrollably in his arms, but she doesn't actually feel the cold against her skin, numb. Kip lays her on the bed, wrapping the blanket around her, piling as much material on top of her as he can. He sweeps her soaking wet hair off her face, wiping a towel over the strands to dry them.

"Look at me," he says, leaning over her. When she doesn't comply, his hands tighten on the pillow under her head. "Kaley, look at me right now or I'm taking you straight to the hospital and you won't have a say in the matter."

She manages to meet his eyes, but her mind remains devoid of thought. His eyes implore hers, searching for answers she won't give him.

"Just tell me what I can do," he says, voice trembling.

Closing her eyes, she rolls away from his stare. "There's nothing you can do."

She can feel his presence still looming over her, but she just wants to go back to sleep. She recalls the many times she wished to feel something, begged the heart in her chest to beat once out of rhythm, and now all she wants is for it to remain still. It could stop and it wouldn't matter to her. It makes her feel smug, like she won, beating life at its own game.

Kip wakes her every two hours, making sure she's coherent before going to back to the couch for sleep. He keeps his distance, his tone removed of all emotion. Each time bothers her more than the last and she repeatedly fights the desire to bite his head off every time he shakes her awake. She just wants to be left alone, and his detachment only adds to her growing anger.

By the time morning comes, she's exhausted. Rolling over, she swallows back nausea, an unsettling feeling taking root in her stomach. Her heart begins to beat rapidly, and she fights bile rising in the back of her throat. Rushing to the bathroom, she heaves over the toilet, but nothing comes up. She sticks her hand in her mouth, forcing herself to puke, and immediately breathes in relief when something of substance comes up.

She's brushing her teeth when she hears voices outside the apartment door.

"…completely insane," Kip says.

Lilly replies. "You don't know anything yet."

"She looks at me like I'm the enemy, like I'm the one who did that to her."

Justin's voice joins. "She's hiding something."

"Why though? What is it she doesn't want me to know?"

"It could be anything. They could have told her they'll hurt someone she knows or hurt her worse than what they already have."

"You don't understand," Kip says, voice pained. "She shouldn't be standing."

"It sounds like she's in shock. We need to be patient, let her open up on her own. Kip," Justin says, emphasizing his point. "Don't push her."

"I haven't, but I'm running out of—"

Kaley turns off the running water of the sink and their conversation comes to a screeching halt. Kip appears seconds later with her favorite pair of pajamas in his hands. She takes them and dresses, ignoring the way he watches her every movement.

"I'm going to go for a walk," she says, finally meeting his eyes.

His body sags. "Kaley, you can't."

"I'm going," she repeats.

He clenches his teeth and the tops of his ears turn red. "You're not going anywhere, unless you want to go to a hospital, and then I will drive you."

"You don't own me," she sneers.

His face morphs, eyes becoming harsh with anger. "Are you trying to kill me? Do you have any idea how hard it is to see you like this?" When she doesn't reply, he places his hands on her shoulders and makes her face the mirror. "Look at yourself," he says. "This isn't okay."

Her left eye is bloodshot, the lid swollen over. The bruising underneath matches her right eye, black with a tinting of yellow branching to her temples. A cut splits her bottom lip in half, scabbed over the swollenness. She seethes, tearing away from his hands. "I never said it was okay. Don't put words in my mouth."

"What am I supposed to think, Kaley?" he snaps, angry.

Kaley shoves past him and into the living room. Lilly and Justin's heads both snap in their direction, Kip hot on her heels as she attempts to put space between them.

"Don't walk away from me, Kaley."

"Don't tell me what to do. You don't own me."

Reaching a breaking point, Kip grabs her arm by the arm and pins her against the nearest wall. Justin says Kip's name in warning, alarmed. Kaley doesn't react, waiting for his next move.

"Is this what you want?" Kip seethes, hands trembling with thinly veiled anger.

Kaley lets out a humorless laugh. "You have no idea what I want."

It's his turn to laugh. "Don't I? This is what you think you deserve?"

"Admit it to yourself, Kip."

His chest rises and falls furiously. "Admit what, Kaley?" he says, voice wavering on tired.

"You don't love me, you want to own me."

He growls, punching the wall beside her head and shattering the sheetrock. Lilly yells his name. "Is this what you want? To push me so it'll prove to you I'm just like them, the men who did nothing but use you?"

His words make her body shake with rage. "It didn't take much, did it?" But even as Kaley says the words, she knows Kip would never hurt her. One hand holds the back of her head and the other anchors her hip, holding her to the wall. But even in their positions, they are gentle. Strong, but steady. Commanding, but tender.

His grip tightens momentarily, only to release a moment later as he steps back. She turns, meeting his gaze.

His eyes are rimmed in red, a level of hurt in his eyes Kaley's never seen before. "I love you for who you are," he says, voice strained. "I fell in love with your broken, chaotic mess. And I fell in love with the girl I knew you could be, the girl you'll be after you learn to love yourself, and the girl that'll come after that. I fell in love with every aspect of who you are. Not just the broken parts and not just the perfect parts."

Much to Kaley's horror, at the point of being unable to stop them, tears spill over his cheeks. Her gentle, strong, steady, commanding, and tender man is breaking before her, and it hurts her in the most unexpected way.

twenty-five

A SOB ESCAPES MY throat, then another, and they continue as I sink to the floor before him. He follows, catching me before I fall, crying with me.

"I'm sorry," he says, voice trembling. "I'm so sorry."

It only makes me cry harder as he holds me, rocking slightly in his arms. He brushes my hair back with his hand, holding me tightly to his chest like he's scared I'm going to disappear before him. *I never knew breaking him would be so easy.*

Unsticking hair from my wet cheeks, he pulls back far enough so I'm forced to look at him. "Tell me what happened," he says quietly.

Lilly hands me a roll of toilet paper as she sits on the floor next to us, and I graciously take it. I hate she's here to witness this. I wipe my nose gently, ignoring the dull ache it causes to flare behind my eyes.

"I guess I need to start at the beginning. A few months ago, I had a client, Cody Landry, con me into sleeping with him for free."

Justin chokes on air. "Cody Landry, the state senator Cody Landry?"

"You are correct."

"Oh, shit." He drags a thumb over his bottom lip.

Lilly's face becomes white because she knows Justin doesn't tend to freak out over pretty much anything.

Kip becomes more alarmed than he already is. "Why, *oh shit*?"

"Hudson's is owned by a co-op comprised mostly of government officials. Cody Landry is one of them," Kaley explains.

"Not just one of them," Justin says, taking a seat on the floor with us. "But the ring leader. Hudson's is one of three locations across the country that provides anonymity for high-profile people to meet up with escorts. One in New York, San Diego, and here. Landry oversees them all."

"Okay, but what does he want with you?" Kip says.

Here comes the hard part. "He's mad I've been taking business out from under him. He slept with me to confirm his suspicions and demanded I work under him as an escort, or pay him back the money he feels like I stole from him."

Kip's face screws up. "He's a pimp," he says, derisive.

Justin drapes his arm over one knee, shrugging. "For a lack of a better word."

For clarification, Lilly says, "And when exactly was this?"

Kip may tolerate discussing my past sexual history, but there's still a part of Lilly that wants to protect her brother. My past and future is divided by one person. "Before Kip."

"When?"

"Lilly, stop," Kip scolds her.

"No, it's okay," I say, knowing she needs the truth. "It was before I even showed up at your house, way before Kip and I ever got together."

This satisfies her, but a glance at Kip tells me he read between the lines Lilly didn't. He swallows and wipes a hand across his mouth. "That's why."

"What?"

Kip pulls back, not enough to let me go, but enough to look at me with a new perspective. "That's why you showed up out of nowhere after four years, because you needed money."

Justin and Lilly's expression are mirror images as their eyes widen, landing on me and then Kip as he sits back.

"I was just planning on asking for it, I swear," I plead with him. "I didn't even know you were out. But then Lilly was kind of distant when she saw me, then she graduated, and then she was engaged. It never seemed like a good time to bring it up, so I never did."

He leans back, giving himself a little space as he sorts through his thoughts. Settling on something, he looks at me. "How much is it?"

I carefully lick over the cut on my lip. "A lot."

He unwraps me from his body and doesn't say a word as he walks to the safe underneath the side table next to the bed. He retrieves a checkbook, grabbing a pen from the drawer, and looks up at me as he sits to write. "How much?" he says, steady.

I begin shaking my head. "I don't want your money, Kip."

Ignoring me, he scribbles on the paper, tearing it off and handing it to me as he walks to me. "Fill it out. However much you need."

I stare at the slip of paper then meet his gaze from high above me. "No."

Clenching his jaw, he shoves it into my hand. "Don't make this more difficult than it has to be."

His face is hard, voice devoid of emotion, and it reminds me of the Kip from last night. The one who kept an emotional wall up because I had pushed him away. I don't like it and I don't want him to believe the money is the reason I'm with him, or the reason I even got with him in the first place.

Standing, I hold the check out between us with both hands, ripping it down the middle as I hold his gaze. "You're not my paycheck," I say, feeling powerful in my act of defiance.

If at all possible, I can almost hear his teeth grinding together as he reins in his temper. "We can end this, stop it in its tracks, if you just let me."

"Do you really think he's going to let me go just like that? He's not the type to give in that easily."

"Neither am I."

I take a step forward, placing a hand on his chest. "It's more than you realize."

He doesn't waver. "How much?" he repeats for the third time.

"A hundred thousand."

Justin cusses and Lilly murmurs God's name in vein, but neither of us look at them.

Kip takes a deep breath, chest expanding under my hand. "It's more than I have."

I had suspected so, but was unsure. At least, until now. "I figured."

Placing a hand over mine on his chest, he shakes his head at me, eyes questioning. "You encouraged me to buy the shop, to start my business, knowing it would eat up whatever money we had left."

I don't have time to speak before he continues.

"Why?"

I thought the answer was obvious. "If I took your money, it wouldn't be any different from taking it from Peter or any of the men at Hudson's, and you mean more to me than that."

"Kaley," he says, holding my face in his hands. "I know what you feel for me is real. You don't have to prove it to me."

"No, Kip. I need to prove it to *me*."

Frustration plays across his face. "It's not your fault I went to jail. It's not even your father's. You have to stop trying to right his wrongs."

I'm taken back, surprised by his ability to pinpoint my motive. "I didn't do anything but encourage you to do what you love. There's nothing wrong in that."

"It is if it came with a price of possibly losing what we have."

His words hit a soft spot in me and I give him a small smile. "I'm not going anywhere."

He looks like he doesn't believe me, but kisses me on the corner of my mouth, avoiding the cut in the center of my lip. "We'll figure something out."

Justin takes the lull in conversation to speak. "What happens if you don't do these things? Work for Landry or pay the money," he clarifies, leaning against the back of the couch now. "What then?"

"Landry kept using Peter as leverage, because he knew Peter would cut me off if he found out I was seeing other people. Once I finally ended things with Peter, I went to him and told him I wasn't going to do it. Work for him, I mean. He demanded I pay him back for working potential buyers out from under him."

"Is that what happened tonight?" Justin says.

"It was a warning. He had a few men kidnap me on my way to the store. They shoved me in an SUV."

"Why don't we just go to the police?" Lilly asks.

Justin shakes his head. "You don't understand. Half the judicial system frequents Hudson's. Even if we managed to convince the police to act, it wouldn't go any higher than the local court system before it would be dismissed."

"And it would out Kaley as an escort," Kip says.

The weight of the entire situation hangs over us as they finally grasp the helpless feeling I've been wrestling with for months. Justin, especially, because he truly knows how corrupt the system is from the inside. His phone rings, breaking us from our thoughts, and he tells us it's Lance as he answers.

"Hey," he greets him over the phone. "Where are you at?"

Lilly stands and retrieves a beer from the refrigerator, holding up a couple in question for Kip and Justin. Justin shakes his head, but Kip gratefully takes the offering.

"I've been trying to get in touch with you." Justin pauses, looking to me before landing on Kip. "Something happened with Kaley. Everything's okay, but you should probably meet us at Kip's place."

Kip doesn't object, taking a healthy swig of beer. Everything hurts as I walk towards the couch, and it's the first time I've felt the pain my body shows. Keeping my eyes adverted, I clench my teeth to mask my discomfort, but it doesn't fool Kip. He swoops me up in his arms despite my protests, settling onto the couch with me on his lap. I quit objecting when he runs his fingers over my scalp. Even my hair feels like it hurts, but the drag of his fingers soothes it.

"Lilly, can you grab a bottle of Tylenol from the medicine cabinet and a glass of water?" I must fall asleep almost instantly because the next thing I know, Kip is nudging me awake. "Take these," he says, dropping two pills in my hand.

I know I was barely asleep for a few minutes, but the light is harsh against my eyes as I attempt to keep them open. Kip helps me drink some water and I immediately let my eyes close, resting my head back on his chest as he resumes running his hand through my hair.

"Sleep. I'll wake you up when…"

"You're telling me you had no idea." Lance's raised voice pulls me from sleep.

Kip replies, "How was I supposed to know she was in this deep?"

"I don't know," Lance says, sarcastic. "Common fucking sense."

"Lance," Justin warns. "We knew she was working there way longer than he did and we didn't have a clue."

Groaning, I sit up. "Stop arguing. You're making my head hurt."

Kip's at my side in a heartbeat, feeding me two more Tylenol and handing me a glass of water. "How do you feel?"

I press a hand to my forehead. "My head is killing me."

Lance bites his bottom lip, attempting to conceal his reaction at seeing my face.

Kip brushes back my hair. "Look at me." I force myself to open my eyes all the way, and he takes in my pupils. "Are you dizzy or nauseated?"

I shake my head.

"Drink more water," he says, pushing the glass of water in my hand. "It'll help with your headache."

I take a swallow to appease him. "Where's Lilly?"

Right on time, she emerges from downstairs with a stack of pizzas. "She's up," she says, placing a box in front of me. "Just the way you like it."

I open the box, revealing a plain cheese pizza with pineapples. "What time is it?"

"Close to twelve. You slept in most of the morning."

My stomach grumbles, and I waste zero time stuffing my face. My headache seems to dissipate with every bite, and Kip's face fills with relief as I shove more food into my mouth.

His momentary look of calm morphs into barely concealed annoyance when Lance sits on the coffee table in front of us. "Kaley, why didn't you tell me everything when I came to your apartment a few weeks ago?"

If Lance's mention of coming to the apartment bothers Kip, he doesn't show it. "At that point, I wasn't working there anymore, so I wasn't worried about it."

"Well that proved to be effective, didn't it?"

Kip shoots him a glare and Lance deliberately disregards it.

"There's nothing you could have done. There's nothing anyone could have done," I say, making it clear for everyone's benefit. "Like Justin said, the police can't do anything."

Justin looks up from the ground. "They'd be forced to if the media got ahold of it."

Lilly sits on the arm of the couch. "What are you saying?"

"We go to the media," he says simply. "Hudson's is a gold mine as far as the media is concerned. With enough public attention, the police and court systems will be forced to act."

Kip folds his hands in front of his mouth before dropping them. "We can't just call a news outlet and hope they listen. We're going to need solid proof."

Justin nods. "We have to figure out a way to expose Hudson's without Landry or anyone there knowing."

"Easy," Lance says. "We get Landry on camera admitting to everything. He's significant enough to garner national attention."

Justin continues to nod, biting his thumbnail. "Kaley, what's the security like at Hudson's?"

"Extensive. You have to apply to become a member or be invited by a member who will vouch for you. You have to sign an NDA and undergo background checks. You're required to leave all electronic devices at the door and pass through a metal detector upon entry."

"There's no way," Kip says, shaking his head.

Lance rapidly sits forward. "We need Ethan."

Everyone looks at him, questioning.

"There's rumors circulating how the attorney general, Ethan Ramsey, has been looking for a way to shut Hudson's down without pissing off the majority of the state's officials. But if we get him on our side, then we can bring it to the public. It'll give us the resources we need and unties his hands."

"That might actually work," Justin says.

"Uh, yeah. That's why I mentioned it."

Kip fights an eye roll. "So where do we go from here?"

"I can make an appointment to see him as soon as I can tomorrow morning, and we'll go from there, but I can't imagine him turning down an inside opportunity to shut down the bar without his name being attached to it," Lance says.

"Should I go?" I offer.

Kip shakes his head. "No."

As much as I can tell Lance wants to shut Kip down, he agrees. "You'll raise too many red flags walking in like that," he says, eyes downcast.

"Lance is right," Justin says, breaking the morose moment. "And we don't want Landry to find out you're talking with the person trying to take him down."

Kip grips my neck. "It'll make everyone feel better."

I roll my eyes, but it hurts so I close them. "Fine."

Everyone says their goodbyes and plans to convene back here tomorrow after Lance talks with Ethan Ramsey. I peek my eyes open and wave bye, and am surprised when Lilly wraps her arms around me. We hold each other, and like our first hug after four years, I fight back tears. There's something about Lilly that's pure, and I've always wanted to be like her in that sense. She says what she means and means what she says.

Kip holds a hand out for me to take. "Bed?"

I don't need to reply as he helps me up and leads me to the bed, situating my pillows for me so long that I have to force him to quit fussing around me. "Just lie down."

He looks like he wants to object, but something in my voice must convince him. He squeezes in as close to me as possible, positioning my head in the crook of his shoulder. Running his hands through my hair, he lets the strands fall between the gaps of his fingers. "You love my hair."

He repeats the motion. "It's everything I'm not."

I tilt my head back on his bicep to look at him. "Pretty?"

He smiles, diverting his attention from the ceiling. "Soft, messy…and pretty."

"Don't worry," I say quietly, feeling the anxiety rolling off of him.

"It's what I do."

I fight the lull of sleep, feeling like the conversation isn't over yet. Each pass of his hand threatens to take me under. The reality of yesterday is starting to take its toll. The gravity of it all, the severity of it, begins to make itself known. Out of nowhere, I find myself choking on my emotions and I keep swallowing to keep them down. I've put Kip through enough today to continue to torture him. I'm just not prepared for the direction of his thoughts when he speaks.

"I'm so sorry," he says, placing his lips to my temple. "I'm so incredibly sorry."

He doesn't have to say for what, and I'm actually grateful that he doesn't. "Me too."

We don't move for a long time, just soaking in each other's comfort.

twenty-six

LANCE CLAPS HIS HANDS. "He's in."

I feel Kip's sigh of relief from across the room. "He's going to help us?" He shifts forward on the edge of the couch, elbows braces on his knees.

Lance and Justin stand idly in front of the TV, as Lilly and I sit on the kitchen counter. "He'll give us the resources we need to make it happen," Lance replies.

"That's all we need," Justin says, mostly to assure Kip.

Kip nods once. "Okay, what's the plan?"

Lance and Justin trade looks and it's obvious they've already discussed it without us. Lance uncrosses his arms, holding out a hand before him. "You're not going to like it but just hear us out."

And Lance is right, because Kip's face goes from curious, to apprehensive, to downright disapproving by the time Lance and Justin finish detailing the plan. It's sketchy at best, but they've pulled off more impossible jobs before. I have no doubt I can do it. I just need Kip to be open minded.

"No." I say his name, but I clamp my mouth shut when he shoots a glare in my direction. "I said no," he reiterates firmly.

Lilly snorts in response. "How long are we going to pretend you have a say in this before you give in? Because I'd really just like to skip to the end where you throw a temper tantrum and walk out. It'll save us a lot of time."

Justin ducks his head, doing a poor job of hiding his amusement, and Lance outright smiles at Kip's incredulous face. "It puts Kaley in the most danger."

Justin attempts to reason with him. "No one else can get into Hudson's, you know that."

Kip stands, holding out his hands before him. "We're literally handing her over to Landry on a silver platter."

"All we need to do is get Landry on audio admitting to pretty much everything and facilitate a transaction to confirm. As long as Kaley is cooperative, there shouldn't be a problem," Justin says.

"Won't it be a little obvious for her to become so willing all of a sudden?"

"It seems that way to us," Lance says. "But if she goes in with a reluctant demeanor, he'll think he's finally pushed her far enough to agree to work for him."

"So basically, she needs to be her normal, stubborn self," Lilly says.

"Exactly," Lance agrees. "As long as she's herself, she'll be fine and he won't suspect a thing."

Kip stares at the floor with his hands on his hips. "When?"

"Ethan agreed to let the DEA take over the case, but he doesn't want to draw it out. As soon as Kaley is healed, we'll take action."

Justin looks at me, assessing. "But we don't want to wait too long in case Landry gets antsy."

They all follow his attention to me, the underlying worry of Justin's recommendation. We're not sure of Landry's next plan of action and we don't really want to wait long enough to find out.

Kip smacks his lips. "I think this is the point I should walk out," he says, meeting my gaze. He grabs his keys and shoves them in the pocket of his jeans, planting a kiss on my forehead. "I'll be back in an hour or so."

I don't object, squeezing his hand once before letting go. He needs to stew in peace and it's probably better for everyone's benefit. Everyone waits for the door to close behind him before letting out a collective sigh of relief.

"That went way better than I expected it would," Lilly says.

Justin wraps his arms around her waist. "I think I can speak for all of us, and say us too."

Lance leans his hip against the counter next to me, looking up at me. His expression is weary, almost coy as he reveals the barest of smiles. "You haven't said much."

I shove my hands underneath my thighs, shrugging. "It's my only option."

It takes him a moment to respond. "You do realize a lot of powerful men are going to be very angry."

I nod, already knowing what he's getting at. "They're going to need someone to turn the tables on."

"Not just them, but the media, too," Justin says.

"It's going to be a witch hunt," Lance says, solemnly.

I force a smile. "I know."

"How bad are we talking?" Lilly asks, hesitant.

"She'll most likely be inundated with charges from all sides. Whatever they can throw at her, they will. Some will stick, some won't, but she's definitely going to be arrested."

"Kaley," Lilly says, part admonishing.

"I know, Lilly," I say before she can continue. "But this is my mess and the last thing I want is Kip worried about it."

She runs her hands over her hair and down her ponytail, something she does when she's stressed. "You're going to hurt him," she says, sorrowful.

I fight the trembling in my bottom lip, gesturing to my face. "I hurt him every time he looks at me."

She doesn't dispute it because she knows it's true. I think she realizes it might be better than any other alternative. She said it herself, Kip deserves the best. And right now, that's not something I can give him.

They leave, wanting to be gone by the time Kip comes back just in case his agreeable attitude disappeared in the meantime, and I take fifteen minutes to feel sorry for myself. I take a shower and cry all the tears of frustration I've been holding in the past few days for Kip's benefit, and allow them to wash down the drain.

I'm so angry at life and the unfairness of it all. I'm angry at Landry and everyone who uses Hudson's to further their miserable lives. I'm angry at my parents for not giving a shit about me whenever everything imploded. At myself, for falling down the rabbit hole to begin with. Even at Kip, for making me responsible for his hurt. This is why I never did relationships, always having to answer for the other person's feelings when I can barely maintain my own. It's worse because his pain makes me hurt, and I can't even fix it.

I hear the door to the apartment open, and I turn away from the door when peaks his head in to check on me. "You okay in there?" he says, sounding pleasantly mellow considering.

"Just finishing up," I say, wiping my eyes even though he can't see them. "I'll be out in a minute."

It takes a beat too long, but he eventually closes the door. I get dressed and brush out my hair, piling it wet on top my head. Kip's back is to me as he watches the coffee pot brew his favorite aroma. Guilt immediately floods through me at the sight of him.

Wrapping my arms around him, I snuggle into the hard planes of his back as he makes another pot of coffee. "Let's go biking."

He looks over his shoulder, a proud smile across his lips. "You can't ride a bike in your condition."

"It looks worse than it feels. I need sunlight and fresh air."

"If I take you in public, people are going to think I'm an abusive boyfriend. Besides, you no longer have a bike."

I frown, remembering where it was left, knowing someone has probably taken it. I want to tell him he shouldn't care what people think but I also don't want people to assume something like that of him, either. "Can we go to our spot then? It's secluded enough to not have to see anyone."

"Kaley, you really shouldn't—"

I pull the travel mug from the cabinet and hand it to him. "We're going."

"Kaley," he tries again.

Ignoring him, I begin packing a couple of water bottles into his backpack hanging by the door. "You're going to take me on a date and cuddle me as I read the new romance novel you got for me and you're going to enjoy it."

He leans on an elbow, watching me with the first hint of a smile I've seen in his eyes in almost twenty-four hours. "And if I refuse?"

"You won't," I lilt.

"How do you know?"

Because you like seeing me happy and energetic despite the circumstances, but I simplify it. "Because you love me." I tug on a baseball cap and sunglasses, pouring his coffee into the mug and forcing it in his hand along with the backpack. "Come on. Chop-chop," I say, clapping my hands together.

He takes a sip of his coffee, eyeing me over the rim. "You're going to be the death of me."

I manage to smile in return. "I don't doubt it." It comes off as teasing, but I know how true it is.

On the hill, he slows his pace to match mine as we hike the trail, but I make sure I keep any discomfort on the down low. We spend the day lounging in the shade, my head in his lap as he plays with my hair as we both read. Eventually, we take a break to eat lunch and cool off in the spring. I kick my feet in the water, scaring away the tiny fish nearby. It's cooler under the trees, but the sun still manages to peek through and heat the rocks beneath me.

"Are you sure you don't want to get in? It feels amazing."

I hold a hand over my eyes to get a better view of him as he splashes water up each of his arms in an effort to alleviate the heat. "And miss this view?"

Kip's smile is blinding white against his tan skin as the sun reflects off the waist deep water he's standing in. "It looks even better up close."

He's the farthest thing from arrogant, but his cocky smirk pulls at my heart strings. He needed this hike as much as I did.

I smile, laughing at his good mood. "Then come closer."

He ducks under the water and I watch him swim in my direction through the clear water. Surfacing, he shakes his shaggy hair, making water shower my bare legs. The sun makes everything warm, but there's a slight breeze that tickles my wet skin and I shiver.

He wraps a strong hand around one of my ankles and I scream. "Oh my God, you're so cold."

Smiling, he pulls me to the edge of the limestone boulder, settling between my legs. The water is shallower where he stands, revealing his abs and the transition to the abdominal v-muscle, and all the way down to the most teasing glimpse of what hangs between his legs.

"How's your head feel?"

"Feels fine," I say, giving a one shoulder shrug. "Hasn't hurt all day."

He pushes a few wry hairs that managed to escape my bun away from my face, eyes smiling as they shift over my face. It's such a nice reprieve from the sad looks he's been giving me. I lean forward and place my lips on his, shivering from the contrast in temperature of his cold skin against my warm skin.

"Are you scared?" he asks, lips grazing mine.

I kiss him again before answering. "I could say no, but you'd know I was lying anyway."

"Can you promise me something?"

His question makes me nervous. "Depends on the promise."

"Will you promise to be careful?"

I smile. "What kind of promise is that? Of course I'll be careful."

His smile dims as he turns serious. "I want to marry you, Kaley." Pausing, his eyes jump between mine, gauging my reaction. I'm not sure what he sees because my mind has gone blank. "I want to marry you and make messy haired kids together. Hopefully, they'll have my temperament and your sense of humor. We'll buy a house and you can decorate the entire thing in weird elephant figurines. I'll pick up the clothes you throw on the floor every morning when I wake up, only to pick them up again when I come home."

He places a hand on my lower back, scooting me even closer to him as he continues, his other hand bracing my neck as I stare at him in awe. "You can go back to school and study art or geography or cultural sciences, I don't care. I'll work my ass off at the shop every day to supply for you and make sure you're happy. I'll complain when you leave the top of the toothpaste off and get it everywhere, and you'll bitch at me every time I leave the coffee pot on."

"Kip, I...I don't know what to say."

"For once, don't say anything." My smile is wobbly as lock my hands around the back of his neck, and I nod. "I know you're scared of us. Everything I just said is making alarm bells go off in your head. But I know you want it, too. You just have to allow yourself to have it."

twenty-seven

"ARE YOU READY?"

I nod. "No."

Kip looks as me, concerned. "Yes?"

"That's what I meant."

He trails his hands over the straps of my dress, using his fingertips to test the position of the wire and tape. "Are you wearing a bra?"

"Justin told me not to because it interferes with the audio."

"Are you comfortable?"

I nearly laugh in his face considering I'm wearing five inch heels, but manage to hold it in. "Yes."

"Do you want to go over the code words again?"

I roll my eyes, halting his hands from checking the wire for the millionth time. Besides, it's distracting. "Stop asking me questions. If I wasn't already nervous, you'd be making me nervous by fretting over me."

"Humor me," he says.

"Run means I'm in immediate danger, jump means we're relocating, skip means I need more time, and hop means whoever I'm with is armed." He takes a deep breath and I smile. "I've got this. All I have to do is talk to Landry, tell him I agree, albeit reluctantly. Get him to confirm some of his business partners, possibly other patrons who hire escorts through him. Then I need to ensure I take someone back to hotel room 315, the floor above us, so we'll have video proving the transaction is trading sexual favors for money."

Kip places a hand over his mouth. As much as I'm acting nonchalant about the task at hand, we know this is going to be a little more difficult than it sounds. I remind myself that I've done this before, conned men into giving me more for less.

Kip's phone dings and he grabs it from the nightstand and reads the text. "Lance said they're set and ready when you are."

"Okay. I left a message with Landry's secretary, letting him know I'll be there at ten, but I want to arrive early."

"He never responded?"

I shake my head. "Nope."

It leaves everything up in the air because he might not even show. Kip is super paranoid that Landry is on to us, but I explained to him how egotistical Landry is, so it's not that surprising he hasn't got in touch with me. He probably was expecting it all along.

Kip hands me my purse, and God help him, he checks my cleavage one more time. "Was that one for your own benefit?"

He smiles, for real this time. "Can't blame a guy for trying."

I take his hand between both of mine, holding it to my lips. "Everything is going to go flawlessly."

He tugs me to him, grabbing my hands and placing them around his neck. "Promise me again."

Every day since I've been waiting to heal enough to go through with the plan, he's asked me to make the same promise. "I will be as careful as I can."

"In the name of our messy haired children?"

I laugh loudly. "That's the first time you've asked me to swear on our imaginary children."

"They're real, just not born yet."

"Did Lance say you can go to the surveillance room?"

He nods. "I'm heading straight there after you leave." His phone dings, breaking us apart. "Landry was just spotted leaving his apartment. He's headed in this direction, about twenty minutes away." Another ding comes through. "And he says everyone can hear me feeling you up, so I should stop."

We bust out laughing, but it quickly descends into silence, and my smile turns sad. He kisses me, not wasting any more time we don't have on words, and I'm grateful. Reluctantly, he releases me. I can't stop myself from kissing him one last time before departing, swallowing back fear as I walk out of the hotel room and away from him.

The smell of the bar hits me first, expensive fragrances mixed in with leather and alcohol. The security guard nods as I enter, but underneath it all, it still smells like cheap sex and cigar smoke. My stomach rolls as I take a seat at the bar. Mondo is assisting a patron across the bar and he glances up, doing a double take when he sees me. He hurries and finishes pouring the drink in front of him, taking the cash and making change before he approaches.

"What are you doing here, Kaley? Last I heard, you were in a relationship."

It doesn't surprise me that he knows my business. He's always had a way of knowing things no one else does without actually being a gossip. "Can I get a glass of wine?"

He looks like he doesn't want to oblige, so I lean forward, picking the pen out of the breast pocket of his shirt. "What are you doing?"

I level him with a stare and he shuts up. On a napkin, I write out a note.

Pour me a glass of wine and then leave the building.

Spinning the fabric around, I watch his face as he read it. He looks from the cloth, back to me, reaching under the table for a glass. I take the moment to look around, downing half my drink in one gulp. Mondo scribbles back on the cloth before moving down the bar, helping another customer.

Is it serious?

One look at me and he continues writing.

Your balls are bigger than mine.

I smile, writing down my next question.

Is Julia here?

He tops off my glass, inconspicuously jotting out a response at the same time. I idly marvel at the talent it takes to do that.

Haven't seen her. She usually comes in late.

I nod in reply, but he takes moment to write something else.

I'm proud of you.

Holding my stare while he takes off his apron, he motions to his coworker he's taking a break, holding up five fingers. The coworker thinks nothing of it, shooting him a thumbs up in return. Mondo leans over the bar quickly, giving me a quick peck on the cheek before departing.

I count the heads of people, speaking the total out loud like Lance instructed me to. "Twenty-eight men and nineteen women."

I keep my eyes trained on the door, waiting for Landry to make his arrival as I sip the remainder of my drink. It doesn't take long before he comes waltzing in, suit impeccable, smiling like he doesn't have a care in the world. He notices me right off the bat, his smile growing as he takes a second to shake hands with a man near the door.

He eventually makes his way to my side of the bar, taking a seat next to me. "Where's the normal bartender who hangs around you like a puppy dog?"

"He's on break."

The other bartender takes a few minutes to finish up his end of the bar before making his way down. "What can I get for you?" he says, placing two napkins in front of us.

Landry holds up a hand, motioning for me to go first. I'm only on my second glass but I really shouldn't have too much to drink. I hold up my half full glass of wine in reply. He orders a scotch.

"I'm glad to see you, Kaley," he says, turning on his stool. "You look amazing."

"It took a while to look like myself again," I retort. Lance and Justin warned me of being too agreeable. It's not in my nature and the last thing we want is Landry catching on.

"My guy is a professional. He didn't do anything that would be irreparable. Most of the work he did on you was just as I said, a warning."

My eyebrows hit my hairline. "Oh, so I should be thanking you."

"Yes, a thank you would be nice," he says, smile pulling to one side. I purposely take a sip of my drink in reply. He laughs, turning all the way around in his stool, placing his back against the bar. "I'm assuming you're here to make a deal."

"You know what they say about assuming."

He waves to someone across the room. "And what's that?"

"It makes an ass out of you and me."

It takes him a moment for it to click and he laughs, eyes twinkling under the recessed lighting. "Would you like to move to somewhere more secluded?"

"Nah, I'm good right here," I say, sweetly.

"I meant, would you like a little more privacy in a booth? I'm not going to do anything to you here, Kaley. This is my place of business."

He doesn't give me the option to reject his offer, standing and helping me down from my stool. We squeeze into one of the booths that lines the back wall, but I'm grateful it at least gives us a view of the bar from where we're at.

"So," he says, swallowing a sip of his drink and smacking his lips. "What have you decided?"

"Since I don't have a hundred grand on hand, I guess I'm only stuck with one option."

"It's a fair one," he says.

"Making me have sex with men for money against my will isn't fair, Landry."

He flattens his tie against his chest with a palm on his hand. "You were already working as an escort before I caught you stealing business out from under me, so don't make me out to be a bad guy."

"And you're the good guy?"

"I'm just a guy," he says, shrugging. "I do business and make money and go home and eat ice cream out the tub just like everyone else."

"You're right. And all your money and expensive paper weights mean nothing when you die, just like everyone else."

He smiles at me like I'm cute and naïve. "But I'm not dead, so I'll enjoy it before I go to hell."

"That's one way to look at it."

"If I work for you, do I get a say in who the client is?"

He narrows his eyes marginally. "You know that's not really how it works."

I lick my lips and point to a man across the room. "He's an accountant at the courthouse and it's rumored he likes to listen to motivational speeches the entire time he has sex."

Landry relaxes into his seat, bracing an arm across the back of the booth.

"And that one," I say, pointing to another man. "He's obsessed with role playing and being spanked." I move onto the next. "Him? He only likes threesomes."

"I run my business by ensuring all my clients are happy, including the ones who are a bit...eccentric."

"I'm not a good liar. I couldn't pretend to be into those things if I wanted to."

"Are you insisting I let you freelance your own clients and pay me a cut?"

I nod. "Yes. As you know, I've made good money from a lot of regulars. We can come up with ground rules, but I don't want to sleep with someone I find detestable."

He purses his lips as he thinks it over. "I can agree with that on one condition. I've already set up a date for you tonight. Go through with it, do what he asks, and we'll come to some type of agreement where you work as you please."

"You were a little presumptuous I was a sure thing, weren't you?"

"He's a close friend of mine."

I'm already dreading his reply. "Who?"

Right at that moment, a figure comes into view, and my jaw hits the ground. "Kaley Monroe, I believe you remember Taylor Moore."

He looks exactly the same as he left, except there's a new layer of hardness in his gaze. Taylor was best friends with Kip since they were fifteen, at least, until they both went to jail. From my understanding, Taylor blamed Kip and Lilly for getting caught. His arrival can't be a coincidence.

"Hello, Kaley," Taylor drawls, sitting on the other side of us, folding his hands together between us on the table. "How have you been?"

"What are you doing here?"

His face remains hard, not a single glimpse of emotion comes from him and it's kind of unnerving. Where Landry is very personable and charismatic, Taylor is the complete opposite. He isn't here to play games. He's here for a reason.

"Cody offered me a job. When I found out it involved you, and that you and Kip were together, I accepted."

Landry smirks. "Taylor is still a little bitter."

"I'm sorry," I say, squeezing my eyed shut once before opening them. "I'm not keeping up. How do you two even know each other?"

Taylor's slow smirk gives me goosebumps, and not the good kind. "Your dad and Cody were close."

My eyes widen when I catch his meaning. "You and my dad worked together?" I ask, Landry.

He cocks one eyebrow, looking smug as he nods. "Technically, your dad worked for *me*," he replies.

A split second of disbelief courses through me, but it's quickly followed by laughter. Loud, uncontrollable laughter. I laugh so hard my eyes water and I attempt to tame them by running a finger under both of them as I wheeze through breaths.

Landry smiles at Taylor. "She is something else, isn't she?"

But Taylor's not amused, not even a little. He doesn't find my laughing fit as cute as Landry does, but I don't take it as an insult. "What's so funny?"

I do one last wipe under my eyes, blinking back the moisture. "This city is huge. I mean, it's like fourth in the nation or something, and my father is still relevant my life from prison. It's seriously unreal."

"Are we doing this or what?" Taylor says, tapping the table between us.

Landry looks to me. "That would be Kaley's decision."

I take a calming breath, reminding myself I'm not actually going to sleep with him. I'm not actually going to betray Kip in the worst way, by sleeping with his ex-best friend who hates him.

"Why does it have to be him?"

"I'm training him to watch over Hudson's while I'm gone, so no more stragglers like you get caught stealing. But also because he wants to."

A glimmer of something I don't like flashes across Taylor's face and I have to stop myself from involuntarily shivering. "Kip went behind my back and set up the raid. We wouldn't be in this mess if he would have brought the problem to me. We would have never gone to jail, we never would've served time. It's time to payback the favor and betray him in the only way I can." He smiles, pointing a finger at me. "You are the key to doing that."

"Have you two been planning this all along?"

Landry takes a drink of scotch, shaking his head. "I decided to hire Taylor after I discovered a couple of girls sneaking work from us, you being one of them. He proved to be a good asset when he kept his mouth shut during the trial and didn't mention my involvement. His motives are all his. I could care less his reasoning as long as he does what I pay him to do."

Taylor stands, shoving a hand in his pocket and holding the other out for me to take. "Are you ready?"

I stare at his hand a moment too long and Landry takes the opportunity to reiterate the consequences of not complying. "I'm using you as an example, Kaley. If I let you off easy, other girls will think they can get away with it too. If you don't do this, there will be repercussions."

Slipping my hand into Taylor's, I let him lead me out of the booth. "I already have a hotel room we can jump to." I focus on the sound of our steps over the marble floor of the lobby to ease my nerves.

He pushes the button for the elevator. "Cody runs Hudson's from his office on the top floor. We can use it." He skims his eyes over the cleavage of my dress and my breath catches. There's no way he knows. "It shouldn't take long," he says, showing no emotion.

Or maybe he's just a pig. "Wouldn't you rather an actual bed?"

"Oh, there's a bed," he says, ushering me into the elevator. "But we don't necessarily need one anyway."

Clenching and unclenching my teeth, I meet his stare in the mirror of the doors. "Let's just get this over with."

"You know, when Cody told me you were escorting, I can't say I was surprised. It's to be expected with a girl like you. But when he told me you and Kip were in a relationship, I laughed because I thought he was joking. Last I remembered, he could barely tolerate you."

"Yeah, well, it went both ways."

The elevator doors open and he leads me into the hall, all the way down to the end. There's no suite number on the door and Taylor produces a key from the inside pocket of his jacket. I try to get a glimpse of it but can't before he puts it back from where he got it from.

"How much are you paying for this?" I ask, taking in the suite. It's larger than any of the other rooms I'd seen before with a desk set in the middle and a bedroom off to the side.

He unbuttons the top button of his shirt. "Most clients would pay roughly two grand an hour, but you already knew that."

I carefully take a step back as he takes one forward. "But you're not?"

"No, I am, but I'm paying much higher than average. Peter Baranski tried to buy you out."

I stutter through a response. "He did what?"

"Cody didn't tell you? Peter offered to pay your debt."

"Then why am I here right now?"

He closes the distance between us, standing toe-to-toe with me. "Because I paid Cody more to keep you."

I suck in an unfulfilling breath, knowing Kip is probably losing his shit right now. Taylor pulls against his erection. "I honestly have no desire to fuck you," he says, bored. "You're pretty, but I could have plenty of willing women at my feet without all the hassle. But the idea of fucking Kip over, literally, makes my blood boil."

"Don't touch me."

Heat flares behind his eyes before they diffuse. "Don't make this harder than it has to be. It'll only make this harder for you, not me."

He reaches for me again and I jerk away. A split second later, I'm pinned against the wall with his hand around my throat.

"I told you we probably wouldn't need the bed."

His hand tightens around my throat and I struggle to take a single breath to breathe. I claw at the hand around my throat, trying to make room to say the one word I need. He pushes his pants to his thighs and I kick as hard as I can, hoping to hit something important. I succeed and he drops me, groaning as he bends over in pain.

I take in one breath or relief before screaming the code word. *Run.*

Stepping around him, my aim is for the door. He reaches out at the last second, grabbing my ankle and making me fall forward. I scream run over and over. Maybe if I say it enough, they'll get here quicker.

"You're getting it now," Taylor seethes as he crawls over my body.

I'm screaming, hoping anyone from the neighboring rooms will hear it. When I begin to feel Taylor pushing up the backside of my dress, I thrash wildly and manage to flip on my back. Everything comes to a screeching halt as he pins my arms above my head, using his weight to push my hips down, his eyes fixated on my chest. All of sudden, I recognize the feel of air over my breast and I look down, noticing the top of my dress is ripped down the middle, exposing my chest and the wire.

The next thing I know, he clamps a hand over my mouth and releases the hold on my arms. Holding a finger to his lips, he slowly releases the hold on my mouth, sitting back. I scramble to my feet and adjust the straps of my dress. He stands, holding his hands in the air in surrender.

"They—"

I don't get another word out before he lunges at me, this time pulling the strap of his belt from its loops and wrapping it around my face. This time, he successfully gets the leather strap between my teeth and he tightens it to where I can only make inaudible noises. He pins me to his front, walking me towards the bedroom, throwing me onto the bed. I immediately reach for the back of my head to undo the buckle, when my eyes land on the gun he retrieves from the end table.

He buttons his pants and shoves the gun into the waistband. He doesn't have to instruct me to sit still as he uses a pillowcase to tie my hands behind my back before he does the same to my feet. Then he punches the bed. Over and over, his fist comes down in a silent fit of rage. He does an about face, sitting on the bed and hanging his head on his shoulders. My panicked breathing is loud and I force myself to inhale and exhale through my nose to calm myself. I don't know what's taking Lance so long.

And as if on cue, the hotel room door busts open with a loud crack. Men in black swarm the room, guns drawn as they land on Taylor, calling out signals to one another as they clear the bathroom and closet. I sag in relief when I spot Lance come in last, followed by an unnerved Kip.

Kip's eyes take two seconds to take in my state of being, then comes completely unhinged and lunges at Taylor. I try to scream around my gag, but it's no use. A few men pocket their guns to help Lance pull Kip off of Taylor, yelling at him to stand down, but Kip doesn't listen as his fist keeps connecting with Taylor in some way, shape, or form. I buck against the sheets, trying to get someone's attention. But it's useless, everyone's concern is on the raging bull—Kip—absolutely losing his shit in the middle of the bedroom.

And then it happens. The sound freezes everyone in the room for a fraction of a second before the second shot rings out. Lance's back is to me, but I can see the recoil in his arms and back as he pulls the trigger of the gun aimed at Taylor on the floor. I scoot across the bed, doing my best to see what happened.

"Call the medic," Lance says, kneeling down.

It's the first time I get a visual. Lance is undoing the bullet proof vest on Kip's chest, but there's two prominent red spots on the plain white t-shirt. There's one on his side, close to his ribs, and the other in his shoulder. Both shots missed the vest by centimeters. Lance undoes his own vest and strips off his shirt, using it as a compress to the one in Kip's side.

Someone finally takes pity on me and unbuckles the belt around my face. Kip's eyes meet mine as he winces against Lance's hands. He reaches for my face, tracing the indention the belt made on my cheek.

"I was thinking about ordering pizza for dinner," he says like it's just another night at home.

Smiling through my tears, I nod. "Okay."

twenty-eight

THE DOCTOR SWINGS THE stethoscope around his neck after checking Kip's breathing. "We'll keep you overnight just for observation, but you should be good to go home in the morning."

"Thank you," Kip says, shaking the doctor's hand before he leaves.

I sit on the edge of the bed by his feet, not wanting to jostle him too much. "I ordered pizza."

He smiles, tired. "Pineapples?"

"None. Are you thirsty?"

"A little."

I refill the paper cup on his bedside table and roll it within his reaching distance. "Lilly and Justin are on their way. She's bringing you a change of clothes. Unfortunately," I tack on, staring at his bare chest.

He starts to laugh, but it ends as quickly as it started in a groan. "Don't make me laugh."

"I'm sorry," I say, pushing his hair from his forehead. "Do you want to watch a movie? There's free pay-per-view."

"No, the sting on Hudson's should be on the news by now." He clicks on the TV and turns it to our local news station.

He's correct because a live clip of Cody Landry being bonded out of jail plays across the screen. The news anchor's commentary details the charges against the senator, calling Hudson's the largest prostitution ring ever uncovered in the country. She goes on to detail numerous other arrests made, showing a picture of the well-known official before moving on to the next. There's ten arrests in all, seven men and three women, and one fatality. They show Taylor's mug shot from his arrest over four years ago, and it displays a slightly younger Taylor than we saw tonight.

Kip's voice pulls my attention away from the screen. "Come here."

"You need something? More water?" I say, already refilling another cup.

"No," he says, pulling me with his good arm. "Lay down with me."

"I don't want to hurt you."

"Not if you lay on this side," he says, his pull on my arm uncharacteristically weak.

"Are you sure?"

"Kaley," he says my name in admonishment, impatience growing.

I can't help but smile at his insolence, secretly loving he's being himself. It takes a full five minutes to find a comfortable spot that didn't cause him pain. "You're so stubborn."

"Strong willed," he corrects me.

"Lance told me you weren't supposed to go in with them."

"He knew there was no way I wasn't going to after I heard everything."

I draw a lazy circle around his nipple. "He also told me you punched his boss when they told you to wait to lock down all the exits."

"He was more worried about the media coverage and how it'd portray his department than your safety. The guy is a total piece of shit."

Smiling, I place my lips to the skin of his collar. "Like I said, stubborn."

He laughs, this time more carefully. "I'm just glad it's over."

Dread fills my belly. "Kip, there's something—"

Lilly comes barreling in, throwing her arms around his neck. Kip smiles good naturedly. "Easy," he says.

"Sorry," she says, hiding her glassy eyes as she pulls back. She hefts a duffle bag onto the hospital bed and rifles through it. "I brought a few pairs of underwear, some shorts and t-shirts, tooth brush and paste, and this three-in-one body wash I found in the shower."

"It's only for one night, Lilly. Unless I shit myself multiple times, I shouldn't need…five pairs of underwear?" he says, counting as she shoves them back in the bag.

She pouts. "I was being thoughtful, okay?"

"It is very thoughtful. Thank you," he says. "Where's Justin?"

She rolls her eyes. "They'll only let two people in the room with you at a time, so he's in the lobby."

"I'll go," I say, sitting up. The way Kip says my name, I already know he's about to protest. "I need some caffeine in me anyway."

"Just…be careful."

The fear in his eyes makes me feel like I'm suffocating him, in return, suffocating me. A few minutes apart will do him some good. Justin looks up from his phone, standing as I approach.

271

"You can go in and see him. I'm going to find the nearest vending machine and grab a drink."

"I'll walk with you." I roll my eyes, but Justin places a hand on my shoulder. "As much as you think you're fine, you're not. It's going to catch up with you."

The waiting room goes in and out of focus and the floors seem to rattle beneath my feet. I focus on Justin's steady gaze. "Which part?" I whisper.

He rubs his thumb back and forth on my shoulder, empathy radiating from him. "All of it."

Those three words bounce inside my head as we walk to the vending area. Justin deposits me by the nursing station but I don't protest because *all of it*. There's so much, too much, and I can't imagine having to deal with any of it. Maybe that's my problem. Justin and Lilly don't stay too long, but I'm secretly grateful they made their visit short. I want to soak in what I can of Kip before everything implodes. I can feel it coming, like an atomic bomb with a clock ticking down.

Kip already has the blanket pulled back for me when I return. "I was getting worried," he says, smelling my hair as I snuggle into him.

"That's nothing new." I lift the lid of the pizza box sitting on his bedside table. "You didn't eat anything."

"I'm not hungry." There's a beat of silence before he speaks. "I think you should see someone," he says. "A therapist or doctor of some sort. Someone to help you sort through everything in your head."

All of it.

"I know," I say, voice quiet.

"Did you...did you just agree with me?"

I smile. "I did. Revel in it while you can."

"I think I will," he says. "I should get a plaque made."

"That's a little overboard."

He chuckles, going back to sniffing my hair. "You don't know how happy that makes me."

"I'm not doing it for you."

"Good."

He turns the channel, settling on a romantic comedy. I idly watch it, mind wandering all over the place. I suspect Kip is doing the same when I catch him staring at the wall.

"What are you thinking about?"

"Taylor," he says, quietly.

I run my lips over his knuckles. "Do you want to talk about it?"

"I just don't know where he went wrong, you know? He wasn't always like that though. I still remember the kid I met outside of Tobey's doing willies on his bicycle. He footed the bills for us when I decided to quit stealing cars and he was the first person I'd call when I was in a bind. We grew up together."

"I don't know," I say. "I think people get an option to choose to be good and he didn't. Being good isn't always easy."

He doesn't reply as he resumes to pretend to watch the movie. I fall asleep in his arms, waking once in the middle of the night to the feeling of being suffocated. Kip doesn't even stir, the pain meds doing their jobs well. I spend the rest of the night letting the tears fall, not able to stop them once they start. I categorize every part of Kip I can. His smell, the rough feel of the palms of his hands, and the way his hair has the slightest wave to it. I've spent more times than I'd like to admit watching him sleep, but I trust now this will be the last time for a while, if not ever.

"Kaley," Lance says, jerking me from my sleep.

Kip yelps in pain. "I'm so sorry," I say, palming his cheek.

He blinks through the haze of drug induced sleep, trailing over Lance and the accompanying police officer. "What's going on?" he says, confused.

Lance gives me an admonishing look. "You didn't tell him?"

"Tell me what?" Kip asks.

Licking my lips, I slowly sit up. "I didn't want to ruin last night."

He winces in pain as he pushes the button to elevate the head of the bed. "What are you talking about?"

When Lance sees I'm not going to answer, he does it for me. "Kaley is being charged with five counts of solicitation of prostitution. We're here to arrest her."

Kip's face turns the deepest shade of red I've ever witnessed on him before. "What? You can't do that? She helped to bring the organization down."

Lance speaks to the officer behind him in hushed tones. The officer doesn't look happy about it, but he leaves the three of us alone. "And she's helped piss off a lot of higher up's. They're spinning it, diverting the attention from all the corrupt politicians to her. They're going to make her public enemy number one."

Kip narrows his eyes at me. "You knew? All this time, you knew and didn't tell me?"

I frame his face in my hands. "I knew you'd fight it."

"Of course I would."

Putting on my best brave face, I say, "I'm tired of fighting."

He huffs out a breath. "So you just give up. After everything you've been through? You're going to throw in the towel?"

"I'm not going to lie down and play dead," I say, defensive. "I'm deciding to play by the rules. I've spent my life trying to find the easy way out and all it's done is get me in more trouble. If the public wants to crucify me, let them."

Red begins to tread the whites of his eyes. "I'll post your bail."

I sigh, kissing him once. "There's no way they're going to release me."

Lance chimes in. "It's already rumored she'll be denied bail."

"Are you fucking kidding me? Heinous people get out all of the time. Hell, Landry posted bail last night and he had over twenty-five counts of pimping and pandering and money laundering, and you're telling me they're going to deny her bail?"

"The attorney general is stuck between a rock and a hard place. He successfully took down Hudson's, but he has a lot of angry people to deal with. They want someone to pay, this is the compromise."

"What compromise? This is a persecution."

"I explained the consequences to Kaley before we went through with the plan. She's okay with it."

Kip places the back of his hand against his mouth, unbelieving of what he just heard. "You never planned on having a future with me, did you?"

"Kip, I want it more than you know," I say, pleadingly. "But if there is ever a chance of us making it, I need to be able to put my past behind me or it's going to follow us."

"We really need to go," Lance says. "I was supposed to arrest you yesterday. Between you and Kip knocking out my boss, I'm not going to have a job by the end of the day."

"Kip," I say, urging him to look at me. "I love you."

He shakes his head, finally dropping his hand away from his mouth. "You can't love me because you don't even love yourself," he says, meeting my eyes. "I tried to love you enough for the both of us, but you're right, I can't do it anymore."

I hiccup on a sob, but somehow am able to swallow it down. He lets me kiss him, but he doesn't touch me, his arms staying at his sides. Tears fall down my face as I step down from the bed, trailing my fingers down his arm, all the way to his fingertips.

"Thank you for being everything I need."

He takes in a shuttering breath, turning his attention to the same wall he spent the night looking at before. "I'm sorry it wasn't enough."

All the air leaves me in one full whoosh, but Lance manages to walk me out of the room to the awaiting officer. He instructs me to turn around and I oblige, mind blank as I go through the motions. Lance grips me by my shoulders, making me meet his gaze.

"Do you hear me?" he says, pulling me out of my daze. "He loves you too much to let you go. He's mad, not stupid. He'll forgive you."

There's so much to be forgiven for and I don't blame him for being angry. Lance brings me to the jail, kissing me on the cheek before releasing me. "I'm going to deposit some money in your commissary and load you a phone card whenever you're in the system." He squeezes me tight as we say our goodbyes.

I'm placed in a holding cell for most of the day before I'm strip searched and escorted through a medical evaluation. The lady asked me nine times if I had any thoughts of ending my life or escaping, and I'm fairly certain she thinks I'm suicidal because I wouldn't stop crying. I'm given a mandatory AIDs testing and I'm assigned a cell with a girl much younger and smaller than I am. Despite her appearance, she's super standoffish and her beady little eyes follow my every move.

I've just finished making my bed when a corrections officer bangs on the open cell door. "Kaley Monroe, you have a visitor."

"How? I was just booked."

He gives me a bored look and I already know he's not going to answer me. He shows me to the visitation room and I immediately recognize Peter's figure hunched over the table. The guard buzzes me through, standing guard at the door as he shuts it behind us. I was told visitation is only on Saturday's so I have no idea how or why he's here. Peter's hand flies across the writing pad in front of him as he looks up. Setting down his pen, he stands to greet me.

"Kaley," he says, nodding.

"What are you doing here?

"Please, sit," he says, pointing a hand at the chair opposite him. "I'll explain everything to you."

"I think I'll stand," I say, folding my arms.

Peter's eyes shift to the guard behind me, and he holds up a hand in his direction. "She's new." He gives me a look. "Sit or be forced to leave. Up to you." He waits for me to sit before he continues. "I'm here to represent you."

"Who called you?" I ask, incredulous.

"Your father, actually," he says, loosening the tie around his neck.

"My father?" I say for clarification.

"John Monroe, the very same."

"Why would my father pay for my lawyer? He has no money."

"That's not for you to worry about. All you need to know, is that I'm already working on negotiating a plea deal."

"Woah, slow down. What kind of plea deal?"

"Well," he says, sliding the notepad in my direction. "They're offering a one-year minimum prison sentence and five years of probation if you plead guilty. Your father will cover all the fines."

I massage my forehead, bracing my head in my hands. "I'm sorry, I'm totally blindsided right now. I need just…need a minute to process."

"We only have a few minutes so you're going to have to process faster. I'm trying to cut the sentence down, but they're being stingy. But I'm positive you won't do more than two years at most. They're itching for retribution but they also know not all of your charges will stick."

"They're revoking my bond on five misdemeanors. Why are they suddenly changing their tune?"

"The public is rocked by the scandal right now, so it's easier for them to get away with more. Especially with half the court system on their side."

"Aren't you on their side?"

"I'm on whoever's side I'm representing. Lucky for you, I'm the best defense attorney in the state."

"Yay," I say, sarcastically. I eye him across the table. "You tried to pay Landry to cover my debt for me?"

"Not me, your father. He cares more than you think, Kaley." He pulls the pad back towards him. "Do you have any names you want to put down for visitation rights so I can expedite them?"

I open my mouth but immediately clamp it shut. I have no doubt Lance is right, and Kip will forgive me at some point. But I can't hold him back anymore. He deserves someone better than me, even if he doesn't know it.

Shaking my head, I say, "No."

twenty-nine

THE SHRILL SOUND OF the phone ringing is drowned out by the cacophony of voices echoing in the room, but my eyes stay trained on the officer as he picks it up, speaking into the receiver briefly before hanging up.

"Inmate Kaley A. Monroe ready for roll up."

I grab my things, mostly books, and walk to the receiving and leaving department. When I open the door, the man behind the desk ushers me forward with his hand. "Are you inmate Kaley A. Monroe 52468-25?"

"Yes, sir."

"Do you have any dress outs?"

I shake my head and my silence forces him to look up at me. "No, sir," I voice.

He goes back to typing on his computer. "We have clothes you can pick from. Do you have a ride?"

I nod. "Yes, sir."

He hands me a slip of paper and instructs me through a set of door. A woman takes my slip of paper and tells me I can choose whatever I like from the basket of clothes on a metal table. She doesn't leave as I dress out of my uniform and change, but I'm beyond accustomed to the strange, voyeuristic feeling of being watched all of the time. I find a decent pair of sweat pants but the only t-shirt I could find was three sizes too big with an image of a parrot on the front. A pair of flip-flops completes the ensemble.

She goes over my discharge papers and I sign them, receiving a copy for my parole officer. "This is your gate money," she says, sliding a white envelope across the surface of the table. When I don't touch it, she taps it. "It's yours."

I fold it and stuff it into my back pocket without counting it. The officer instructs me through a set of double doors, pushing the buzzer to let me through. They open, revealing the tiny lobby, and past it the doors leading to the parking lot.

"Good luck," she says, monotone.

I walk through the lobby and push open the heavy door that leads to outside, bracing against the sting of the cold against my skin. Taking a deep breath, I breathe the air of freedom for the first time in over a year, and yet nothing but dread fills my lungs.

A car honks and I whip my head in its direction, catching Lilly's hand raised outside the window of her car. I duck my head against the wind as I trudge to her car. The locks sound a second before I open the passenger door and get in.

"It's so cold," I say, rubbing my hands together.

She throws her arms around me and I squeeze her back. "I know. That's why I didn't get out the car."

Sitting back, I take in her frame, smiling at the sight of her round belly. "Can I touch it?" I say, already touching it.

She smiles, watching me rub a hand across her stomach. "She's crazy active right now. She hates the cold."

Right at that moment, a distinct bump knocks the palm of my hand and I scream. "I felt her."

Lilly smiles, amused. "She refuses to move for Justin so be honored."

"I'm so rubbing it in his face," I say, giving her belly one last pat.

"You have to be starving," he says, starting the car.

"You have no idea."

"We can stop somewhere and eat before we hit the road."

"I can't believe Justin let you drive this far without him."

She rolls her eyes. "If I have to hear about 'my condition' one more time, I'm going to murder someone. Luckily, he got stuck working an extra dayshift at the hotel today, so he didn't have a say."

"He doesn't know you're picking me up, does he?"

She gives me a 'come on' look. "He's pretending like he's too busy to notice so we don't fight about it. Besides, it's not like I would do anything that would put us in harm. We'll stop halfway to stretch and wear our seatbelts."

We find a burger joint close by and choose a booth closest to the kitchen to get warm. A waitress takes our drink orders and I nearly die an early death at the taste of carbonation. One sip and my eyes water, but it's so good at the same time.

"Oh, how I've missed you," I speak to the drink, stroking the side of the glass.

Lilly stares longingly at the glass too. "Me too. Me. Too."

"Not even a little?" I ask, holding the straw in her direction.

She holds up a hand to block her view of the drink. "Don't tease me. I dream of carbonation and caffeine and sugar and all of it combined. I want to bathe in it."

Slowly, I pull my straw back. "Pregnancy has made you crazy."

"I'm hungry," she defends. "All the time. To top it off, I only crave what I can't have."

I laugh at her outrage, but she slowly breaks into a smile. We order two of their largest burgers with fries and two different types of pies right off the bat. And I go ahead and order a second drink.

"You look good," Lilly says, sincerely.

I look at my reflection in the window, cringing at what I see. "I look like shit."

"No you don't. You look healthy."

"Healthy is another word for fat. Just call me fat."

She laughs. "This is fat," she says, pointing to her belly. "Argue with me some more."

"Nope," I say, holding up hand. "I've been around pregnant you all of thirty minutes and I can already tell that's not something I want to do anytime in the near future."

Both of us forget about arguing the second the food arrives, too busy stuffing our faces to talk at all. Every bite makes my taste buds feel like they're actually exploding and I have to stop myself from moaning with every bite. To Lilly's credit, she eats like she hasn't had anything but day old bologna the past year too.

She actually does moan, cradling her belly as she finished chewing her last bite. "That was so good."

I bob my head in agreement, wiping my mouth with a napkin, disgusted with how much sauce and grease comes off. "Literally, the best thing I've had in a year."

"Kip ate like a bear for months after he came home too, stocking up like he was preparing for hibernation." My reaction at hearing his name must read all over my face, because her face becomes slightly panicked. "I'm sorry. I didn't think. I mean, I didn't—"

I wave a hand in the air, shoving one more fry in my mouth I don't need. "It's okay. How's he been?" I say, nonchalant, not feeling it in the slightest.

"He…works a lot," she says, rubbing her belly absent mindedly. "But he's good."

I nod my head repeatedly. "That's good," I say. "He likes to stay busy."

"He does," she agrees, dropping the conversation.

I'm partially pleased and saddened by it. I want her to tell me everything. How he's doing, who he's doing it with, does he miss me? But the other, more rational part knows I have no right to ask. I haven't seen him since I left the hospital with Lance that morning and I never replied to his one and only letter. Over time I had added Lilly to my approved visitors list, but she knows where I stand when it comes to Kip. We don't talk about him. It's almost easier and harder at the same time.

Once we're back on the road, it starts to drizzle. "You still haven't told me where you're staying," she says, kicking up the windshield wipers.

"I wasn't sure until a week ago," I say. "Lance found an apartment I can sublease with the current tenant, and they'll let me turn in my first month's rent after I get back on my feet."

"That's great," she says, truly meaning it. "Do you know who it is?"

I shake my head. "No idea."

She can't hide her cringe and I laugh. "I'm sorry," she says. "I should be positive. I bet he or she is wonderful."

"That was a pathetic attempt at being optimistic. You should stick to what you know."

"In that case, I hope it's not someone like Mrs. Cecile. God forbid you stay out past ten."

"How the hell do you know about Mrs. Cecile?"

She hesitates a moment. "Kip and Lance have both filled me in enough to know she needs a hobby."

I smile. "Thanks," I say.

"For what?"

"For picking me up and pretending my new roommate can't be worse than Mrs. Cecile."

She smiles like she's proud of herself. "You're welcome."

For the rest of the way, she gives me a rundown of everything that's happened since I've been gone. Justin finally quit smoking, for real this time, and his brother, Jacob, got accepted into grad school in the city. Her firm is being super supportive with paying her through her maternity leave after not even working there a year. The baby wasn't planned but not a terrible surprise for them. Cal is getting in more trouble than ever lately since Mr. Wilson has been battling some serious health conditions.

"But he's grown fond of Kip, so I'm hoping some of Kip's good influence will rub off."

"Doubtful," I say, smiling. "It did nothing for you."

"It's so annoying. I know he's a good kid. I don't understand why he acts out so much."

Life can change so much in a year. I shake my head, amazed by it all.

Lilly programs the address Lance gave me into her phone and she volunteers to come inside to meet my new roommate with me. It's on the west bank but it's a clean apartment complex with a pool and playground set. The apartment is up six flights of stairs and I begin to worry about Lilly on the second floor.

"Are you okay?"

She holds her side, waving away my concerns. "Like I said, I'm fat," she says breathlessly. "It takes a little more effort."

"You don't have to come up. Really. I'm sure my roommate is fine." She gives me a murderous look and I hold my hands up in surrender. "Let's just take a break."

We do this every two floors until we reach the top. By the time we knock on the door, I'm afraid she's going to scare my roommate into revoking their offer on the apartment. The door swings open and a very pretty redhead greets us.

"Hi. You must be Kaley," she says, smiling sweetly. "I'm Beck."

"Hi," I say, waving. "This is my friend Lilly. She wanted to come along to ensure you weren't a serial killer."

She laughs, opening the door wider. "That's not a problem. My boyfriend might be offended though."

"Your boyfriend?" I say. "Lance didn't tell me there were two tenants."

"Oh, I don't live here. This is my boyfriend's apartment."

When Mondo comes into view, my confusion morphs into understanding. He leans a forearm on the doorjamb as he uses the other to tug Beck to his side. "No serial killers here, I promise."

"How...why...what?"

He laughs. "Lance tracked me down two weeks ago and said you would need a place to stay when you were released."

"But how did he know who you were or even that we know each other?"

He shrugs, dumbfounded. "He told me you'd know." Lilly and I trade looks, just as baffled. "Something about the government seeing your porn?"

I bust out laughing and tears come to my eyes as all three of them stare at me like I've lost my mind. "Inside joke," I explain once I have myself under control.

Beck smiles, dubious. "If you say so."

Mondo waves us in and he shows us the layout of the apartment. It's a two bed, one bath, but it has a balcony off my bedroom so that's a plus. There's not much to it, still very much a guy's apartment, but Beck is super friendly and open to Mondo sharing an apartment with a girl, which I'm more than grateful for.

Lilly lounges in a foldout chair on the balcony, cradling her belly as she rests. "This isn't too bad."

"No, it's not bad at all," I say leaning my forearms on the railing.

After a moment, she asks. "Are you okay?"

I smile at her over my shoulder. "I'm okay. Strangely tired, but okay. I don't feel like it's set in yet."

"Do you need any money?"

I shake my head. "I have enough for about a week, but hopefully I can find a job soon." As I say it, I remember how hard it was for Kip to find a job with a criminal record and the same dread from earlier returns.

"You need clothes and food and necessities. Why don't we go shopping?"

Smiling, I look at her. "Do you not have anything to do today?"

"I took the day off to spend with you," she says, taking a good five minutes to heft herself up. "Besides, I know *you* don't have anything to do today, so you're stuck with me."

We spend the day bargain shopping. I buy a few sets of clothes but I'm honestly more excited about having bras and underwear that fit and aren't plain white. I also buy food for the apartment, hoping Mondo likes some of the stuff I pick out since I can't afford rent right away.

It's a good day. Probably the best way I could have spent today. I've felt like I waited for this day for forever but dreading it at the same time. Everything didn't fall into place last minute. Lilly and I stayed in contact for most of my prison sentence, as was

Lance, but I knew I wasn't going to be able to stay with either of them when I was released. Both offered, but neither felt right. Once Lance realized I was serious, he told me he'd find a place, and he's somehow found Mondo. Apparently the government does see all. Creepy.

thirty

I DROP THE APPLICATION into the slot in the door of the boutique. It's been two weeks since I've been released back into the real world but there's been no luck with jobs. It's too early in the year for the summer rush to begin and too late for anything seasonal. I don't imagine I'll be getting a call back anytime soon. My parole officer is going to be thrilled.

I take the bus back to the apartment, aggravated at another day wasted. Sometimes I feel like I'm not even real. What if I'm having one really long, detailed dream about getting released, but I'm actually still back at the prison, sleeping the days away. I do the same thing now, so it's hard to tell.

I come home to an empty apartment. Mondo is gone most of the time. If he's not working at the bar down the street, he's at Beck's, and if he is home the chances are he's sleeping. I unzip my jacket, pulling my arms free, when a feeling washes over me. It's hard to describe, but it's a sense of anxiousness and nostalgia mixed into one. I've thought about it more times than I've wanted to, but now it feels like I'm going to die a slow and painful death if I don't go.

Hailing a cab, I ignore the voice in the back of my head that it's not worth the money. Especially because it's so far out of the city. I sit in the back of the cab, butterflies erupting inside me. It's like they know where we're going and they're just as excited as I am. I tip the driver for the speedy delivery and hop out, surprised by the amount of hikers who are out in the chilly air.

I choose the path of least resistance and hike the beginner trail to the spot. The smells of the trees are different than I remember but it's probably because it's still considered winter. Each time I round a corner and someone comes into view, my heart stops for a split second before resuming its pace. I remind myself that the odds of seeing him are slim to none and I didn't see his truck in the parking lot. I looked…twice. Not that I don't want to see him, because that would be a lie. But I don't know if I'm ready to, or if I'll ever be.

I mean, I assume we'll bump paths eventually. Lilly has been coming over almost every day to chat. If she's not eating all of my food, she's chatting my ear off about all the gross things pregnancy does to the human body. Don't even get me started on the sex stories. All those years in college, when I'd have to drag every last detail from her is long gone. I don't think I ever want to hear another description of Justin's penis.

By the time I make it to the top, I realize I came wholly unprepared. I'm dehydrated and I didn't stop to think about water in my mad rush out the door. I lick my lips, reminding myself I can get a drink from the spring. Cutting through the trees, I start to get nervous that I forgot where the spot is for a moment. A few vague details stick out to me, and I'm relieved when I finally break through the foliage and onto the plateau.

I breathe in deep through my nose, releasing it through my mouth. All the anxiousness and doubt about where my life is headed unravels, leaving a sense of serenity. I walk towards the edge of the cliff, looking down at the riverbed below. It's shallow because it's been an uncharacteristically dry season, so there's ground showing that wasn't visible the last time I was here. Taking a seat on the edge, I smile what feels like the first real smile in a long time.

When I feel a presence next to me, my eyes snap open, landing on the one person who can make all the butterflies in my belly go bat-shit crazy. He doesn't look at me, just stares out over the ravine, dangling his legs over the side. I can't even pretend to not be magnetized by him. My eyes wouldn't leave him even if I tried.

He seems like he's aged more than a year's worth of time. His hair is cut short again, but his trademark bandana is still in place. He uncaps the water bottle in his hands and takes a drink, wordlessly handing it me. Remembering how thirsty I am all of a sudden, I take a gulp. It's spring water. I can taste the difference—untouched by man.

"Thank you," I say, taking another swallow before handing it back.

His hand touches mine, and I don't have to look up from our connection to know he's finally looking at me. I can feel the blood in my cheeks as I force myself to meet his eyes, letting the water bottle slip from my fingers to his. His gaze isn't angry or hurt or even disappointed. He's always surprised me and now is no different.

We sit like that for minutes, hours, I'm not sure. But we don't speak. I don't know why, but it doesn't feel like there's anything to be said. It's nice to not feel pressured to overanalyze this, but it also kind of scares me. Maybe a little part of me pretended like there was still a fraction of a chance he'd wait for me or that there would still be something between us.

I knew it wouldn't be fair to ask him that. Not then, not with what we were dealing with, or with what I was dealing with. Kip was right when he said I needed to love myself and I've spent the last year reading as much as I can to understand who I am. Self-help books and psychology textbooks, any and everything I could get my hands on. If prison does anything, it gives you a lot of time to think about who you are. If you don't already have an existential crisis, sitting in prison will give you one.

"I come here almost every day." he says.

My heart warms at his confession. As much as it was his spot before he brought me here, it feels like our spot. His skin tells me he's telling the truth, not that he would have a reason to lie. It's tan, way darker than I've ever seen it before and his hair is also a brighter blonde than when I left. After un-shamefully looking at him for longer than what should be acceptable, the corner of his lips tip up, and right then I know, I *know*, we have much more to say.

"Do you have a ride back?" he says, standing.

The sun is beginning to set, taking the minimal amount of warmth with it. Oddly, I haven't felt the sting of cold since I've been here, but now it's starting to seep in.

I shiver, standing as well. "You know how I am with preparing. I'm probably just going to call a cab."

He stares out at the landscape, thoughtful. "It's going to be hard to find a cab to come all the way out here on a Friday night. You should just catch a ride back with me."

"Are you sure? My apartment is on the west bank."

He meets my eyes, tilting his head in a nod. "It's not a problem."

We walk through the woods to the trail. Even though it feels good to be in his presence, my heart won't slow. It's done nothing but beat heavily in my chest since he sat down next to me and it's slowly driving me crazy. Going down is always easier than hiking up, and we reach the parking lot in no time. There's only one vehicle in the parking lot and it gives me pause.

"Where's your truck?"

"I still have it, but it's on its last leg. I bought this truck to get around in."

It's shiny and still has the brand new smell when I climb in. He cranks the ignition but the rumble I remember is gone, replaced with a silent hum. The station plays a slow country tune as I buckle up.

"Better?" he asks, pushing some of the air vents in my direction.

I hold my palms over the heat to defrost them. "I didn't realize it had gotten so cold."

He pushes a button and the seat warmers begin to really make a difference, and I lean back into the seat. The trees zoom past the windows, the headlights illuminating them for a brief moment in time before they fade into black again. It's as if we're cocooned from the world. The interior of the truck muffles outside noise way better than the old truck, making the ride feel intimate. More intimate than when we were sitting at our spot. My stomach rumbles and the sound is magnified in the silence.

Kip smiles, looking over the arm he has braced on the steering wheel. "Are you hungry?"

It's funny how I keep forgetting basic human needs today. "Actually, yeah."

"Want to stop and grab a bite to eat?"

I want to, so badly, but it's not in the funds. I splurged that day Lilly picked me up, but I can't afford to do it again, not even if it's with Kip. "No, it's okay. I have food at home."

He nods once but doesn't reply. I can't tell if it bothers him I said no, or he doesn't care either way. We don't speak again until he parks in front of my apartment building.

"This it?" he says, looking up at the building.

I nod. "This is it. At least, for now."

Bracing his arm against the arm of the seat, he runs his fingers over his mouth a few times, looking from the window to me. He doesn't speak, just looks at me, not a hint at what's hiding underneath the surface.

Getting the feeling he's not ready to depart yet, I ask, "Would you like to come check it out?"

There's a split second of silence before he puts the truck in park. "Yeah," he says. "If that's alright."

"Yeah, totally," I say, not even trying to disguise the eagerness in my voice.

He follows me up the stairs and I pretend like I don't feel his eyes boring a hole into the back of me. I hold the door open as he passes through, locking it behind him. Shrugging out of my jacket, I turn the heater up a few notches.

"Living room, kitchen, hallway," I say, motioning to the tiny apartment.

He stands awkwardly by the door, hands shoved in his pockets. "Can I have something to drink?"

"Um, sure," I say, slowly. His request is odd but I suppose he's thirsty. "Is water okay?"

He nods and I walk to the kitchen to fix him a glass. I open the fridge to retrieve the pitcher, when I feel his presence behind me. I stand, looking at his close proximity over my shoulder.

"What are you—"

He braces a hand on the open door, ducking his head to look at the contents in the fridge. "I thought you said you had food," he says, accusing.

Caught off guard, I stumble over my words. "I do. I keep my food in my room so my roommate's girlfriend doesn't eat all of my food."

"Show me."

"What? No. Kip, you're being ridiculous."

He doesn't respond, just simply walks down the hallway. Pushing the first door in, he correctly guesses my room, looking around the tiny area. He inspects the room, looking at me in question. "I don't see any food, Kaley."

At this point, I'm angry. Stomping to my bed, I pull a box of food out from under my bed. Bread, snacks, chips, peanut butter, and pop tarts are shoved inside. He's not appeased, so I stand and open my closet door, revealing a mini fridge with drinks, cold cuts, and cheese. "Happy now?" I say, arms folded across my chest.

He looks a smidge embarrassed. Running a hand across his face, he sits on the edge of the bed. I give him a sympathetic smile, sitting next to him. "You literally can't help yourself," I say.

He shakes his head slightly, a touch of a smile on his lips. "I'm sorry."

I shrug. "It's okay. If I'm honest, it makes me feel good that you care."

His eyes implore mine as he digests my words. "I was mad at you," he says, voice low.

I nod, meeting his eyes. "I know."

"You refused to let me visit you and you never replied to my letter."

It's not necessarily a question, but I can tell he doesn't want to have to ask me why. I could not reply and he won't push, but only because I shouldn't have to be pushed. He deserves answers and he knows it.

"I was scared to see you," I say, forcing my voice to stay steady. "I knew if I saw you that I'd cave."

"Cave to what?" he says, confused.

"I would have asked you to wait for me."

He breathes deep through his nose before looking away, finding the wall across from my bed way more interesting. "I would have," he says. "After I was done being mad, I would have waited for you."

Placing a hand on his shoulder, I use it to brace my chin on. "I know. And I would have been selfish enough to do it."

He tenses, knocking me from his shoulder as he stands. "So making me believe you didn't care for me at all was better? You think it was less painful not knowing where we stood? For days and weeks I waited for you to give in, finally deciding that you must not want to be with me at all."

"I had already put you through enough," I say, surprised by the sudden strength in my voice. "I needed to figure out my shit."

"I know what prison is like. If there was ever a time to rely on someone, it was then," he says.

"Exactly," I say, feeling vindicated. "If I could make it through that without using someone else as a lifeline, I could make it through anything." I take a moment to swallow down my rising voice. "Kip, you deserve someone who is whole; someone who loves you because they want to, not because they need you."

It's like I punched him in the gut, his face morphing into hurt. "Is that all I was to you? A lifeline?"

"At the time, my feelings for you were so interwoven with feeling like I couldn't survive without you. Not only for your sake, but for myself, I needed to sort out which was which."

He stands with his hands on his hips, anxiety stretched across his features. "And?"

My heart beats furiously in my chest and I stand, putting distance between us as I walk to the door to the balcony. It's easier to reveal my feelings if I don't have to look at him and I can pretend I'm speaking my thoughts out loud to myself.

"I realized I don't need you. I can spend the rest of my life without you and I'll be okay. Life will go on, I'll get a job, and find my own place. Maybe, somewhere down the road I'll meet someone and love them the way you deserved from the beginning, because I'm finally secure enough in myself to be able to." I pause, breathing out a deep breath before continuing. "But I also can't imagine not having you in my future. I will survive if I have to, but I don't want to."

Finding courage somewhere deep inside me, I turn around to face him. He's sitting again, back to staring at the wall. I wasn't sure how our reunion would go, or if it would happen at all, but I feel so much relief at getting everything off my chest. He's not ready to make a decision about us, and I respect that. I wouldn't expect any more than he's already given me.

"I'm starving," I say, walking to the fridge and pulling out contents, holding up a bottle of mustard in his direction. "I'm going to make me a sandwich. Want one?"

He eyes the bottle, a slow, knowing smirk bracing his lips. "Yeah."

thirty-one

I HOLD THE PHONE to my ear.

"Kaley," Kip says, before I can speak.

I attempt to clear my eyes of the fog of sleep. "Yeah? Is everything okay?" My brain is awake, but my body is not.

"Lilly's having the baby. Her water broke an hour ago."

That does the trick. Sitting up, I knock over a bottle of water by my bed and it spills across the floor. I cuss.

"Are you okay?" he says, concerned.

"I'm fine, I'm fine. What hospital is she at?"

"Providence. Don't rush. You still have plenty of time."

"Okay. I'll be there in a bit. Thank you for calling me."

There's a pause on the other end of the line and he says, "See you soon."

I've always felt like I get the slowest cab drivers at the most inopportune times and tonight is no exception. It takes over an hour to get to the hospital but all my stress is for nada because Lilly, Justin, and Kip are all playing a game of poker when I arrive. They all look up from their hands when I knock on the door.

"I told Kip there was no reason in calling you this early," Lilly says, smiling. "It's all a waiting game."

"I knew she'd want to be here," he says, a tad defensive.

"He's right," I say folding a leg under me to sit next to her on the bed. "I don't want to miss a single second."

Justin throws a pile of poker chips to the center of the bed. "You might rethink that. The doctor said it could be hours and hours before we make any progress. Sometimes it can be close to twenty-four."

"Twenty-four?" I exclaim.

Lilly laughs. "She'll probably come sooner, but there's no telling. My contractions are sporadic."

I stare at Lilly and Justin's smug grins before turning my attention to Kip. "Why *did* you call me?"

He shuffles the cards and deals them out, including me in the next game, and Justin drops a handful of poker chips into my hand.

"What are we playing for?" I say, inspecting my two cards. Two jacks.

Lilly smiles devilishly, tucking her cards beneath her hands. "I'm still undecided on a middle name," she says. "I'll *consider* the choice of a middle name of whoever wins. I check."

Kip checks.

"A consideration? That's it?" I say, lighthearted. I tap my cards. "Check."

Justin checks, dealing the flop. There's a collective beat of silence as we assess our hands. Lilly folds, Kip bets a couple chips, I call, and Justin calls.

"What are the names?"

Justin flips the next card, revealing the turn. I watch Kip and Justin's reaction, but their facial expressions don't change. The cards do nothing for me, but there's a pair of tens that give me worry.

"Justin wants Marie, which is his mother's middle name. She's never liked me," she clarifies.

He looks up at her under his lashes and I catch his hidden smirk. "She likes you," he says.

Lilly rolls her eyes and begins to speak, but her breath catches as she leans to her side, face frozen in concentration.

"Another contraction?" Justin asks, rubbing a hand over her back.

She nods and breathes through it, sitting up again. Or as much as she can, considering her belly. "And Kip wants Rosaline, Rosie for short," she says like nothing's amiss.

I toss in a bet. "Why Rosaline?" I ask, watching Kip as he contemplates calling my bluff.

"Lillian translates to Lily, the flower, and Rosaline to Rose," Lilly says, disdainful.

Justin folds and draws the river. It's a jack, so I bet higher, looking to Kip for his next move. "You have a thing for flowers?"

He debates, glancing at me before calling. "They're pretty," he says, revealing his cards. He has a ten and a three, beating my three of a kind.

I make a face, showing him my cards. "I almost had you."

"But you didn't," he says, pulling his stack of chips across the bedding. His words ring a level of truth I'm not sure he realizes.

Lilly breathes through another contraction, but it doesn't last as long as the last one, and she deals. "You know how much I hated my nickname growing up," she says to Kip.

"I know," he says, smiling. "But it suits you."

We play the next hand and I fold before the river, immediately regretting it when I realize I would have had a flush. Justin wins, a tad too gleeful as he gathers his chips.

"Can I add my own middle name suggestion?" I say, ready to go all in with my next hand.

"Absolutely," Lilly says. "Anything is better than theirs."

"Portia."

It takes a moment, but everyone's eyes light up, and Lilly laughs. "I like that."

Justin releases his bottom lip from his teeth, eyeing Lilly's excitement before looking at Kip. "I think all bets are off," he says.

Kip's lips thin as he fights a smile, but he doesn't comment as he tosses his cards in to fold.

We continue the game, but end up taking more and more breaks as Lilly's contractions progress and a nurse comes to check on her. Justin ends up winning, but I think he's well aware his name is last in the running. I step out to grab refreshments, pausing when I hear footsteps echoing mine out the door.

"Is it okay if I tag along?" Kip asks, a touch sheepish.

"Yeah, of course," I say, letting him catch up to me before resuming.

"Where do you think the cafeteria is?"

"I don't know. I doubt it's open at this hour though."

A smile hints behind his eyes, but he doesn't let it shine through. "I think I saw vending machines by the elevators," he says, digging in his pockets for dollar bills.

The selection is limited, but I make do with a bag of peanut M&M's and a soda. It's basically what I've lived off of for the past year anyway. I devour the bag by the time we make it back to the reception desk. Instead of heading into Lilly's room, he takes a seat in the sparse waiting area. There's an awkward moment where I'm not sure if I should sit or stand. The last time we were in a hospital together, I was breaking both of our hearts. It feels like yesterday and forever ago all at once.

Kip pats the chair next to him. "You look tired," he says.

"You did wake me up in the middle of the night," I say, gulping down the caffeine in the can.

His eyes wander around the waiting room, but there's not much to look at. A couple of oil paintings hang from the opposite wall along with a TV mounted in the corner. Everything is muted, neutral tones, and it reminds me too much of being inside the walls of the prison.

"I remember how exhausting it was to get through the day after I was released. It felt like everything drained the energy from my body. Going to the bathroom seemed like work."

I smile and nod, hating how right he is. "Sometimes I feel like I'm not really out," I say, focusing on the TV. "It's hard not to sleep the days away."

He nods in understanding, eyes empathetic. "Have you found a job yet?"

I shake my head and sigh. "No, but I'm sure things will pick up in a month or two when it starts to get warmer."

Shifting in his seat, he follows my gaze to the TV. "I could use some help at the shop," he says.

I smile openly as he continues to stare at the news report. "You don't have any help by now?"

"I do," he says, tapping his thumb on his thigh. "Andie has been working for intern hours, but she's going to be leaving soon after she graduates in May."

I squelch the roar of my heart, reminding myself I have no reason to be jealous. Whether or not I have a right to be is irrelevant. "Thanks for the offer, but I think I'm going to keep looking."

He stills his movements and I see the flicker of something flash across his features before it's gone. "Okay," he says, resuming tapping his jean clad thigh.

"It's not that I'm not grateful," I say. "I just need to do things on my own. I'm already a step behind. I owe Lance for finding an apartment for me, and then I owe Mondo for letting me delay first month's rent. The last thing I want is to owe you something too." *Especially when I already owe him so much.*

He looks at me again. "You would be doing me a favor. I don't have anyone lined up. You don't have to stay forever, just until I can find someone else."

I breathe deeply, not wanting him to feel slighted by turning down his offer twice. "I'll think about it," I reason.

He nods once. "Okay."

A young couple walks in the sliding glass doors. The guy has his hands full with a baby bag, duffle bag, folder full of paperwork, and a very pregnant significant other waddling next to him. He's frazzled, cheeks flush as the girl smiles at him adoringly. "Breathe," she says, cradling her belly as they make it to the registration desk. He smiles, but it's only momentarily because the woman behind the counter starts asking questions and he does his best to answer them.

"I want that," I say, too afraid to tear my gaze from the couple. But I can feel the way Kip's eyes roam over my face as he turns his focus to me. My cheeks burn from the blood rushing to my face, but I manage to keep my cool.

"I thought you wanted a hammock on a beach."

"Eventually," I say, smiling. It's a mixture between amusement as the couple begins to argue over whether or not the other remembered to pack an extra baby blanket and because my old dreams seem so naïve now. "But prison gave me a lot of time to think. Fairly early on, I knew I wanted more from life than I was living. At the time, I wasn't sure what it was, but it didn't take me long to figure it out."

I hear him swallow before he speaks. "There's something about staring at the same walls every day that makes you look at life differently."

Licking my lips, I finally meet his eyes. "I'm going to meet Jackson tomorrow."

He attempts to not be surprised, but his eyes give him away. "How did this come about?"

"I wrote to Paula and explained everything to her. My dad, when I found out, the money...everything. It took a little while, but she wrote me back."

At first, her letters were formal, clouded in niceties. There was a part of her that was weary, and rightfully so. But overtime, they grew more friendly and she opened up about Jackson's day-to-day life. He's a bookie, preferring to read unlike his brother who loves to play video games. Eventually, she expressed gratitude for the money I sent to them, but also made clear how she wouldn't have accepted it if she had known how I was getting it. We wrote back and forth for months before she broached the subject about meeting Jackson once I was released.

"It was actually her idea," I say, steadying my thoughts.

Kip places his hands over mine in my lap, and it's then I realize how bad I'm twisting them. "This is great, Kaley. There's no need to be nervous."

I release my hands. "I just want him to like me."

He gives me an encouraging look. "He will."

His reply doesn't necessarily ease my worries, but it's still nice to hear. I stand, ready to make my way back to Lilly's room when he says my name.

He stands, placing a hand on my upper arm as he looks down at me. "I'm really proud of you."

"Thank you," I say, giving him a small smile in return.

We spend the rest of the night metaphorically dancing around each other. The pull we used to have is back, but somehow it's stronger yet more welcome this time. Before, I used to force myself to distance myself from the butterflies in my belly, but now they give me hope. And every time his eyes meet mine, they reveal exactly what I'm feeling. Whether it's playing cards, bantering with Lilly, sitting in the hall with me as she goes into labor, or holding his new baby niece in his hands, his eyes hold hope.

"Did you decide on a name?" I say, peeking over Kip's shoulder at the burrito wrapped human.

"We did," Justin says, shit eating grin in place. He hasn't stopped smiling once, even as Kip ribs him for nearly passing out while Lilly was in labor. The nurse had a field day relaying the story to his entire family. His mom and dad laughed, but no one got a better kick out of it than Jacob. Through it all, Justin hasn't stopped smiling.

Lilly, looking drastically less amped on endorphins but happy all the same, smiles. "Portia Rosaline Knight, but we'll call her Rosie."

As ecstatic as I am they picked my name, I'm even more happy they picked Kip's. He cradles the baby to his chest, smiling down at the sleeping baby in his arms. "She does have some rosy cheeks," he says, stroking his finger gently across her cheek.

For the millionth time, his eyes meet mine and my heart gallops in my chest. The image of him already doting on the little girl in his arms reaffirms my beliefs. He's going to be an amazing husband and an even better father, and I want to be there to witness it.

thirty-two

MY HANDS TREMBLE AS I knock on the screen door, balancing the pan of store-bought banana pudding in my hands. I should've picked a dessert with a better track record, but I figured I was safe since I didn't actually make it.

Footsteps pound on the floor from the other side of the door and I hear a young boy's voice call out. "Got it," he yells, opening the door. "Hi!"

"Hi," I say, smiling in greeting. "You must be Danny."

He nods enthusiastically. "And you're Kaley, Jackson's new sister. Not my sister," he clarifies, pointing a thumb at his chest.

Paula has watched Danny since he was a baby while his mom works at an overnight clinic. They live next door so Jackson and Danny have literally spent their whole lives together. From my understanding, they sometimes forget they're not actually related.

"Technically, no," I say. "But we can still be friends, right?"

"Cool," he says, swinging open the screen door.

More footsteps pound down the hallway and Paula comes into view. "I told you not to answer the door if I'm not around," she admonishes him.

"It's just Kaley," he says, defensive. "We knew she was coming."

She pulls him back from the doorway by the collar of his shirt. "I don't care. Unless I give you permission, don't open this door. Not even for the president. Got it?"

He nods, pouting.

"Go set the table," she says, scuffing his hair. Finally, able to greet me, she knocks her hair out of her eyes, smiling. "I'm so sorry. He never listens"

"It's okay. I completely understand. I mean, I'm not a mom, but I get it."

Holding open the door, she takes the dessert from my hands and hugs me. "It's nice to meet you after all this time."

"You too."

"Come in. Jackson is still upstairs getting dressed, but dinner's almost ready."

The house is shotgun style, each room leading into the next with a staircase lining one side of the hallway. I follow her through the living room, through the dining room where Daniel is shuffling around plates, and into the kitchen. The furniture is sparse and the carpet is worn to the plywood underneath in some areas, but it's as well maintained as possible. Other than the few random toys strewn about, the house is immaculate.

"Smells good," I say, trying for small talk.

"Is spaghetti okay? I guess I should have asked if you were allergic to anything."

"No, spaghetti is perfect. Can I help with anything?"

She deposits the pan in the fridge. "Oh, no. You're a guest. Besides, there's not really anything left to do."

Paula and I wrote back and forth a lot over the past year, so there's a level of familiarity between us. I wasn't sure what to expect meeting her would be like because my main worry was always Jackson, but I'm glad there's not any awkwardness.

She smiles big. "He's so nervous."

Her words bring such relief. "Really?" I say, not caring that I'm giving away just how anxious I am.

"Really. He won't admit to it," she says, resuming her stirring. "But he's spent all day playing video games."

I give her a confused look, leaning against the counter next to her.

"He only plays video games when he doesn't want to think about something. Almost every time we have to leave for IPV, he spends the night playing them. It's mindless."

"IPV?"

"Intrapulmonary Percussive Ventilator. It's a type of therapy to help release the mucus from his lungs and airways. It's never fun."

"Does he have to do that often?"

"Not too often. We do most of his therapies at home."

Danny comes barreling back into the kitchen, screeching to a halt at Paula's feet. "I'm done setting the table. Can I go outside?"

"We're about to eat. Why don't you go see what's taking Jackson so long? Tell him it's not nice to keep guests waiting."

Danny doesn't look particularly happy about Paula's instructions, but he manages to keep his expression in check as he spins on a heel and runs back to the mouth of the stairs.

"Danny has one speed and it's full throttle. If he's awake, he's running or jumping or trying to fly," she says with a laugh.

I smile. "Something tells me Jackson is the opposite."

She nods. "That boy could read his life away and wouldn't think twice about it."

My eyes travel to the medical supplies stacked on the kitchen counter next to the pantry. There's bottles upon bottles of vitamins and supplements, tissues, and prescriptions. There's an obvious attempt to keep it all organized in plastic containers and daily pill reminders. A clip board hangs on the wall to keep track of what medications need to be taken when and how much. Most of today's prescriptions are already accounted for but the laundry list of prescriptions for tonight still takes up a quarter of the page.

Two sets of footsteps pound down the stairs, one noticeably quicker than the other, and it's to no surprise Danny emerges first. Jackson follows not far behind, but at a much more leisurely pace. His eyes immediately find mine.

"Hi," I say, doing my best to smile through my nervousness.

He waves. "Hey," he says, eyeing me.

The kitchen is quiet as he stares at me and I try not to fidget under his gaze. It's assessing, but not in a bad way.

"We share the same dad."

"We do," I say.

"Do you like him?"

Caught off guard, I look to Paula and she looks just as taken aback as I am. Jackson understands we have the same father who is now in jail because he's done bad things, but I was not expecting to be asked my opinion on the matter right off the bat.

"I think…I think it depends on the day. Sometimes I'll remember a good memory of him and I'll catch myself missing him. Other times I feel like I can't remember a single good thing about him. So…I'm not entirely sure," I answer truthfully.

"What about today?" he says, inquisitive.

Paula opens her mouth to speak, but I give her a look to let her know I'm okay with his questioning. I have a feeling Jackson isn't looking for a particular question, but he's looking for an openness from me. Maybe these are things he's conflicted about himself and he wants to compare thoughts on the matter. All I know is however

I react is going to determine how much he feels like he can trust me.

"Today," I say on a sigh, releasing the tension from my body. "I kind of like him because he made us siblings and that's pretty cool."

He barely tilts his head to the side, a peek of an approving smile in his eyes. "After we eat, do you want to play Mario Kart?"

"I haven't played in years so I doubt I'm any good."

"It's okay, neither is Jackson," Danny says, a smirk already in place.

"I beat you once," Jackson says in defense, moving towards the dining room.

"I had a broken foot, it doesn't count."

Jackson gives him a dumb look. "What does that have to do with anything?"

They're voices trail off as they discuss the difficulties of playing video games while injured.

I take a sigh of relief. "That went well," I say.

Her eyes are round as she meets my eyes. "I had no idea he was going to ask you those questions, I swear."

I laugh. "It's okay. I think I passed."

She nods in agreement. "I think you did, too."

I help Paula carry the food to the kitchen counter and dish out the food for the four of us. Paula says grace and the conversation moves from video games to books and onto school work. Jackson is home schooled, in part due to the risks he'd face in public school due to germs and infections. Danny seems to think Jackson does nothing but read all day, but Paula assures him Jackson does the same work from home.

Jackson asks me what kind of books I like and his face screws up in disgust when I tell him I've been on a romance kick for the past year. He prefers sci-fi and dystopian, but he'll read an occasional Western if he's feeling up to it. We agree to trade books and I promise Paula to keep my recommendation PG. Throughout dinner, I notice Jackson doesn't eat much. He pushes his spaghetti around and picks apart the noodles with his fork. As we're finishing up, Paula tries to get him to take a few more bites, but is met with resistance.

"I'm really not hungry."

"Two more bites," she insists.

"Paula," he draws out, sulking in his chair.

I can tell Paula wants to push him and probably normally would, but for the sake of not arguing while I'm here, she lets it go. "Fine. You two can clean the dishes and I'll put Mario Kart on in the living room."

I follow Paula up the stairs to grab the gaming system. Jackson's bedroom is small but it looks even smaller with all the medical supplies stacked along an entire wall. It's so much, way more than I realized he needed in the first place. There's different machines and tubes. A device is mounted to the wall above his bed with a bag of some type of fluid connected to it.

Paula's eyes follow mine. "Sometimes I forget what it looks like," she says. "This is everyday life for us, but through new eyes, I'm sure it's overwhelming."

"It's weird, because he doesn't even look that sick."

"No, he doesn't. But CF is sometimes hidden that way. Some days I forget he's sick at all, and others it's all I can think about."

The weight of Jackson's disease seems to sit on her in this moment, almost like it wants to pull her under.

"It's not easy doing it on your own," I say.

She shrugs, a sad smile on her face. "It's not my disease, it's his, and he still manages to wake up every day with a smile."

"But he's your responsibility. That's scary enough with a healthy kid, let alone one who needs constant monitoring."

She looks at me, like *really* looks at me, and gives a tiny shake of her head. "You're not going anywhere, are you?"

Not sure how to answer, I say, "Right now? This instant?"

"No, I mean ever. You're not going to disappear."

It's not a question this time and I give her a genuine smile. "No."

She nods once and turns around to gather the gaming system. I've never hooked up a gaming system in my life—I can barely hook up my DVD player—but Paula is an expert and has it up and running by the time the boys are done with the dishes.

We play Mario Kart way past their bedtimes, but Paula doesn't complain. She even joins in for a couple of rounds. No one is a match for Danny, but he humors us and loses a few. I spend the majority of my time learning who Jackson is and how he interacts with the people closest to him. He's doesn't laugh much, and in a way, it reminds me of Kip. His smiles tell everything. Especially when Danny says something Jackson finds completely idiotic, his smile reveals everything.

It's close to midnight before Paula suggests it's time to say goodnight, but neither of the boys complain. I watch Jackson do his nighttime ritual and hook his feeding tube to his port before bed. There's a level of maturity in him that I'm sure is a product of his upbringing. Once they're in bed, I help Paula pick up the living room. We'd used the couch cushions to sit on the floor, closer to the TV, and there's popcorn and snacks strewn about.

Paula plops down on the sofa as I call for a taxi, lounging next to her. I didn't realize how tired I was until just now, and I fight to stay alert.

"Why does Jackson call you by your first name and not Mom?"

She smiles. "I kept Danny from a really early age and he always called me Paula, so Jackson just repeated what he heard. It kind of stuck."

"He seems so level headed."

"He is," she agrees. "I don't know where he got it from because God knows I'm not."

I laugh. "And there's no way he gets it from his father."

She shakes her head, smiling. "That's for sure."

We're quiet for a few minutes before I find the courage to speak. "You never mentioned how you met my dad."

"Why do you ask?" she says.

"I've just been wondering," I say with a shrug. "And if I'm being honest, I don't see you as being the type to have an affair with a married man. You're so…nice."

She laughs out loud. "I'm sure there's lots of people who would dispute that." There's a beat of silence before she continues. "If I tell you, it stays between us. I don't want Jackson to know. At least, not until he's older."

"Okay," I drawl, suspicious.

Sighing, she gives me a knowing look. "I amassed a lot of student debt after college. I come from a fairly poor family, and I wasn't prepared for the interest to start rolling in so quickly after graduation. I wasn't able to make ends meet on a teacher's salary and pay off school loans." She swallows down an emotion I can't pinpoint. "An old classmate of mine recommended working at a bar downtown. She said she'd been doing it for years, all the way through college, and she was debt free. She convinced me it was safe."

It doesn't take a genius to figure out where she's going with this, and my heart lodges firmly in my throat. I frequented a counselor, Sanya, in prison to help me organize my feelings and guilt I had accumulated inside of me. I hadn't realized the extent of damage sleeping with men did to me until I was forced to. Sometimes I feel like I'll never be able to distance myself from my past, but Sanya had helped me figure out how to balance putting it behind me, while still being okay with it being a part of who I am today. It's obvious Paula has held the same struggles.

"I didn't hate it," Paula continues. "And I loved the money. I had only been working there a few weeks when I met your father. He was handsome and charming, very affectionate. It didn't take me long before I fell in love with him, or at least, the lifestyle he afforded me."

"And then you got pregnant," I say.

"So the story goes," she says, smiling. "John wanted me to get an abortion, but I just couldn't. Once he realized I wasn't going to terminate the pregnancy, he agreed to pay for everything I needed as long as I kept my mouth shut. And he did for a long time."

"Until he went to jail?"

"Correct."

"But…that doesn't make any sense. He still has money. I know because he paid my legal fees."

She shakes her head. "It wasn't ever about supplying for us or taking care of Jackson's medical bills," she says.

It dawns on me. "It was about saving face, more particularly, saving you from spilling information about Hudson's."

She nods. "At least, that's my guess."

I lean back, staring at the blank screen of the TV. It's funny how my opinion of my father can change from minute to minute. I hadn't lied when I told Jackson I wasn't sure as to my opinion on my father. Sometimes I think he did things out of the goodness of his heart, and then something will remind me of the terrible things he's done. He's in jail for killing people, selling drugs which probably killed more people and ruined lives, but it's so conflicting with the man I knew all of my life.

313

I still remember him taking me out to eat when I brought home good grades and how excited he was to gift me something I really wanted for Christmas or my birthday. He used to help me with my math homework and teased my mother for lack of cooking skills.

I don't like him as a person. I don't like what he's done to people or to Jackson, his own son. Everything was always with conditions with him. Maybe I'll never figure him out or maybe I'll visit him one day to ask him why he's so shitty face-to-face. Or maybe I'll leave all the questions behind and forget he exists. For now, I'll just focus on building a relationship with Jackson and be grateful for what my father has given me.

thirty-three

IT'S BEEN A COUPLE of weeks since I've seen Kip. Every time I've visited baby Rosie, he hasn't been around. Even though I never asked, Lilly assured me he was just busy with the shop and filling an order for Marty. I've stayed away from our spot on the hill, afraid I'll push him away if I don't give him space. Kip's not one who responds to pressure well. He has to come to a conclusion on his own before he'll act on it. He needs to decide how he feels about me without me there to muddle with his feelings.

And I get it. When I'm by myself, my feelings are all over the place. I miss him even more in the real world than I did in prison. He feels so close, yet so far away at the same time. I pretty much spend the entirety of my days thinking about him and trying not to. I'm able to distract myself in small spurts, but my thoughts always find a way of reminding me how much I want to see him.

I slouch in my seat, trying to relax on my day off. The sun is shining and it's almost mid-sixties outside, signaling winter is almost over. All the windows are open, letting in the fresh air. Breathing deep, I try to dispel the restlessness inside me. I must not be doing a good job because Beck and Mondo both laugh at my sour mood.

"Why don't you just freaking call him?" Beck says, lounging against the couch. Mondo is busy doing push-ups on the terrace. They coordinate their days off to spend them together. They're not particularly affectionate, because they don't feel a need to reaffirm their feelings for one another by constantly touching. Sometimes I wish Lilly and Justin had the same outlook.

"I don't want to smother him," I say, absentmindedly flipping through a tabloid magazine.

Mondo hefts his body into a sitting position, breathing heavy. "Maybe he's waiting on you to make the first move."

"I don't want to have to feel like I have to persuade him to want to see me. If he wanted to be with me, he would."

Beck grins. "He's probably waiting on you to do the same."

Mondo sits on the edge of the couch, wiping a rag over his face. "Wasn't most of your two's relationship one sided?"

"It was not," I say defensive, looking up from my magazine.

"But he feels that way, doesn't he? Lance told me you hid everything from him. You most likely wounded his pride a little bit."

I huff. "Since when did you and Lance become so close?"

"He's paying Mondo to keep tabs on you," Beck says, like it's no big deal.

My eyes widen on Mondo but his glare is on Beck. "Thanks for that," he says.

She shrugs. "Girls got to stick together. Plus, I told you I would tell her if you didn't."

"Well, Lance needs to worry about himself and keep his mouth shut." I pick up my phone and send him the middle finger emoji, telling him to mind his own business. Sometimes it takes him hours or even days to respond since he's out working on a job, but he'll get the message.

"Don't worry," Monday says. "He wants to know the basics. Whether or not you're staying busy, did you find a job, have you gotten off your ass and confessed your love for Kip yet."

I groan, dropping my head back against the cushions of the chair. "Not that it's everyone's business, but I've already told him I love him. He knows I want to be with him and he hasn't done anything about it."

"Like I said," Beck says. "He's probably waiting on you to *show* him that you mean it."

Mondo and Beck share a smile before Mondo resumes his workout on the patio. I focus on the spread of trendy shoes in my hands, but the words seem to blur together. Their opinions replay in my head and a strange niggling sensation starts to make me doubt myself. What if they're right? What if Kip's been waiting for me to prove that I'm in this?

I glance up and find Beck's eyes flick over me, a meaningful smile tugging at the corner of my lips.

"Do you know something I don't?" I demand.

"Other than the fact you're obtuse when it comes to relationships? No."

"Funny."

"Listen," she says, giving me her full attention. "You see that man right there?" She points to Mondo doing crunches. "He's never told me he loves me. But I don't need him to, because he shows me every day that he does. Words are great and all, but they don't mean anything if you don't back them up."

Emotions clog my throat and I force them down with a swallow. "What if he doesn't want to be with me?"

She shrugs. "Then you'll know you did everything you could to make it work. You said it yourself, you can live without him."

I nod, agreeing with her. I've been delaying the inevitable. At some point, Kip and I will either move on together, or apart, but we can't stay in limbo forever.

"I'm going to go," I say vaguely as I stand.

Mondo shoots me a salute. "We'll be here when you get back."

Beck winks at me and it's their way of saying they'll be here for me no matter what. Somehow, I've found friends who love me despite my stubbornness and I couldn't be more grateful. My phone dings and I read Lance's reply, which is basically him telling me to fuck off with a random eggplant emoji he uses just to be annoying.

For the first time in my life, I finally get a cab driver that understands my need for urgency and I tip him well once we arrive to the hiking trail. I take the amateur trail just because it's the quickest. There's a lot of people hiking today, the weather urging people outside to enjoy it.

I've probably never hiked the hill quicker before and I'm slightly out of breath as I make it to the top. Once again, I didn't prepare and bring any water but I don't bother to stop at the spring as I head toward our spot. Kip says he comes every day but I'm not sure when exactly. It's after lunch so there's a chance I've already missed him. I debate calling him, but decide I'll wait it out instead. I need to show him and I can't do that over the phone.

I clear the trees and come to halt when I reach our campsite. We always nestled our tent between two, outlying trees. They stand apart from the woods, solitaire in their spots next to each other.

And someone—more accurately Kip—has strung a hammock across the expanse of space between them. I walk toward the strung rope, running my fingers over the mesh, testing its strength before I sit on it. In the middle, there's book in a zip lock bag. It's the latest novel from one my favorite authors. Carefully and slowly, I ease my weight onto the hammock, and let out a sigh when I swing my legs off the ground. All I can do is smile.

Mondo and Beck were right; he has been waiting for me.

I crack open the first page of the book, truly relaxing for the first time that I can remember in over a year, and begin to read. I spend the day in a mixture of absolute bliss and anxiously waiting for Kip's arrival. I end up taking a break to get a drink of water after the thirst becomes too much. I return to the hammock, half expecting Kip to be there but remind myself to be patient when he isn't.

I must have fallen asleep because the sound of shuffling feet across the dirt rouses me awake. It takes a few seconds, but my eyes adjust to the fading light of the sun. Sitting up, my eyes land on the sight of Kip's figure a few feet away. He's looking at the sunset, but he turns his attention to me when he hears me shift.

"Hey," I say, smiling through the haze of sleep.

He smiles back. "Hey."

"Thank you," I say. "For the hammock and the book."

He doesn't speak, just nods slightly as he holds my stare.

"Do you want to sit with me?"

He hesitates for a split second before carefully rocking his weight into the sling with me. We nearly tip but we shift our weight in the nick of time to prevent catastrophe, laughing once we get it under control. There's no way not to be plastered next to each other and he sweeps an arm underneath my head to get comfortable.

"You smell like motor oil."

He sniffs his shirt, cringing. "I'm sorry," he says.

"I like it," I say.

He looks at me, a sense of peacefulness in his eyes. "That's weird."

I laugh and a real smile peaks out from his lips. "It's...comforting," I say, smiling at him.

Holding my stare for a split second longer, he uses the arm under my head to wrap around my shoulders and pull me closer to him. He sniffs my hair and I can hear the smile in his voice when he speaks. "I've missed your smell too."

His confession sends a jolt of endorphins through my system and I breathe through the onslaught of emotions. "I want to be with you, Kip. I know I can do better this time. I can love you like you deserve to be."

It seemed impossible, but he pulls me even closer. "There's nothing wrong with the way you loved me, Kaley. It was the way you tried not to love me that was the hard part."

I look up at him, adoring the way his lashes make the best backdrop to the blue of his eyes in this light. I feel an urge to convince him how good we can be together. "I can make you happy."

"Kaley, falling in love with you was painful—excruciatingly so—but it was also the happiest I've ever been." He brushes my hair out of the way and places a kiss to my lips. I'm too stunned to reciprocate at first. "You make me happy," he says against my lips.

"I'm sorry I made it so difficult," I say, ready for the feel of his lips on mine this time when we kiss.

"It's okay," he says. "I have a feeling this time is going to be even better."

acknowledgements

Marlon, without a doubt you pulled triple duty while I worked relentlessly to finish this book. You never once complained and every day you encouraged me to do whatever I needed to pursue my dreams. You're with me every step of the way, and there's no way I could do this without you. Thank you, once again, for proving to me that there is a such thing as unconditional love.

Alicia, thank you for being the most supportive friend. You're my sounding board for everything and you always give the best advice even when you're busy or stressed out. Everyone deserves an Alicia. I don't know what I've done to deserve such a kickass friend.

Murphy at Indie Solutions, thank you for your patience and allowing me to cram this manuscript in last minute. You still managed to do everything last minute and during a huge life-changing decision. I know no one would put up with me like you do. I can't think of anyone I'd trust more on editing my work and who can make me laugh through the horrendous task of edits.

And Kristin, too. You're the best proofreader. I don't know how you do it, but you make edits mildly tolerable.

Sara, thank you for believing in me to make this book happen. Sometimes God puts the right people in your life and you are one of them for me. You help me in more ways than one and I love your face. I will also officially retire "creamy thigh sauce." At least, until you miss it and ask me to bring it back. Until then...

Portia, you are literally the best. I could go on and on about how much you do for my sanity, but I know how you are with feelings so I'll keep it short. We'll be best friends when we meet, I'm sure of it.

CeeCee, thank you for loving me enough to tolerate me. You always give a different insight to my stories and I seriously value your opinion so much. It's why I kept asking you to beta and you came through for me even though you were hesitant.

Wendi, thank you SO FREAKING MUCH for fitting me in last minute. You're a lifesaver and my saving grace on this one.

Elaine, thank you for always catering to my last-minute changes and doing ARCs at the drop of a dime.

Dani, thank you for beta-ing the switching of POVs and encouraging me to move forward with the concept. I'm positive I wouldn't have stuck with it if you hadn't insisted it was good.

Mom, for supporting me in my pursuit of writing even though it has tons of cuss words and sex scenes. I love you too.

ALL MY PEEPS IN THE BACK. That's my BSers who would take forever to thank by name. Every. Single. One. Of you complete me. When no one else gets it, y'all do.

And thank you to everyone who has read my work. There's a lot of books out there. A LOT. So the fact you picked mine means the world. Thank you:)